xoxo
Victoria Ashley

D1519721

RECKLESS
ROCK STAR

NEW YORK TIMES AND *USA TODAY* BESTSELLING AUTHOR
VICTORIA ASHLEY

Editor: Charisse Spiers
Photo Credit: Wander Aguiar/Wander Book Club
Model: Colton Benson
Formatted by: Nancy Henderson

CHAPTER ONE

MADDEN

Taking a moment to catch my breath, I reach for the bottle of water sitting on the stool behind me and pour it over my head to cool off.

My entire body is drenched in sweat from head to toe, and the crowded room full of people is making it hard to breathe.

It always seems so fucking hard to breathe when my name is being yelled out by strangers expecting something great from me. Maybe it's the pressure of living up to everyone's expectations that puts this heavy weight on my chest, making me *feel* as if I'm suffocating.

After tossing the empty bottle into the crowd, I turn back around and drain the glass of whiskey that's been begging me to drink it since three songs ago. I haven't had a chance to do anything other than focus on the music and please the crowd. I hate to admit that I need liquor to help me get through the night. Actually, I need it to help me get through most nights.

It's the new norm for me. A bad habit I'm afraid I won't be able to break or even want to.

Taking my guitar off, I quickly pull my drenched shirt over my head and shake out my hair with my hand. Whistles fill the room and female fans are going crazy at the sight of my abs and chest on display for them.

I have no doubt that hundreds of images of me shirtless will end up on social media in ten seconds or less with the hashtag: #takeitoffmadden.

It's been trending since the first time I stripped out of my shirt on stage, undid my jeans and poured water down my pants to cool off from the beaming hot lights. There were so many zoomed in shots of my crotch that night I couldn't go anywhere for over a week without someone glancing down south instead of at my face.

I take a few seconds to hype up the crowd before replacing my electric guitar and nodding to the other band members that I'm ready.

The screaming of hundreds of fans surrounds us as we prepare for our last song of the night. It's a song they're familiar with and always end up singing along to until the very end. They always do, no matter what state we're in or how big or small the venue is. This is the song that made *RISK* known and put us on the radar two years ago.

I wrote this song after getting my heart stomped on by a girl who I believed would be with me 'til the end. She made me believe we were perfect together—that nothing or no one could tear us apart. Then one day she decided I wasn't what she wanted anymore. Suddenly, I wasn't enough to keep her out of someone else's bed.

It fucked me up for the longest time, but in the end, it led me to where I am today. In a way, I guess I should be thankful. But honestly, if I had to choose between love and fame, love would win every fucking time.

"All right now. We're going to end the night with a little something you all know well. Sing along and add it to your social media. Hashtag that shit with RISK and I'll watch them later."

The screaming dies down and quickly turns into singing as I get into *Without You*.

I'm lost in the song and feeling it, just like every time I have to sing these lyrics, when I look out into the front of the crowd and notice some asshole grab a girl's wrist and yank her back to the point that she loses her footing and falls over.

My voice becomes angrier—deep and intimidating as I watch him yell and point in her face after grabbing her arm and yanking her back up.

But I really lose it when he grabs her face and gets in it, digging his nail into her forehead as he points his finger at it. "Fuck that... hold up a minute. Stop the music." The room quietens down as I walk to the end of the stage and point directly at the prick less than ten feet from the stage. "Hey, you. Is that your girlfriend there?"

The big guy nods his head and yells. "Yeah, the dumb bitch is drunk."

I clench my jaw over his choice of phrasing, wanting nothing more than to kick this motherfucker's ass for being so rough with her. "Come here."

The dickhead begins walking forward with a cocky grin, as if he thinks I'm taking his side.

"Not you, asshole. I'll deal with you later." I point at the pretty little brunette he left behind in this savage-ass crowd of guys. "Your girl."

He looks pissed when our security team guides his girl up to the stage to join us.

Not giving a shit that I'm holding up the final song, I grab my stool and pull it forward for her. Then I grab her hand and walk her over to it. "What's your name?"

"Melody. Oh my god. Oh my god. I can't breathe right now." She's so excited to be near me that she's shaking and actually having a tough time catching her breath as she anxiously fans herself off. "I can't believe you touched my hand. Or that I'm up here right now. Holy shit! My friends are never going to believe this. You're Madden Parker. *The* Madden Parker."

Grinning, I grab her chin and run my thumb over her bottom lip, wanting her asshole boyfriend to see how a man is *supposed* to handle a woman. "I'll make sure you get some pictures to show your friends."

I release her chin and take a step back. Her eyes roam down my wet chest, checking me out. "What's your boyfriend's name?"

Her lip trembles. "Brad. His name is Brad Jacobs," she answers.

I back away and look out toward *Brad*, who doesn't seem to have that cocky grin on his face anymore now that his girl is up here with me. He knows he fucked up.

Crouching down, I keep my gaze right on him as I speak.

"Now, let's fucking continue, shall we?"

Once I jump back into singing the lyrics, the rest of the band begins playing, joining in. Just as expected, the entire room is singing along to the song *I* wrote. I'll never get over that feeling. Not ever. No matter how stressed this lifestyle can get sometimes.

When we get toward the end of the song, I grab Melody's hand and pull her up to the front of the stage, stepping in close to her. I'm so close that I can feel her heavy breathing hitting my neck.

"Here's to Brad Jacobs. Everyone join in. You know the deal."

"...*fuck* Brad. She's better off without you..."

As soon as the last lyric leaves my lips, I wrap my hand

into the back of Melody's hair and pull her in for a kiss, while giving Brad the middle finger with my free hand.

I bite her bottom lip and suck it into my mouth, making sure that Brad gets a good look of his girl's mouth being devoured by me.

The crowd continues to repeat the chorus, up until I finally pull away and run my thumb over her lip, wiping the wetness from my mouth away.

From the veins bulging out of Brad's neck and forehead, I'd say my little show worked and he's pissed. The asshole should know not to push females around. That's how you get your ass kicked *or* your girl taken; possibly both.

And since I can't cause another scene and end up in jail right now, due to commitments and such, kicking his ass is out of the question. The least I can do is make him leave here feeling like a loser.

"Brad will be kicking his own ass for not treating you with more respect. Maybe he'll change his ways now," I whisper against her lips. "If not, then leave his ass behind and find someone else who will."

Melody stands there speechless, most likely in a state of shock as she runs her tongue over her lips and nods. She's in a daze. It's the effect I seem to have on women these days. Funny the kind of power a little fame will give a person.

I release her hair and nod behind her. "Wait for us backstage and we'll get you some pictures before you leave."

"Holy shit... thank you!" She backs up slowly, keeping her attention on me, until Landon Beckett, our drummer, grabs her shoulder, causing her to turn around and look at him.

She must be freaking out over Landon too, because I hear him laughing as he guides her backstage.

"What the hell was that?" Hendrix Drake, our bassist, walks across the stage and tosses a fresh water to me. "This

VICTORIA ASHLEY

shouldn't surprise me. You're always doing some crazy shit on stage. I'm sure a new hashtag will pop up soon."

"Yeah... well, her asshole boyfriend shouldn't have pushed her around in front of me. He's lucky I didn't jump off the stage and kick his ass." I open the water and take a quick drink, before pouring the remainder of it over my head and face.

"Dude is pretty pissed. Check him out."

When I look out into the crowd, I immediately notice Brad pushing people out of his way and yelling at them. "Fuck it. People talk no matter what. Might as well give them something to talk about, right?" I slap Hendrix's back and hand him my guitar, before jumping off the stage, making my way through the crowd.

Female hands go crazy, groping me as I make my way toward Brad and tap him on the shoulder.

"What—" He turns around and I swing out my elbow, connecting it hard with his jaw, causing him to fall back. This douchebag is really pushing his luck here tonight.

Brad is quick to jump to his feet and come at me, tackling me down to the ground. He's bigger than me, but as soon as my head connects hard with his, I'm able to push him off me and get back to my feet.

I get a few more swings in before security breaks us apart. Aaron drags Brad away as Travis shoves me toward the back of the room and away from everyone. At least, I assume it's Travis until I hear my cousin Chance's Australian accent and finally look up to see his copper reddish-brown hair and blue eyes.

"Are you trying to end up in the back of a squad car again, Mate? You're being reckless. Maybe wait until you get the wanker alone, yeah?"

"I'm good." I shake the grip he has on me and pull out a cigarette, turning to Travis as he approaches and attempts to reach for my shoulder. "I'll be on the tour bus, chilling the fuck out. I need some space for a bit."

He throws his arms up, not wanting to get on my bad side, most likely. "Fine. I'll let the guys know."

Once outside, I take a huge breath of fresh air and run my hands through my wet hair. I really need this right now. It's not often that I get even five minutes away from the chaos, and I'm hoping I can get at least ten while everyone else is drinking and unwinding a bit.

Lighting up my smoke, I hop onto the bus, Chance following behind me.

My cousin had a short-lived career as a soccer player in Australia until he tore his ACL his first professional game. I grew up not really knowing who he was, since he moved away when he was five—before I was born—but have recently become close to him after learning he was back in the U.S.

Whenever *RISK* has a concert in California, Chance and his wife come from Hermosa Beach to watch it. "Where's Aubrey? Is she here? How are the kids?"

He shakes his head and searches through the mini-fridge as if he owns it. "Nah, she had a girls' night with Adele. Said to say hello for you. They're great, Mate. Finally got Bree to say Dada." Without asking, he opens a sandwich he finds and tears into it. "Hope you weren't planning on eating this sandwich with your name on it."

"I saw. Pixy too." The thought of little Chance, Bree and that damn goat of theirs, eases my mood just a bit. With a half-smirk, I shake my head. "Nah, you're good. I can't stomach shit right now anyway." I run a hand through my hair again and exhale. "I didn't see you before the show. Was wondering where your ass would pop up. Thought maybe you changed your mind about coming."

"Nah." He stands and slaps my shoulder, popping the last bite into his mouth. "You never know when I'll pop up. That's part of my charm, Cousin." He eyes me over, slipping out of his brown leather jacket and getting comfortable while he eats It's a few minutes before he asks, "What's wrong?"

"Everything." I take a long drag off my smoke and exhale, my mood quickly going back to shit. "The camping trip coming up is fucking with me."

"Maybe's she's moved on by now."

"Nope. She hasn't. Her many texts on my phone proves she hasn't." I flex my jaw. "And I'm pretty sure she's going to be there again."

"And I'm sure you'll be fine. You can handle her." He stands and grips my shoulder, before shrugging his jacket back on. "You're stronger than you think."

"Appreciate it, man. But I don't know. It's easy for a guy like you with a happy family to say. I envy you, dude. What you have—that greatness—inspires me to work for the same. I'd be home right now instead of this concert if I had what you do."

"Which is exactly why I'm heading out. As eventful as it was to watch you give that wanker a good beating, I'm ready to get back to my family. Just don't worry and things will work out." He pats his pockets, probably in search of his keys, before making a face as if he just remembered something. "I almost forgot. I plan on framing this." He grins and pulls a rolled-up paper out of his pocket, before tossing me a marker and unrolling what appears to be a poster of me getting arrested. "Sign it right there across the top, Cousin. Make it pretty for my junk art room."

"You had a picture of me being shoved into a police car made into a poster?" Can't say I'm surprised. It is Chance Bateman, after all. If anyone knows about posters, it's him. He's only had thousands of him purchased.

He nods as I laugh and sign it for him. "Not just *a* poster. About a couple hundred of them. One is included in the landscaping package I offer my customers. They appreciate the extra gift. Most get a good laugh out of your facial expression as you're struggling against the police."

I can't tell if he's joking or not about giving them away to his customers, but I wouldn't put it past him. "Of all the pictures out there of me on the internet, you just had to find the worst one."

"What can I say... it's a gift." He rolls the poster back up and shoves it into his pocket. "I told Aubrey I'd try to make it back before it gets too late, so I'm out."

I nod. "No worries, man. I'm glad you came." I offer him a half-smile. "Thanks for the laugh. I needed it."

"I knew you would from those tense-ass texts you've been sending the last few days." He winks, before hopping off the bus, singing "Fuck Brad" under his breath. And just like that, he's gone.

Once I'm alone, I wait a few seconds before grabbing my phone and powering it up as I head back outside and lean against the bus.

I have a shit-ton of notifications, from *Instagram* and *Facebook* tags to tweets on *Twitter*, but I ignore them all and go straight to Jake's missed call, returning it.

He picks up. "Hey, man. What the hell is all this shit on *Facebook* and *Twitter* about you kissing some girl on stage? There's this new hashtag: #fuckbradshesbetteroffwithoutyou." He stops for a second to laugh. "Good concert, I'm guessing?"

I laugh and blow out smoke. "The same as usual. Some asshole pissed me off and I had to act on it. You know me..."

"Thank fuck you didn't end up in jail this time. You have an important trip to make soon. You're still making our annual trip next week to my dad's cabin, right?"

"Yeah." I take another quick drag before tossing the cigarette. "I'll be there. I haven't missed one yet and I don't

9

plan to start now. The band will be fine without me for a bit, and I suppose jail will be too," I add as a joke.

Jake laughs. "It's Thursday through Tuesday this time. You staying the whole time or you got some shit with the band to take care of? You know they can come too. We'll make room like last year."

"I'll be there Thursday, and there's no way I'm leaving early. I'll make it work. I always do. I'm flying to Temecula on Tuesday, so I don't get stuck doing some shit that will keep me from making it. I'm not giving Jason the chance to keep me in LA for the next week doing signings, photoshoots, and whatever else he can think of. The guys might show up toward the end again.

"Sweet. I'll tell the crew. They're going to be happy, for sure. Things have been blowing up for you and the band over the last year. A small break will do you some good."

"Yeah, I can't wait." I walk back toward the building, so I can get Melody those pictures that I promised her. I stop at the back entrance and ask the dreaded question I already know the answer to. "What about Alana?"

He sighs. "Yeah, man. You know she comes every year. Nothing is different this year. Sorry."

"Shit..."

"It's been three years. Maybe's she's moved on by now."

"That's what you said last year and look how that turned out. The entire trip was miserable for both of us, because all she did was cry and beg me to take her back. I can't handle that shit again, Jake. I can't fucking do it. She ripped my heart out, and if I fall for her again it'll only end up being the same shit."

"Then bring a girlfriend. Show her that you've moved on, and then she'll have no choice but to do the same. It'll make this trip a hell of a lot easier. Trust me, you'll be doing us all a favor. That girl isn't giving up easily, because she believes no one will ever replace her."

A girlfriend? He knows more than anyone that none of my past relationships aside from Alana have lasted longer than one damn night.

"Jake—"

"I know you don't have a girlfriend, dickhead. Fucking borrow one. Do whatever it takes. Shit... I have to go. Jess just got here and she wants dick. See you on Thursday."

Before I can say anything else the asshole hangs up on me. He doesn't get it. There's not one girl I've slept with who hasn't fallen for me. I can't ask them to pretend to be my girl-friend. They're too attached. That shit will not end well.

I stand outside for a few more minutes, thinking about what my best friend suggested.

Borrow one.

That's something I've never thought of before...

CHAPTER TWO

MADDEN

Running my hands over my face, I sit up and release a slow breath, trying to piece together what all happened last night after I got back to my hotel room.

The naked body beside me has me cussing under my breath and reaching for the bottle of Jameson to my right.

"Well, this should be interesting..." I take a few swigs straight from the bottle, before I toss the sheet aside and throw my legs over the side of the bed.

From what I can remember, Alana sent me a few messages that resulted in drinking my ass into oblivion. Melody was there, and with every passing thought about my ex and how she fucked me over, the more I needed to take out some of my aggression on someone.

Based on the items of clothing scattered across the hotel floor and the three condoms in the bedside trash, I'd say I found a way to do that.

But it's nights like these that always seem to get me into trouble when the morning rolls around and the girl beside me decides we belong together and she's going to follow me around on tour.

I really need to get my shit together and stop letting that bitch send my mind into overdrive every time she decides to text. When it comes to her, I need to stop worrying, and stop thinking about what we had or could have had. We're history.

Just the thought of seeing Alana soon has my chest aching and feeling tight again. The last two trips have been complete hell because of her and I refuse to let her ruin it for me this year.

What she doesn't get is that this trip is my only time to get away and just chill with my friends with no worries. The only time I get to truly be *me* and feel like myself.

I get *one* time a year to do this and she can't even give me that because she's selfish and used to getting what she wants.

Alana broke my heart and trust. She made the decision to walk away from *me*, yet she's the one that can't accept we're over and move on, because she knows no one will ever treat her or make love to her as good as I did.

Sitting here naked, and against my better judgment, I reach for my phone and read the messages that Alana sent me. This won't be the second or third time I've read these, but more like the hundredth time. I guess I'm just a glutton for punishment.

10:02 P.M.
Alana: We need to talk at the cabin about us getting back together. I don't know how many times you expect me to apologize for what I did but I'm sorry and I mean it. I miss you so damn much.

10:18 P.M.
Alana: You kissing that girl on stage hurt, but it didn't

fool me one bit. Just admit that you're not over me. Not over us. Please, Madden.

10: 40 P.M
Alana: Will you just answer me for once? This is getting a little old. We both know you're reading my messages.

11:12 P.M
Alana: Okay... fine. Ignore me now, but we both know that once you see me you'll remember how much you truly miss me. You can deny it all you want, but we get so close to getting back together every year on this trip. I won't give up until it happens this time. See you soon.
🤍 **Alana**

Everything went blurry after that, landing me right where I am at present, full of rage and regret. Not even my multiple texts to Chance last night helped distract me like I was hoping before I was able to make the mistake I did.

I growl out in frustration and toss my phone at the wall.

Melody stirs beside me, so I stand up and slip on my jeans, before disappearing into the bathroom.

Turning on the fan, I reach for my pack of smokes and light one up, before taking a seat on the edge of the tub.

This might be the last stop on our tour before I fly out to my brother's, but we have a photoshoot that I need to get my shit together for.

The thought sends me over the edge with anxiety.

I need this break more than anything right now, and it pisses me off to no end that Alana is set on ruining it for me.

It's because of her that I end up naked next to strange women with no control over my dick. Honestly, I should've blocked her a long time ago, but every damn time I tell myself I'm going to do it, I don't. I can't.

A part of what she said is true. I haven't gotten over her yet... over us. That's kind of hard to do when I've known her since I was twelve and we dated for seven years.

That's why *not* going back to her has been the biggest battle of my life. Keeping myself occupied with countless women who I know have no chance in hell of hurting me has been my way of moving on, but it doesn't fill the void.

She was my best friend, and she cheated on me and then walked away as if what we had built over the years meant nothing to her.

I can't allow myself to ever get crushed by her again, because there's a chance I won't survive this time.

A knock at the bathroom door has me on alert. I know what's coming next.

"Madden... you've been in there for a while. Want me to get you anything, or maybe run you a bubble bath? I don't have anywhere to be today. I'm all yours for whatever you need me for. We can spend the entire day together."

They all want to take care of the broken rock star.

"Shit..." I mumble under my breath and toss my cigarette into the toilet. "I'm fine, Melody. Just give me a few."

"Okay," she says through the door. "I'll be out here waiting. Take your time."

Releasing a breath, I walk over to the sink and splash some water on my face, before taking a good look at myself in the mirror. The dark circles under my eyes are a sign of how I truly feel: exhausted.

I have to prepare myself every time this happens to turn into the dick I always told myself I'd never become once we made it big.

But I have to do something to keep these girls from

falling for me and wanting more. I learned that after the first year of touring.

When I open the door, Melody is splayed out across the bed, naked and waiting for me. She holds up a condom and bites her bottom lip. "Ready for round four?"

"I can't."

She gives me puppy dog eyes and crawls across the bed to get closer to where I'm standing. "You went pretty hard last night, but I'm sure you have more in you. I'll make it easy for you and even do all the work. I think you earned it after last night."

Needing it more now than before, I walk over to the bedside table and grab for the bottle of Jameson again. I tilt it back, probably longer than I should, before turning to face Melody as she grabs for my dick.

"No sex." I clench my jaw, because I know I'm an asshole. "Last night should've never happened. I was wasted and barely even remember bringing you back to my room."

"That's okay." Not giving up, she slides her hand into the top of my jeans and begins stroking my semi-hard dick. "I'm sure you remember our kiss on stage though, right? The whole world saw it. We can start over fresh today. No biggie."

Growling out my frustration, I grab her hand and pull it away from my now hard dick. "That kiss was only to piss Brad off and we both know it. I was a dumbass and drank too much and that's the only reason you ended up in my bed. Let's not turn this in to something more than it is or ever will be. You were just a distraction that I needed at the time. I used you."

Her eyes go wide before she reaches for the clock on the table beside her and tosses it at my head. "You're a huge asshole. Do you know that?"

"Yes," I say stiffly.

I stand here like an ass and watch as she scrambles to grab

her clothing and get dressed. "I should've known better than to fall for your smooth talk last night. Hello. I mean, you're a rock star for crying out loud. What the hell was I thinking? Madden Parker doesn't fall for women. They fall for him and end up broken."

She stops in front of me and tosses my shirt at my face. "Oh yeah. I remember now. I was thinking you were a better guy than Brad, but apparently all men are assholes. So, screw you for making me like you, *asshole*."

The door slams behind her so hard that the pictures on the wall shake.

I have no doubt that Landon and Hendrix will be making their way to my room soon, now that they know she's gone.

And I'm right, because as soon as I take a seat on the bed and place my face in my hands, the door unlocks and opens.

"You look like shit, dick." Landon steps inside and looks around the room. "What... Did you fuck her against every surface in this room? It looks more like shit than you do."

"I couldn't tell you, because I don't remember." I look around the room to see tables and other shit knocked over or out of place. "But I'm guessing... yeah. I fucking did."

Hendrix pokes his head inside but doesn't bother joining us in the chaos I created last night. "Both of you dicks need to shower. Our photoshoot is in less than an hour."

I nod and empty out my suitcase, wanting to get this shit over with so I can escape for a while. "I'll meet you guys at the bus in thirty."

"Alright, man." Landon stops at the door and turns back around. "And lay off the Jameson. You're already teetering on the edge of being smashed and it's nearly noon on a fucking Sunday."

With that he leaves me alone to get ready.

And as soon as I'm alone again, my mind turns into a whirlwind of messed up thoughts...

I TAKE A SLOW, deep breath and reach for my guitar case, before grabbing my suitcase and hoping that it's going to be a clean exit from the restroom.

I haven't had a second to even think since the moment I stepped off that plane, because I've been surrounded by screaming fans and paparazzi, despite my attempt to keep hidden by this hoodie.

My flight landed over an hour ago—the one I chose to take over driving in hopes of clearing my head—and I'm not surprised one bit that Logan hasn't shown up to pick me up yet.

I get that his job is demanding and keeps him busy, but shit, I haven't seen him in over eight months. You would think he'd put his job aside for ten minutes and remember that his baby brother is waiting for him at the airport.

He's the one who suggested he pick me up in the first place when I offered to take a taxi from the airport. He gave me this five-minute spiel about how he's my brother and there was no way in hell he was going to leave me to take a taxi when he could provide me with transportation himself.

The moment I step outside and get ready to reach for a smoke, a group of females run at me, holding up their phones and snapping as many selfies as they can get with me in them.

Keeping my cool, I lean in and pose for a few, before I take off walking and pull out my phone to see if Logan has messaged me back yet. I smile when I see a missed text from Chance. Followed by one from my brother.

7:10 P.M.
Chance: Hope you're feeling better today, Mate. Thanks to you I didn't get any sleep...again. Just for that I'm going to order a few hundred more of those

posters and leave them on unsuspecting cars. You're welcome...

7:12 P.M.
Logan: I'm in the usual spot. Where the hell are you?

Apparently, Logan messaged me back eight minutes ago and I missed it, due to the little photoshoot.

I take a second to text Chance back with a middle finger emoji and light my smoke, before I quickly make my way around the corner to see my brother leaning against his SUV, dressed in a slick blue suit.

His blond hair is smoothed back to perfection and his face is freshly shaven just like every time I see him. Brings me back to the old days.

My lips tilt up into a smile when he looks up from his phone and notices me coming at him. "Damn, big brother. Looking slick in those fancy-ass lawyer suits these days. I may need to borrow one to get in with the ladies."

Logan grins and pushes away from his Audi. "I think that leather jacket and guitar case gets you in with the ladies just fine, little brother. We both know you don't need a damn suit."

He meets me halfway, leaning in for a hug, before he looks down at his phone again and begins typing out a message, cussing under his breath.

"Busy day?"

"Yeah." He nods and rushes to open the hatch. "Sorry, I'm late. Things haven't slowed down since I crawled out of bed this morning. There's too many assholes fucking up and expecting me to fix their mistakes, and I do. I never get a break." He slaps my back and laughs, before shutting my things in. "As if I have to tell my famous little brother what that's like. Shit. I see your photos all over social media these days. Can't get online without seeing your face pop up."

"I suppose Natalie has seen a lot of me too?"

He laughs and waits for me to join him in the vehicle before he responds. "Oh yeah. She's seen them all. She spends a lot of time on social media when things are slow at the hotel. She thinks you're a fucking mess. Oh, and a huge manwhore."

"So, her opinion of me hasn't changed much then?"

"Oh, hell no. Not at all." He throws the vehicle into reverse. "We'll grab some takeout on the way to my place. Natalie won't be coming over tonight because she's stuck at the hotel late."

"Hey, takeout is what I live off of. I'm good with whatever."

"Good, because that's all you're getting."

This is where it begins.

It's two days of uninterrupted sleeping at my brother's and then I'm heading out to the middle of nowhere—no reception or interruption from the outside world—with hopefully a *girlfriend* at my side.

Sitting here next to Logan over the last hour has me thinking back to Jake's suggestion of borrowing a girl.

Logan is busy all the time with work and from what I can tell, Natalie has been needing a break from the hotel she manages. To top it off, Natalie is the one person I'd never have to worry about falling for me, or vice versa.

She's basically my only option of forcing Alana to stop with all the texts and move on already. She needs to see that I've moved on from her and that's exactly what I am going to give her.

A few hours later, I'm sitting on the couch messing around on my acoustic guitar that I keep here, when I decide to just get it over with and ask my brother for his help.

"Alana messaged me again."

He stops what he's doing to turn away from his computer. His face falls, and he swallows before speaking. "She's still at it?"

I nod and set my guitar aside. An ache fills my chest, because talking about Alana is never easy. "She texts me after every single concert talking about how much she misses me and wants me back. She's going on the trip again this year and said that we need to talk. It's dragging me down and fucking with my head. I can't do it anymore, Logan. I can't."

"Hell no. Fuck that." He leans his head back and slowly exhales, before gripping the arms of his chair. "She messed you up in a way that even scared me. I never want to see you go through that again. Not happening."

"And I never want to. Trust me. I want to move on and forget about her, but I can't unless she does first. I hate it. I hate that she has that power over me, but she does."

He flexes his jaw and rolls up the sleeves of his fitted shirt. "What does she want from you? It's been three years, and you haven't fallen back into her trap yet. Apparently, she needs to see you've moved on or something."

"I can't settle down with anyone and you know it. It's not in me anymore. If a girl I've known over half my life can lie to me the way she did then how in the hell am I supposed to trust a random girl I just meet?"

"I don't know how to answer that, but you'll never learn to trust another girl with that attitude and negative thinking."

"Maybe I don't want to."

It's quiet for a bit as I think of how to go about asking about Natalie.

"You making it this year? Jake asked about you this morning and I told him I wasn't sure."

He laughs as if I should already know the answer. I do,

and that's what I'm counting on. "You know I can't take time away from work to go on a trip to the middle of nowhere. I haven't been able to make that trip in three years."

"What about Natalie? She hasn't met the gang yet then?"

He shakes his head. "Nope. I'm not sure when she will either. There's too much going on here for me to worry about that."

"How about on Thursday?"

He gives me a dumbfounded look. "I just told you I can't make it. How would she meet everyone?"

"What if she came with me on the trip?"

He laughs, before his face turns serious. "What, as your *fake* girlfriend or something?"

I lean forward and place my elbows on my knees, wanting him to see I'm dead serious about this and need it to happen. "You know more than anyone that nothing would ever happen between the two of us. She'd be the perfect one to help get me out of this situation with Alana's crazy ass."

"I don't think so. No. Nope."

"I wouldn't ask you if I didn't think it was necessary. I have no other options and you know it. Alana won't stop until either we're back together or I've dropped dead from alcohol poisoning."

"What the hell? Don't say that shit." He's quiet for a few minutes, as if he's thinking it over. "What would she have to do if I agreed to this? And..." He shakes his head and re-rolls his sleeves. He always does this when he's nervous. "She'd have to agree to it too. So, *if* she agrees... let's say she does; then what would be involved in being your girlfriend for the trip? Give it to me straight or the answer is a big hell no."

"I don't know. Me wrapping my arm around her shoulder by the bonfire... dancing with me. She'd definitely have to kiss me from time to time to make it look real, but *no* sex if that's what you're asking."

"Well, shit, Madden. You've put me in a tough spot." He runs his hands over his face and stands up, looking distressed. "No groping. Definitely no tongue or I'll kick your ass. You know I will. And the only reason I'm agreeing to this fucked up insanity is because I don't want you getting wrapped up in Alana and getting hurt again. Also, because there's no way in hell that Natalie would ever fall for you—she doesn't even really like you." He laughs, as if it's the last thing on earth that would ever happen. And it probably is.

"I'll take it, big brother. You know she'll be safe in my hands. Then, later, if you decide to take the trip next year, we can just tell everyone that we broke up because I was on the road a lot and you were there to pick up the pieces. Her hero in a fancy suit."

"Well, good luck talking Natalie into it tomorrow." He sits back down and begins typing on the computer again, answering emails. "I'm sure she'll get a kick out of this."

Yeah, and knowing Natalie I'll probably get kicked for asking...

CHAPTER THREE

NATALIE

I take long, slow breaths in an attempt to keep my cool as I hop on the elevator and ride it up to the third floor for the third time in an hour.

I swear, if these jerks get locked out of their room one more time because they decided it was cool to party in the hallway and keep calling me up to let them back inside as if my job is a joke, I will most likely end up getting fired tonight for hurting someone's pride.

The elevator opens to one of the drunken idiots standing at the door, apparently waiting on me, because he immediately begins walking beside me, clearly checking me out on our way down the *long* hallway. It's way too long right now if you ask me, and I'm two seconds away from losing my cool and calm attitude.

"Are you single?" he asks immediately.

I clench my jaw. "Not a chance."

He flashes me a flirtatious smile that does nothing but piss me off more. "Maybe we should change that."

"Maybe we shouldn't," I hiss. "Now stop talking."

"Someone's a little bitchy. I bet that means you're aggressive and angry in bed too. Are you?"

"Maybe. But you'll never find out."

"Maybe not, but I'm always up for a challenge, beautiful. And since you're already here and all, maybe we can..."

When I feel him walking too closely to me, I stop and place my hand on his chest, pushing him a good distance outside of my personal space. "Back up, creepy little stalker, unless you and your friends want to experience the most miserable night of your sorry existence."

He throws his hands up and laughs, as if he's having fun getting rejected. Apparently, he's one of those assholes who get off on the chase.

The closer I get to the room I take notice of just how quiet the hall is. It was extremely loud the last two times I came up here, which tells me Douchey here most likely called me back up here just to try getting in my pants.

Getting more frustrated with each step I take, I quicken my pace and turn the corner to look down the hall, seeing that it's empty.

It's completely vacant, which means this little player wannabe isn't locked out of the room at all. His idiotic friends are inside, most likely cheering him on to see how far he'll get with me.

I stop in place and reach into my pocket, before turning around to face this little pretty-boy who I want nothing more than to punch in the balls right now.

Stepping up to him, I place my mini pink stun gun to his dick and lean in to press my lips to his ear. "Since you didn't know I was carrying this cute little thing, I'm going to give you a chance to apologize before I roast your tiny manhood."

Stiffening up, he slowly lowers his chin to look down and see what's currently threatening his precious little package.

"Oh shit. Oh shit. I'm sorry. I didn't mean any harm. My friends and I are just drinking and having fun. Fuck, and for the love of God, do not use that thing on my dick."

I tilt my head and smile, because I'm the one amused now. "Good boy. Now run along and tell your friends not to bother me or the staff again for the rest of the night. If you get locked out again, you're shit out of luck. You can sleep in the hallway. Got it?"

He nods his head but doesn't speak. He's still too focused on his pride getting hurt.

"Good. Glad we got that taken care of." I bump him out of the way with my shoulder and begin walking the opposite direction. "Oh, and by the way... I *am* very aggressive and angry in bed too. You would've never been able to handle me."

His eyes go wide, before he grabs his dick and begins swearing under his breath.

Smiling, I shove the stun gun back into my pocket and step into the elevator. Pete would probably rip me a new asshole if he knew I was still carrying this thing while on duty, but I feel much better being here at night knowing that me and my crew have some sort of protection. You never know what you're going to find in the middle of the night at a hotel, and security isn't always close enough by to get to a situation in a timely manner.

I tend to pull it out more when I'm on edge, and this dumbass picked the wrong time of day to mess with me. Once ten p.m. hits, it's best not to provoke me unless you want an extremely furious woman to deal with.

That's exactly why I do everything in my power to be out of this place before then, but sometimes, like tonight, I have no choice in the matter.

Gigi called off, Hilary couldn't get a babysitter, and Amy doesn't get back from vacation until tomorrow, so Kayla and I had to split her shift. It's now almost one a.m. and close to time for me to get out of this nightmare, which I've been at since noon.

Kayla gives me an irritated look once we meet up at the front desk. "I wish they would just fire Gigi already. This is getting ridiculous. Do you know that my shift starts at nine a.m. and ends at five? How do they expect me to function during the daytime rushes when I have to be here right now to cover this bitch's shift?"

I shake my head while clocking out, and then reach under the desk for some of my things. "I know. I've been here all day and I'm tired of this crap too. I'll talk to Pete tomorrow —*after* I get some rest—and tell him that he needs to hire someone else because we can't keep doing this anymore."

"Don't you have some vacation days to use up soon? There's no way I can handle this crap job without you unless he gets us someone else."

"Yeah, I have to use them by next week or I lose them. You know Logan though. I likely won't be using them, because I'll have no reason to. I'll end up stuck here, taking on late shifts and filling in for incompetent employees."

"I hope so."

"Well, that's real nice. What a friend you are."

Kayla laughs and reaches for her bottle of soda. "I'm sorry, but it's true. I need you here with me, so I'm sort of glad that Logan is always too busy for you."

"Hey!"

"Again, I'm sorry. But you know it's true. You two have been dating for almost two years now and he's never taken you anywhere. I mean at all. Not the movies. Not out dancing. Not on any vacations. Nothing. Just dinner that he always seems to get rushed through. It's a little pathetic. My worst boyfriend was better than that."

I lean against the desk, somewhat feeling sorry for myself

now that I've had to listen to it come from someone else's mouth. "Yeah, well... I knew what I was getting into with him when we met. I can't complain now, and I won't. He's a good guy and he treats me well. What else could a girl want?"

Kayla gives me a *duh* look and leans in close to me from the opposite end of the desk. "Some excitement. How about that for one? Some wild, crazy sex on occasion. There are two. A guy who takes her places to meet his friends... That's three. Should I keep going?"

"Okay." I stand back up and release a frustrated breath, wishing that she'd stop pointing out all the obvious things I've been trying to deny. "I guess. But I'm sure he will when he's not busy. Besides, none of his close friends live around here. He hasn't seen them since we've been together."

"Isn't that trip you're always talking about coming up this weekend or something? Let me guess. He's not going again?"

"Yes and no. His little brother is at his house now and I guess he's heading out on Thursday."

Kayla is quick to perk up at the mention of Madden. "Whoa! Whoa! Whoa! Madden Parker is here in town and you failed to mention that to me?"

"He's a manwhore, Kayla. Trust me, you don't want to meet him or else you'll end up in his bed with a broken heart just like every single girl he's slept with."

"And your point is?"

I laugh and begin walking away. "You don't want to be one of those girls. Everyone thinks they can handle it until experiencing it. I've heard it takes years to get over a guy like Madden Parker."

"With looks like that I wouldn't care if it took ten years, as long as I got my one night with that man."

"Bye, Kayla!"

"Yeah. Whatever." She waves me off with a dreamy look in her eyes. "I'm daydreaming now. Just go so I can be alone in my thoughts of that sexy as hell rock star since you won't bring him here for me to meet. Or will you?"

The front desk phone rings and I'm thankful for the distraction.

"Good luck with that."

"Ugh. You're lucky." She throws her head back and grunts, before picking up the phone.

I seize this opportunity to get the hell out of here before I end up stuck here longer talking about my boyfriend's playboy of a brother. I just can't deal with that right now.

Remembering I have to drop off the phone charger that I borrowed earlier, I head across the street to *Sunrise Motel* and walk to the adjacent bar. I'm immediately greeted by Carla, the bartender, whom I met a couple years ago when first starting at *Brightside*.

"Hey, babe!" She extends her tatted-up arm out to reach for the charger when I hold it out. "Oh good, you brought my charger back. I have less than ten percent battery power left."

"Sorry, I thought I'd have it back sooner. It's been a hell of a night."

"Want to talk about it?" She leans over the bar and places a fist under her chin for support. "I'm not going anywhere anytime soon. Lay it on me."

I smile, grateful for her always being willing to listen and offer up advice. "As nice as that sounds, I'm beat. I'm barely keeping my eyes open as we speak."

"You sure?" She reaches up to play with one of the old school curls on top of her head. "How about a drink to take the edge off?"

"Tempting... so tempting, but I should go. Maybe tomorrow tonight."

"Sounds good." She winks and moves to plug her charger in. "Have a good night, babe. Get some rest."

"Later, Carla."

Once I get to my car and start driving, I realize just how tired I truly am, and decide to head to Logan's place instead of mine since it's closer.

I seriously don't know if I can make it the extra ten or twelve minutes to my place, and knowing Logan, he gave his bedroom to his brother since I told him I wasn't coming tonight.

That means I'll have to squeeze my way onto the couch beside him, while at the same time doing my best not to wake him up and disrupt his sleep.

His day starts in less than four hours and he needs every minute of sleep he can get. He's insistent on making that clear every time we have a sleepover. As much as it annoys me, I get where he's coming from. His job is very demanding and stressful.

I do my best to be as quiet as possible as I stand on his front porch and dig through my messy purse for the spare key.

It's so dark out here that I have to use the flashlight on my phone while trying to hold my purse and dig at the same time. It's not an easy task and my brain is too exhausted to think straight right now.

"Thank fucking goodness!" Once I finally find the key, I turn off the flashlight and drop my phone into my purse so I can unlock the door and quietly creep inside.

I can see the shape of Logan's body spread across the couch and covered up by a sheet, so I carefully strip down to my underwear and bra and climb over him to get to the back of the couch.

Then I carefully lift the sheet and shimmy my way under it, before I wrap my arm around Logan and snuggle up against him.

He's shirtless, so his warm, muscled body feels fantastic against mine, and I find myself running my hand over his arm and leg until I finally begin to doze off.

"...wake up."

I snuggle in closer, too out of it to understand anything. "Shhh... go back to sleep, Logan."

He struggles to lay on his back, before he whispers something that I can't understand.

All I want to do is sleep, so I rest my head on his chest and run my hand down his hard stomach, resting it inside the waistband of his briefs.

"... not Logan."

The words *not* and *Logan* somehow register in my mind and I pull my hand out of Madden's underwear and shoot up so fast that I end up elbowing him in the face.

"Ouch," he grunts.

"Oh shit! I thought you were your brother. I didn't... Why are you... Shit!"

I'm already ducking behind the couch and doing my best to cover up when Madden sits up and looks over the edge with a smirk. "Nice undies."

"Shut up, Madden!" I whisper-yell. "You always sleep in the bedroom. You were supposed to be Logan."

He laughs quietly, reaching over to grab for a cigarette. "Well, I'm not." He doesn't even bother grabbing for his pants to cover up after he throws the sheet off and stands up. He just walks to the backdoor and opens it, standing there in the dim lighting with his perfectly sculpted body. "I need a smoke after all that groping you were doing."

"I wasn't groping." I reach over the couch and yank the sheet around me to cover up. "It's not my fault you and your brother are built alike."

He lights his smoke and takes a drag before speaking. "We're not. I'm bigger and harder all over. Trust me, babe. You can tell the difference."

"I don't even know why I'm talking to you right now. All I want to do is sleep. I had a long, shitty day. I'm tired and I can't function right." I shoot him a dirty look that he most likely can't see very well from where I'm standing and make my way to Logan's bedroom door, my heart racing with adrenaline. "Let's just forget this ever happened. It was a mistake."

I feel like such an idiot as I step inside Logan's room and shut the door behind me. I should've checked first instead of just assuming that Logan would be on the couch, and as exhausted as I was the only thing on my mind was sleep.

I just want to sleep.

I take a few seconds to clear my head of Madden's hard, half-naked body before I crawl into Logan's bed and snuggle up behind him.

A feeling of guilt takes over, because now that I'm snuggled up behind Logan and I'm aware of what I'm doing, the difference between their bodies is extremely clear.

This only proves just how out of it I was when arriving here tonight.

I move in closer, needing to touch the right Parker Brother right now. *My* Parker Brother.

"It's hot in here, babe," Logan mutters, while shaking my arm off of him. "You against me is going to keep me awake. I need my sleep."

"Sorry," I whisper, before backing up a bit to put some space between our bodies. My stomach twists into knots as I stare at the back of his head in the darkness, wanting nothing more than to hold him or to have him hold me. To feel some kind of comfort after such a long, hard day of hell at the hotel.

There's my clue. That's how I should've known it was Madden on the couch and not his brother.

He actually didn't complain about me being too close. If I had been more aware, I would've caught that.

Maybe I should've just stayed on the couch where I was at least warm and cozy. In my mind it was Logan at least, and I liked that Logan... a lot.

CHAPTER FOUR

MADDEN

WHEN I ROLLED OFF THE COUCH THIS MORNING, THE FIRST thing I thought about was Natalie crawling into bed with me —or should I say the couch—last night, thinking I was my brother.

I could've had so much fun with that, and given her a reason to agree to come with me tomorrow, but I figured if I let her hand go where we both know it was headed, she probably would've kicked my ass and gave me a definite no.

To be honest, it felt nice having her snuggled up against me with no expectation of sex. She was so warm and soft, and her touch felt genuine, unlike the girls I've been with since Alana.

She might not have known it was me, but it still felt good to just lay there and accept the comfort her touch was bringing.

I was awake for a good ten minutes before I forced myself to wake her up; before things could get more confusing or Logan came to find us snuggled together on the couch.

Had that happened, there's no way in hell he'd still agree to me borrowing her for the trip. Not if he actually saw with his own two eyes how we looked together.

No fucking way.

I'm positive the two of us looked hot as hell lying there on the couch, half-naked and tangled up together. It *felt* hot at least, and *she* sure as hell looked hot. My brother has been holding out on me.

When I opened my eyes and looked behind me, she was lying there with her thick strands of mahogany colored hair falling over her delicate face. Her full lips were slightly parted and pressed against my shoulder.

Would it be wrong to admit that seeing my brother's girl half-naked when she jumped up and elbowed me made my dick twitch with excitement?

Yeah, I thought so. It's probably best to keep that shit to myself.

It's half past two, so I'm at the coffee shop getting some bagels and coffee to bring to Logan's office.

I want to see him again before I head out to ask Natalie about the trip. I have to make sure he was serious when he agreed to this. Plus, I need him to tell me what time she goes into work so I can catch her, since she was already gone when I woke up this morning.

With a smile, the blonde cashier slips me my receipt and then a piece of blank receipt paper. She can hardly stand still. "Can I get your autograph?" she whispers excitedly. "I've been waiting for you to come back ever since I missed you last time. Everyone here talked about it for weeks and rubbed it in my face. I was so pissed I had that day off."

I tilt my head up and lift a brow as she frantically searches for a pen, completely missing the one that's right beside the register. "Looking for this?" I grab the pen and take the cap off with my teeth, before jotting down a quick message and signing it. "Here you go, Lindsey."

I wink and toss the pen down, before scooting the receipt paper across the counter to her.

With a quickness I haven't witnessed in a long time, or maybe even ever, she grabs the pen and shoves it into her shirt pocket. "Holy shit! I'll be keeping this *forever*. Thank you, Madden! You've just made me one happy barista. Everyone else here can suck it, because I'll be getting them back for last time. *Screw* them for rubbing it in my face. Wasn't cool at all."

I nod my head, grab for my order, and exit the coffee shop before anyone else takes notice of me being here. I'm thankful for her being quiet, and pretty positive it was solely because she wanted to be the *only* one there to get to see me this time, since apparently, she missed out last time.

Sometimes this hoodie is an acceptable disguise, but when someone has the chance to look at me straight on, it's obvious who I am.

I'm doing my best to make it through this last day before I finally get to be where I know no one will give a shit about my autograph or taking photos with me. The one place I can be myself and not have to impress anyone.

There I can be the same ole Madden Parker who plays guitar by the bonfire for the simple fact that I enjoy playing for my friends and have since I was sixteen.

When I enter the law office Logan works at, a few cute women check me out as I make my way past the front desk and to my brother's office, but none of them make a show of it, which makes me happy. I'm sure they've been told to act professional if I come in, thank God.

Logan is on the phone when I step into his office, so I quietly shut the door behind me and toss the bag of bagels at him.

He misses and gives me a stern look as I set his coffee down in front of him.

"Like I said—I'll see what I can do. I'm a lawyer, not a fucking miracle worker, John. Yes... I know this, and I always do, don't I?"

I stand back with my arms crossed and watch as he paces his office with a flexed jaw. He does this for a few minutes before he finally ends the call and takes a seat on the edge of his desk.

"Shit, it's been a stressful day." He breaks a small smile when he notices my eye. "Who did you get the shiner from?"

"Your girlfriend."

"No shit?" He laughs and reaches into the bag. "I take it she said no then?"

"Nope." I grab for my own bagel and bite into it, before continuing. "I haven't asked her yet." I point at my eye. "This happened when she accidentally crawled onto the couch with me late last night and then realized she was cuddling the wrong Parker Brother."

He narrows his green eyes at me while taking a sip of his coffee. "And that's exactly why I know I don't have to worry about her. Now you on the other hand..." He sets his coffee down and stands up to roll his sleeves up. "What did you do to get punched in the fucking eye?"

"Not let her grope me." I say teasingly. "She didn't take it too well, as you can see. Clearly, my body is irresistible."

He clenches his jaw, *clearly* starting to rethink his previous answer of letting her go on the trip. It's time to stop pushing him before I ruin my chances of him trusting me with her. Without Natalie I'll be shit out of luck.

"She slipped her hand under the waistband of my pants and when I woke her up she freaked out and got me good with her elbow. It was an accident. And then she gave me the usual attitude and joined you in bed. Calm your fancy slacks, big brother. Nothing happened."

"Yeah, well... I didn't think so."

"When does she go into work? I was hoping to catch her there, so she has a little time to consider it before I leave. I'm heading out tomorrow evening, which doesn't leave much time for her to agree."

He looks down at his watch. "In about twenty minutes. But she gets really pissy if you bother her when she first gets there. She usually has a lot of shit to catch up on from the night before. Trust me, it's best to wait until later."

I grin and slap his shoulder. "Thanks, brother, but I'm sure I can handle her."

"You're lucky I love your ass and want what's best for you, because this is an extremely fucked-up request. If anyone else asked to borrow my girl I'd probably kill them with my bare hands."

"Good thing I'm not anyone else then, brother." I stop at the door. "Oh yeah. You might want to tell me her favorite dessert, aside from rock hard abs that is..." I lift a brow as I watch him tense up again. "I'm joking. I need to butter her up a bit if I'm going to have any chance of her saying yes. We both know this."

"Caramel cheesecake from the bar across the street from the hotel. The one Carla works at." Clearly annoyed with my mouth, he huffs and rerolls his sleeves again. "You're going to send my stress level through the damn roof today, Madden. Get out of my office before I change my mind. You've got five seconds."

I hold my bagel up to him and say, "You're welcome for the bagels, dick," before I disappear out his office door.

One of the women checking me out when I first walked in flashes me a seductive smile and bites her bottom lip as I walk past the front desk.

She clearly wants what I'm packing, but unfortunately, right now I'm not in the mood to take some hot secretary into the bathroom and bend her over like the last time I visited this place. It ended messy and I can't do messy right now.

Plus, I have something way more important on my mind, so I keep on walking, not stopping until I'm getting into my old truck. Once inside, I head toward *Sunrise Motel* and hope like hell that getting Natalie some cheesecake from Carla is going to be good enough to make her hate me just a tad bit less than normal.

When I step into the bar, Carla is wiping down the counter while in conversation with an elderly man. "Take a seat, babe, and I'll be right with you," she says without looking my way.

"How's my favorite girl?" I take a seat on the nearest barstool and grin when Carla's head shoots my way, her eyes widening when they land on me.

She smiles and tosses her towel down. "Holy shit! I was wondering when I'd see my favorite rock star again." She rushes over to give me a hug, before examining me. "You look *good,* Madden. Much better than the last time I saw you."

"Yeah, well, that's because it's been almost a year since I've seen that crazy bitch Alana." I take a seat again and Carla moves back behind the bar. "I can't say that for long, though."

"Shit. It's that time again, isn't it?"

I nod. "Yup. But that's the reason I'm here. Well, other than coming to see you, of course."

Her smile widens. "Let me guess... you need some advice?"

"What I actually need is cheesecake?"

"Really?" she questions, giving me a suspicious look. "You don't even like cheesecake."

"It's not for me. It's for Nat."

She places her hand on her hip and narrows her eyes at

me. "Explain," she motions to my face, "because I'm not sure I like that look."

"I'm going to ask Nat to come with me," I say simply. "As my *girlfriend*."

"Whoa... okay. I was *not* expecting that." She leans over the bar, her questioning eyes meeting mine. "I'm completely missing something here. Natalie never told me you two were a couple now. What about your brother?"

"We're not a couple," I clarify. "She's still with my brother. Nothing about that has changed, Carla." I stand up and smirk. "Except the fact that Nat is going to be my pretend girlfriend for six days. At least, I hope." I nod toward the cooler. "So, I'll be needing that cheesecake to butter her up."

Her mouth drops open as she stands up straight. "Do I need to tell you how bad of an idea this is?"

"Nope. I've got it all under control, babe. Now are you going to help your favorite rock star out and give me that cheesecake I asked for? Might want to make it the biggest piece. I need all the help I can get."

Shaking her head, she walks to the cooler and grabs the biggest slice of caramel cheesecake she can find and sets it down in front of me. "Just be careful, Madden. The last thing you want is for things to get messy for you and your brother. Pretending to date someone isn't as easy as it may seem. Feelings sometimes get involved. Are you ready for that possibility?"

I toss down a twenty and grab the back of her head, planting a firm kiss on her forehead. "Nothing to worry about, babe. Nat practically hates my guts anyway. What could possibly go wrong?" I hold up the container while backing toward the exit. "Thanks for always having my back. I'll see you when we get back."

Once back inside my truck, I set the cheesecake down and make my way across the street. When I pull up in the parking lot of *Brightside Hotel,* a text from Alana comes through that has me wanting this to happen more than ever now.

I *need* Natalie to agree to this.

3:10 PM
Alana: I think I should sleep in your room again this time. It'll give us some private time to talk. I can cuddle and rub you like old times. I miss that more than anything. The way your body feels beneath my fingertips. I miss you, Madden, and I know you miss me too. See you soon.

I squeeze my busted-up phone, before tossing it into the backseat with a growl, and then reach beside me for the container of cheesecake.

I have a feeling that Alana is going to be the cause of me having to replace my phone yet again. It's pretty much on its last leg now, and all it'll take is one more time of me throwing it for it to die.

Those shitty cases and screen protectors are nothing compared to my anger, apparently.

I step out of the truck, already lighting a cigarette to help calm my nerves. I quickly finish it before I walk inside and begin my search for the one woman who can hopefully get me out of this mess with Alana.

She's not at the front desk, and since no one else is, I take a seat in the chair and answer the phone when it rings. "Brightside Hotel. What's up?"

"Ummm..." a confused female voice says. "You're not Natalie. What are you doing answering the phone?"

"It rang," I say simply. "Where is Natalie, by the way?"

"Is this Logan?"

"Do I sound like I have a stick up my ass?"

"Well... no. Ooh! Ooh! Wait!" her voice turns to excitement. "This is the sexy little brother, right? The lead singer of *RISK*."

"You'd be correct."

"Do not leave. I repeat, do not leave! I'm heading down to the desk. Oh my god!"

Before I even have a chance to say anything the ecstatic girl hangs up on me.

I look down at the phone and shrug. "Well, all right then."

I hear footsteps coming up behind me right before I hear her angry voice. The same one she used on me last night before rushing off in a hurry.

She's probably still embarrassed, and I don't blame her. She almost groped my dick. Maybe I should have let her...

"What the hell are you doing behind the desk, Madden? Are you trying to get me fired?" Natalie moves around to face me and snatches the phone from my hand with a scowl. I can't help but to notice once again just how cute she is when she's angry. "And you seriously answered a phone call? Get up out of that chair. Hurry, there's cameras for fuck's sake."

She gives me an annoyed look and pushes my chest, until I finally stand up from the chair and look her over. "Is this what you consider foreplay, because I think it's working."

"You're an idiot. What do you want?"

"I brought a peace offering." I smile, sliding the cheesecake across the desk. "Calm down. I'm only messing with you because I know my brother doesn't know how to have any fun. And I thought you could use this."

Her attention focuses on the container as I tap the top of it. "Is some small rodent going to jump out at me if I open it?"

"No, but I can arrange that if it makes you happy. What would you like? A baby bunny? I don't think that's going to fit in this container, though."

"What would make me happy is for you to tell me what you want so I can get back to work. Really, Madden, I'm extremely busy and this day is not starting out well for me. I have too much crap to do and I'm close to choking someone. Do you want that someone to be you?"

Her ice-blue eyes pierce into me as she slams the phone down.

Shit, my brother was right. I probably should've waited a bit to show up. I'm positive she hates me even more right now. The simple act of me breathing seems to be pissing her off more by the second.

But it's now or never.

"I need to ask you a favor and it's important to me." I flex my jaw, giving her a serious look. I may joke and mess around with her a lot, but she needs to see that I *do* have feelings too. "Just promise me you'll consider it before saying no. Please. I need you to promise."

Her blue eyes roam over my face, softening a bit once she realizes just how hard this must be for me to do. "Yeah, okay. I promise. Is everything okay?"

I swallow and open the container of cheesecake, hoping that it'll at least help me out and let her see that I'm considerate when I want to be.

I just haven't *wanted* to be in a while.

A small smile crosses her face once her eyes move from me to her favorite dessert. "You asked your brother what I like?"

I nod. "I did."

"Go on," she says softly, before clearing her throat and trying to pretend that I haven't impressed her. "Ask me, so I can get back to work."

"Okay. I need you to go on the trip with me and pretend to be my girlfriend in front of my old friends. Specifically, Alana... my ex."

She must be stunned, because she can't seem to speak for a good ten seconds. "Wait... what?"

"Be my girlfriend for six days. Please. I *need* you to do this for me, Nat."

She lets out a nervous laugh and begins organizing things on the desk. "You're insane, Madden. I can't do that."

"Why not?"

"Because I'm dating your brother. That's why. Can't you choose some random girl you've slept with or something? I'm sure they'd do just about anything to spend time with you."

I shake my head and walk behind the desk to get her to look at me. "I can't ask anyone else. Every girl I've slept with has become obsessed with me and hates me for not wanting a relationship. I need someone who won't fall for me and I know I can count on that when it comes to you."

She looks up at me from the desk and laughs. "So, I'm the only girl in the whole damn world who won't fall for *the* Madden Parker? Is that what you're saying?"

I nod my head. "Yes. You're the only one so far. Everyone else is blinded by the fame."

"Holy. Shit. It is you."

Natalie and I turn away from each other at the sound of phone girl's voice.

A cute short-haired brunette pushes her breasts up and quickly fixes her hair to get my attention. "Can we just get married so we can do this thing?"

"See what I mean?" I point out.

"Really, Kayla?" Natalie rolls her eyes and turns her attention back to me. "Okay, I get your point. But I'm sorry. I can't just leave. I have a lot of work to do around here, and besides that... I'm dating your *brother*. I can't just show up where all your old mutual friends are and act as *your* girlfriend. It would cause a mess later."

Her co-worker's eyes widen as she shakes her head in confusion. "Say what?"

I move in closer to Natalie, wishing I could do something to change her mind, but I know that I need to be careful. Usually the brushing of my lips over any girl's neck is enough to change their mind, but I can't do that with *her*. So, my words will have to do. "You and I both know that Logan doesn't plan on going anytime soon. None of our friends even know you exist. Of course you can show up as *my* girlfriend. No one would know any different."

"Oh wow." Kayla swipes her finger across the cheesecake and sucks it off. "This is entertaining. I'll be asking lots of questions once this is over, and FYI, the marriage offer still stands. Please keep going."

Natalie narrows her eyes at her co-worker and begins walking toward the exit door. "I'll be back, Kayla. I need some fresh air. I can't breathe in here."

Not ready to give up, I follow Natalie outside and grab her waist before she can get too far from me.

She quickly turns around and gets in my face, our bodies so close that her breasts swipe against the front of my hoodie. "Thanks for pointing that out, jerk. I feel like such an idiot now thanks to you."

"Whoa!" I grab her arm and stop her from trying to walk away again. "What the hell did I do? I'm not the enemy here. Talk to me."

Her face is red, and when she speaks, she's so angry that she sounds out of breath. "You just had to go and say it out loud. That's what you did." She turns her head away as if ashamed, so I grab her chin and turn it back toward me.

"What? That our friends don't know about you?"

She doesn't say anything, which tells me I'm right.

I flex my jaw, feeling like an insensitive jerk. "I didn't

mean to make it sound as bad as it did. I'm sorry, Nat. I just meant that work is Logan's priority right now."

"Doesn't matter how you said it..." She removes my hand from her chin and backs away from me. "It's the truth. I've been with Logan for almost two years and his friends have no clue who I am. The truth is, I've been wanting to go on that trip since he first told me you guys all get together every year no matter what your lives are like, just so you can all be together like old times. That seems important. These people seem really important, and I haven't had the chance to meet any of them yet."

"You can meet them with me."

"Then what? What happens if Logan decides to go next year? Do I pretend to go with you again? The rock star's girlfriend? Or do I end up being that girl that switched teams and started dating the other brother?"

I shake my head and push my hood back. "Next year I'll have moved on. We tell them that I was on the road too much and Logan was there for you. No hard feelings. It's an easy fix."

"And as your girlfriend, what does that entail? I have to kiss you? Have sex with you?" She laughs. "This all sounds ridiculous."

"Nah. Of course not." I lift a brow as her eyes meet mine. "Just the kissing part. But just in front of people like any happy couple would do."

She bursts out into a fit of laughter.

"What's so funny about that?" I lean against the building and pull out a smoke, waiting for her response. She's really finding the whole kissing me thing to be funny. That's a damn good way to destroy a man's ego.

It takes her a minute or two, but she finally stops laughing. "I can't imagine *ever* wanting to kiss you. And I sure as hell can't imagine your brother wanting that either."

"He already does." I take a long drag and slowly blow the smoke out while talking. "He's already agreed to it."

She freezes and her face turns from one of hurt to anger, before she rips the cigarette from my hand and flicks it across the parking lot. "The answer is no. Now leave me the hell alone."

With that, she pushes the revolving door with force, disappearing inside.

Once I'm alone, I rub my hands down my face, feeling like crap for upsetting her over this shit.

I've never seen her this upset since I've known her, and I have to admit that it has my chest feeling heavy.

I feel like a fucking asshole, and that's not how I wanted this to go, but apparently the truth made me one.

If Logan would step his game up and treat Natalie better none of this would've happened, because she wouldn't have had a reason to feel like crap just now.

I have to admit that even I think it's weird he hasn't taken Natalie to meet our old friends, or at least mention her to them.

I might not be the right Parker Brother, but I'd like nothing more than to bring her to them.

She's beautiful.

Smart.

Independent.

Confident.

Honest and feisty as hell.

All the qualities I would look for in a woman I wanted to spend my time with. And I especially love a woman who can put me in my place. She's done that more times than I can count over the years.

That's another reason it'd be believable as her being mine. My friends know me well, and most of the girls I've slept with since Alana wouldn't even come close to being believable relationship material.

They'd see right through it after only the first day.

"Shit. I'm screwed."

A part of me wants to go inside and talk to Natalie, but doing that will piss her off even more, and probably lead to her using her stun gun on me.

It almost happened once.

After a few minutes, I push away from the building and head toward my truck.

I have no idea what to do to make her change her mind, but I need to figure it out, and fast...

CHAPTER FIVE

NATALIE

I'M FUMING RIGHT NOW. THE PARKER BROTHERS THINKING it was perfectly okay to make this decision without me makes me want to slap them both straight.

Who do they think they are to discuss *me* without my knowledge? Especially when it includes me being borrowed by one of them as if I'm someone's property.

I feel like such a fool right now. Like I don't know my own boyfriend at all.

Logan agreed to this?

He actually agreed to me going away with his womanizing, rock star little brother without any worry of what could happen for six days. That doesn't sound like him at all. It doesn't make sense.

If he truly cared about me, he'd want to keep me *away* from Madden, not place me right in his arms when he knows how easily women fall into bed with him.

Without even realizing what I'm doing, I'm slamming things around on the desk, letting my anger out, when I hear a few screams of excitement from a group of teenaged girls sitting in the lounge pointing outside and pulling out their phones.

They weren't down here when Madden was inside, but now that he's walking through the parking lot with his hood down, he's recognizable to anyone within a visible distance.

There's no way possible that man can go anywhere and not be noticed by at least one person. Even without the fame of his band.

He's extremely *hot*.

His dark hair, perfectly sculpted body, and sexy, full lips make him impossible to miss. Yes, I hate to admit it, but it's true.

No one with eyes could deny it.

Madden Parker is every girl's weakness.

But for me... he's also my boyfriend's brother.

His brother who's quick to just give me away, apparently.

I shake my head and turn away from the fangirls, trying my best not to pay attention to them, but I find myself watching them as they run out the door and chase down Madden before he can hop in his truck.

I've never seen anything like it. Girls cling to Madden as if they need him to breathe.

"Do you see those girls?" Kayla huffs. "They have no shame at all. Chasing that poor, sexy rock star down and jumping all over him like Girl Scouts selling cookies."

I give her a 'did you really just say that' look while plopping down in the chair Madden easily made his not too long ago. When I came out of the office and saw him sitting here, my heart jumped at the memory of last night and how good it felt to be snuggled up against his body.

Yeah, I didn't know who he was, but that doesn't change the fact that I enjoyed the way his body felt against mine.

That's another reason this whole idea is a bad one.

A very bad one.

"You asked the guy to marry you, Kayla. You have no room to talk." She shrugs when I look up at her and then goes back to watching Madden and the girls outside the door. "You gonna get back to work or run out there and attack him with photos too?"

"Now that you mentioned it... I didn't have a chance to get one." She quickly digs into her back pocket, grins at me, and rushes out the door.

"You've got to be shitting me," I mumble to myself while throwing my arms up.

Did she really think that was an invitation for her to join them outside like a groupie?

I find my attention lingering back over on the little show outside, until the hotel phone rings, pulling me back to my duties.

"Brightside Hotel, Natalie speaking."

There's a grunt before a gruff voice comes through the line. "I need to cancel a reservation for tonight, and I need a refund on my account too."

Really? This asshole has bad timing.

"I can cancel your reservation, sir, but I can't issue you a refund. The room must be canceled with a twenty-four-hour notice for you to not be charged."

"Bullshit! Don't you give me that shit," he screams, causing me to pull the phone away and cuss under my breath. "I'm not paying for something I'm not going to use."

"Sir, it's hotel policy and has been from the very beginning. That was explained to you when you made your reservation, and you agreed. I'm sorry—"

"Put a manager on the phone, girl. I'm not going to sit here and waste my time on a nobody like you that's not going to give me what I want."

I growl and grip the desk, trying my best not to snap on

this asshole. "I am the manager, sir. Sorry for the disappoint-ment, but as I said before—"

"I'm not paying shit for that room, and if I find a charge on my account, I will call my lawyer and sue this shitty hotel for stealing from me..."

I pull the phone away from my ear as he continues to scream at me, as if it's going to get him what he wants. I'm dating a fucking lawyer, I know that's not how it works.

"Need me to deal with someone for you?"

I hadn't even realized Madden came back inside, but when I look up, he's standing in front of the desk with his eyebrow cocked, listening to the dickhead's angry voice coming from the phone.

From the look on his face I'd say he's not too happy. "Give me the phone."

"I'm good. I handle assholes like this daily."

Releasing a breath, I place the phone back to my ear and cut him off. "Feel free to contact the owner and tell him that his policy is shit, but I can assure you that you still won't be getting your money back, because now we have a room to fill and no time to do it, so have a great day, sir."

With that, I hang up the phone, slamming it down harder than I should.

The day has barely started and I'm already over it. This place has done nothing but stress me out ever since I was promoted to manager. I'm seriously going to lose my shit if I don't get away soon.

"What happened to your army of groupies?" I look around and don't see the three girls or even Kayla, which surprises me.

"I gave them some of my clothing and they took off in a hurry to most likely post all over social media."

I stand up and check him out, noticing that his hoodie and belt are now gone, and I can't help but to be slightly entertained by this. "Nice. But where's Kayla? I need her here working."

He leans against the desk and crosses his arms, giving me a good view of his sculpted biceps. "She's outside making a call to your boss to let him know that she'll be covering your shift for the rest of the day."

He has to be joking, so I play along with him. "Oh yeah? And what did you have to give Kayla to get her to agree to that? One of your socks or both?"

"My underwear," he says with a serious face. I laugh but stop when I look up to find his expression unchanged.

"Are you for real?"

"I can show you if you'd like, but I'm not sure my brother would appreciate that. Now, let's get the hell out of here so you can pack. I'll help."

He reaches out and grabs the cheesecake before reaching for my hand as if he's just won.

"Whoa!" I pull away as he helps me to my feet. "I'm not going, Madden. Don't make me explain myself again. Please, just leave before I really lose it. I'm pissed at you Parker boys. Did you miss the conversation we had outside less than five minutes ago?"

"What if I apologize? I'll apologize the whole way there if you'll just say yes."

"Go, girl. It's covered here," Kayla says as she steps inside. "Pete just hired Jennifer back and she needs the hours. Get the hell out while you can. Seriously, run."

I let out a breath of frustration and turn back to Madden. "Getting someone to cover my shifts without my permission isn't helping you any. Now go."

He looks disappointed but doesn't make a move to leave. "What do I have to do to make you say yes? Name it and I'll do it. I don't give a shit if it's ten thousand dollars. It's yours, Nat."

"Well shit. I'll go, but I can't promise we won't be married by the end of the trip." Kayla smiles and takes a seat in the chair, bringing her eyes to rake over Madden's body. "You're one fine man. I don't know who could ever say no to you."

"Stay out of it, Kayla." I turn back to Madden and try my best not to let his good looks sway my decision. Everything comes so easy for him that I'm sure he's forgotten what the word *no* sounds like. "I don't want your money, Madden. I just want you to leave so I can get things done. I don't want to talk to you or your brother right now. Got it?"

His jaw tightens, but he doesn't say anything as he turns around and leaves. The disappointment on his face right before he walked out the door unexpectedly made my heart sink, and I hate it. I'm supposed to be pissed at him, not feel bad for him.

"A little harsh, aren't we?"

"No." I take a deep breath and slowly release it. "They had no right to make plans behind my back. I'm pissed the hell off."

"Oh, come on. You and I both know you want to get away and meet Logan's friends. You're just as curious as I am to find out if there's some girl there that he's been hiding you from or something." She shrugs, picks up the phone when it begins ringing, and then hangs it up. "Going with Madden can't be all that bad. He may not be the right Parker Brother for you, but at least he's willing to bring you with him instead of hiding you away like some dirty mistress."

I'll admit it. I've thought about that before. That maybe there's some girl from Logan's past he's not over yet and that's why he hasn't introduced me to anyone. Going with Madden just to find out is somewhat tempting, but it's not that easy. Madden is not easy to resist. I don't want any reason to be tempted by him. "You're insane, Kayla. Do you know that?"

She nods. "So I've been told a time or ten."

I can't help but to smile, even though I feel like exploding inside. As much as I hate to admit it... getting out of here and away from the real world for a bit sounds nice.

It's the whole part about being *Madden's girlfriend* that I don't think I can handle. It's already hard enough to pretend that I don't notice him.

Logan is extremely handsome, don't get me wrong. But Madden... Madden is unexplainably attractive with his powerful features and mysterious personality. He's completely alluring and almost impossible to turn away from. And he's a likable guy on top of that, even though he's mastered driving me crazy over the years.

The only way *not* to fall for him like millions of other women have is to keep him at a safe distance and pretend as if his presence has no effect on me. That whole 'dating his brother' thing should make it easy.

He may very well be right. I'm possibly the *only* woman who hasn't fallen for him yet.

How the hell am I supposed to go away with him to the middle of nowhere for a week and not let my physical attraction for him show?

"...yo." Kayla snaps her fingers to get my attention. "Are you going to take care of room three-ten or do you want me to? They just called and said the mini-fridge stopped working again. Have you even been paying attention?"

I shake my head. "I'll take care of it. Just watch the front desk and don't leave it alone this time."

"Yeah, whatever." She waves me off. "Next time I have to pee I'll just grab for an empty bottle and do my best to not make a mess on the floor."

I roll my eyes and back away toward the elevator. She's always such a smartass. "You know what I mean. I'll be back."

I'M EXHAUSTED by the time I get done working for the night, and even though I'm still mad at Logan for what he did behind my back, I head toward his house instead of mine.

We have a lot to discuss, and knowing him, he'll be headed to bed soon to make sure he's well rested for work tomorrow.

This crap needs to be discussed in person and not over the phone. He needs to know just how much he's embarrassed me by agreeing to this without talking to me *first*.

Who the hell just loans their girlfriend out for a week?

The thought has me angry all over again, so I push it aside the best I can as I pull into Logan's driveway and park.

From the number of unanswered messages that Logan sent me today, he must know I'm angry with him, because he steps outside and closes the door behind him.

"I'm sorry, babe." He meets me halfway as I step out of my vehicle. "The only reason I even agreed to let Madden borrow you for the trip is because I knew you'd say no. I would've discussed it with you first, but I thought it'd be funny if you kicked his ass for asking." He places his hands on my shoulders and begins rubbing them. "You know I love you and I'd never do anything on purpose to upset you."

I take a step back and look up at him before I speak. "Yeah, well, it's pretty embarrassing to find out from your boyfriend's brother that your boyfriend agreed to let another man pretend date you. I felt and looked like an idiot in front of Kayla today, Logan. That's not cool at all."

"I apologize for that." He bows his head and pulls my chin up until our mouths touch. "Forgive me?"

His kiss is almost enough to make me forgive him and forget about this whole situation, but I can't help but to ask something. This question has been eating at me since Madden walked away.

"Why is it so important to Madden that I go with him on

this trip?"

Logan releases my chin and exhales. "His ex keeps screwing with his head and won't let him move on. She broke him and he's afraid she'll break him again if he doesn't give her a reason to let go of him."

I shake my head and bring my eyes over to the front door. "But there are pictures all over social media of him with other women. Isn't that enough proof that he's moved on?"

"Those pictures are proof that he *hasn't*. She's smart. Alana knows they're just enough to numb the pain for a night or two. He hasn't dated anyone seriously since her. They've known each other since they were kids. I'm not sure he'll ever *really* be over her and she knows it."

My heart sinks as I think back to some of the stories Logan told me about his brother when we first started dating. About how he didn't leave his apartment for weeks and drank himself to sleep each night, waking up covered in his own vomit.

If it wasn't for Logan looking out for him, he might've died from alcohol poisoning on two different occasions, but luckily, he barged into his place in the middle of the night and rushed him to the hospital.

The thought of that makes me feel guilty for telling him no when there's a chance he could unravel and hurt himself that way again. I can't imagine the pain he must've been feeling to let things get that far.

"So, she goes every year too?" I ask softly, guilt beginning to eat at me more.

He nods and runs his hands through my messy hair. "She does. And every time Madden returns from the trip he falls back into a depression for a few weeks or longer, yet he refuses to give up the time with his friends and the break away from the fame. His life is chaotic, and it's not like he can just leave whenever he wants to hang out with them. You know? Besides, he loves these trips and won't give them up for anything. Not even a broken heart."

I nod. "Yeah. I get it."

"Come on. Let's get some rest." He grabs my hand and pulls me toward the house. "I'm tired and need some sleep, and I'm sure you do too. Tomorrow is going to be hell for us both probably."

When we step into the house, Madden is sitting shirtless on the couch playing his acoustic guitar.

He looks away from the strings just long enough to make eye contact with me before he closes his eyes and gets lost in his music, as if he's the only one in the room.

Seeing the passion on his face is actually quite beautiful, and I find myself telling Logan I need a glass of water before I join him in the bedroom, but really, I just want a moment to watch Madden play.

A moment that I don't end up getting, because he sets his guitar aside when his phone pings with a message.

His face hardens and I catch his jaw flexing before he tosses his phone aside and steps past me to grab a beer from the fridge.

"Who was that?" I question as he tilts the beer back while gripping his hair with his other hand.

"My ex," is all he says before he walks away and steps out back.

I stand here and watch him through the sliding glass door as he kneels down and grips at his hair, like he's in physical pain.

A part of me wants to go outside and make sure he's okay, while the other part tells me it's best to just leave him be to handle his situation the best way he knows how.

Once inside Logan's room, I strip down to my underwear and crawl in bed with him. He immediately begins kissing my neck, while sliding his hand down my panties, but I can't seem to concentrate on him, because all I can think about is the look that was on Madden's face as he read the message from his ex.

I've never seen a man look so broken before, and I can't help but to think that maybe saying no to him was a mistake.

"Loosen up, babe," Logan whispers in my ear, while slipping a finger inside of me. "You're so tense."

I close my eyes and lean my head back as he begins sliding his finger in and out, but still all I can concentrate on is Madden, and his pain is eating away at me. "Stop..." I push his shoulder until he rolls over onto his side of the bed with a huff. "I feel bad."

"About my brother?" He sounds frustrated as he rubs his hands over his face. "He's a big boy and I'm sure he'll be fine without you. As much as I want him to stop hurting over her, I'm not sure I can handle you being away from me until Tuesday. And besides, you don't have to do anything you don't want to do. You gave him a firm no, but if you change your mind, I'll support that too. I trust you."

I stare up at the ceiling, trying to gain control of my thoughts, but it's impossible.

They're all mixed up and I know there's no way I'll be able to make the right decision without sleeping on it first. "I'll figure it out in the morning. I think I just need to get some sleep first."

He leans over to give me a quick kiss before he rolls back over to his side of the king-sized bed. "I think that'll be best for us both. We'll talk about things over lunch tomorrow. We can meet at our usual spot. Sound good?"

I nod.

"Goodnight, Natalie."

"Goodnight," I whisper; although with the way I'm feeling, I know I'll be up for hours.

And I have a feeling Madden won't be sleeping at all...

CHAPTER SIX

MADDEN

I KNEW AFTER RECEIVING THAT TEXT FROM ALANA EARLIER that sleep wouldn't be an option. I tossed and turned for all of thirty minutes before I said fuck it, hopped into my truck, and headed for Carla. I knew she'd be working all night and that she wouldn't judge me while I sat here and got shitfaced.

"You ready for another one, rock star?" I slide my glass toward her in response. She hesitates before filling it with more Jameson. "Keep this up and I'll be giving you a ride home. *That* or I'll be calling your brother to pick you up. We both know how he'll feel about that."

"I'm good, Carla. I'll figure my shit out." With my gaze on her worried eyes, I tilt the glass back, emptying it halfway. "I have a high tolerance these days. I'm going to need at least another five of these before I'm completely fucked. I'm counting on you to make sure they're in front of my face before the night ends."

"You sure you don't want to talk about it?" She motions around the mostly empty room. There are only two other people hanging around and they're too busy talking to drink. "As you can see, I have the next hour to fill. Help me speed the time up, gorgeous."

"I'm fucked. Nat refuses to go with me on the trip." I slam back the remainder of the whiskey, before setting the empty glass down and sliding it her away again. "Alana is going to *ruin* me once again, and I'm going to let her, because I'm a sucker for love even when it kills me."

"Then *don't* let her, Madden." She exhales and leans her elbows down on the counter. "Ignore her the entire trip and maybe she'll realize it's truly over."

"I can't do that, Carla. I've tried and failed every fucking time."

"Then don't let Natalie say *no*. Tell her why you need her, but don't forget what I said earlier. Things could get messy if you don't know what you want."

"I do," I say stiffly. "I just want Alana to move on."

"Okay. Well, if your brother isn't holding Natalie back and you're sure you won't fall for her or vice versa, then it's on you to make sure she says yes." She reaches for the bottle beside her and refills my glass. "You're not easy to say no to, Madden. If I wasn't afraid of falling for you—let's face it, all women do—I'd go my damn self. I'd show this Alana bitch just how much she screwed up by hurting you. *Biggest* mistake of her life."

"Thanks, babe. Appreciate that."

"I'll be right back." She slaps the dark wood, before turning away to mess with her phone or something else over by the register. I can't tell which and I'm not sure I care at this point. My head is too screwed up to think straight.

After checking on her other customers and doing a few things, she returns with a glass of ice water, practically shoving it in my face. "Drink. You're going to need to sober up a bit for this."

"For what?"

"To get what you want..." she nods behind me when someone walks in. "...from her."

I turn around to Natalie standing there in a leather jacket, looking fully awake. I thought she'd fallen asleep hours ago. After she went in my brother's room it was completely silent. "Hi, Carla." She offers a genuine smile before slipping out of her jacket and taking a seat beside me. "I'll have a Sprite, please."

"Coming right up, babe." Carla smiles and lifts a brow, sliding Natalie's glass in front of her. "I'll be cleaning up a bit. Holler if you two need me."

The moment Carla walks away, I set my gaze on Natalie, trying to read her. I can't tell if she's pissed she's here because of me or not. "I suppose Carla told you I'm drunk and needed you to come save me?" I stand up and slip into my jacket, not wanting to give her more reasons to hate me. "I'll give you gas money for the hassle, but I'm fine. I can drive myself. I've only had three drinks."

She shakes her head. "I texted Carla."

"Okay..." I take a seat again and reach for what's left of my drink, curious about why she left my brother sleeping to go out to a bar at one in the morning. "Get into a fight with my brother?"

She huffs. "He fell asleep hours ago. I doubt he even realizes I'm gone." She rolls her eyes at the last part. "I noticed you left a while ago and wondered if you were here drinking, so I asked Carla. I almost didn't come but I couldn't sleep."

"You don't have to explain that shit to me. I doubt I'll sleep for a while," I admit. "I've had too many sleepless nights to count."

"Me too," she says softly. "Too much stuff on my mind that I can't shut off."

"You're dating my brother, so I don't doubt that," I joke.

"I remember what it was like being around his uptight ass every day. Does he still get mad about fingerprints on the coffee table or the toilet paper roll being put on wrong?"

She laughs into her soda, nearly spitting out what she just drank. "*He's* the one who puts the toilet paper roll on wrong and then complains about it as if it was me. Every. Single. Time."

"Then I can see why you're here. My brother drives me crazy too."

"He *doesn't* drive me crazy. That's not what I... that's not why I'm here, okay. I just wanted to make sure—"

"I'm not passed out drunk somewhere choking on my own vomit?" I know my brother told her about those days. I also know she probably judges me because of them. Everyone does. "Because I'm not. You don't have to worry. I don't need a babysitter. You can go back to my brother with a clean conscience."

"Didn't say you did." She stands up and turns around to look behind her. "I was hoping to release some energy to help me sleep. How about we play a game of darts and then head out together?"

I can't tell if she really wants to play darts with me or if she's testing me to see how drunk I am before letting me drive home, but I stand up anyway and follow her to the back of the room. Anything to get my mind off Alana is a good thing right now. If I'm being honest with myself, liquor barely does the trick unless I'm passed out.

"We'll play a quick game of 301."

"501." I hand her a set of darts. "501 and I'm in."

"Fine. 501 it is." She grabs the set of darts and walks over to setup the game. "Either way it'll be quick."

"Why is that?"

She smiles as she gets into position. "I have pretty good aim. Just ask Carla."

"She does!" Carla hollers as if she's been listening to our entire conversation. "You don't have a chance at winning, Madden."

"Okay, show me." I motion for her to take her turn. I'm surprised when she hits a double bullseye, followed by an outer bullseye and then a double twenty. "Impressive. I'm guessing you beat my brother's ass in darts a lot. He sucks at most activities. Always has," I say, amused.

She doesn't say anything to that, and instead just yanks her darts out and gets out of the way for me to take my turn. My scores are far less impressive with a single twenty, a nine and an eighteen.

"Not too bad for someone on the road a lot. I'm guessing you don't get to play darts much."

"I don't," I admit. "I barely have time to breathe when I'm on the road. Every day feels like I'm suffocating with no escape. This trip... with my friends... is my only escape, and even *that* isn't an escape anymore thanks to my ex."

Her face falls and I can tell she feels sorry for me. "You can't just avoid her? Maybe pretend she's not there and just talk to your other friends? She'd have no choice but to take the hint."

"She won't. The moment I get there she'll be all over me as if we never broke up in the first place. She'll beg me to take her back because she *knows* I'm dead inside without her. Alana knows me better than anyone. She always has."

She swallows, before turning away and hitting another double bullseye, followed by two double twenties.

Good thing I'm not trashed, because Natalie was right, this game won't last long. I need to take Carla's advice and not let Natalie say no before my chance is up. I need to give her something to think about before this night is over.

Feeling the pressure consume me, I toss my darts at the board, not giving a shit what I hit and then turn to face

Natalie. "And like an idiot, I'll let her in and leave feeling emptier than when I arrived. *That* is why I need you, Nat. So that I'll stay away from her this time. So I won't let her fuck with my mind like every other trip."

She's quiet and I can tell I have her thinking about it. I'm not sure if it'll be enough to change her mind, but I hope it is.

"You're right," she says moments later, her forced smile making it clear she's trying to lighten the mood now that it's so fucking dark. "Logan sucks at darts. We've only played a few games but if I'm being honest, he can barely hit the board."

"Still?" I laugh and concentrate a little too hard on my next throw, wanting to prove to Natalie I'm better than my brother. "Bet he's never hit a double bullseye. Or a single for that matter."

She watches as I pull the darts from the board, her expression slightly impressed with the ninety points that come off my number. "You're right, he hasn't. I don't think he even tries because he's always too preoccupied with his phone or lost in his head. That's why I come here alone sometimes and play with Carla when she's not busy."

"Must suck."

"What?" she questions, stepping up to the line.

"Dating someone who doesn't ever *play* with you. Having fun is an important key in relationships. Love is the most important aspect of course, but if you can't have fun and laugh and play together one of you is bound to get bored and move on. That's why I like to have fun too. I want my girl to be satisfied in every possible way."

She swallows, her eyes lingering on me for a few moments before she clears her throat and throws her darts at the board. "Game over."

Yeah, apparently that might be the case for me. I gave her something to think about and now it's up to her.

"I CAN'T DO THAT, Jason. I'm already on the road," I lie through my teeth, not giving him any reason to believe he has even the slightest chance of me canceling my trip. "I'm thirty minutes out and about to lose reception. Cancel the appointments. I won't tell you again."

"Come the fuck on, Madden." His angry growl comes through the phone, but I'm so used to it now that it doesn't even faze me. "We both know this trip of yours is no good for you or the band. You come back liquored up with your head so royally fucked that you can barely function for weeks. Just turn your truck around and drive your ass back to LA."

"Not happening."

"Stop fucking with me. I've already made commitments for the band and we need you here. You can go to a cabin in the middle of nowhere next year. I'm sure your friends will understand."

He's already been in my ear for the last twenty minutes and just the sound of his voice is starting to piss me off now.

"Fuck off, Jason. I've been going on this trip every year for the past eight years and a pissed off manager isn't going to stop me. I'm not in violation of any contracts. Cancel the shit and I'll see you in a week."

"Madden..."

Before the asshole can piss me off any more, I toss my phone against the wall and make my way into the bathroom.

His argument about my head being royally fucked has me thinking about last night again.

I'm not gonna lie; it was rough as hell after I received that text from Alana. Four simple words had the power to unravel me on the spot, and the last thing I wanted was for Natalie to witness the unraveling and then to find me half-drunk at the bar afterward.

Alana: I still love you...

Doesn't she understand just how much she's fucked with my head since she walked away?

Doesn't she understand that I'll never trust her again?

I figured my silence would be enough to make her see that, but clearly, I was wrong.

It's only made her try harder, her desperation clear and escalating with each text.

She believes her words will be enough to change my mind about us or she'd have given up already, but they'll never be enough to suffer through the pain she inflicted again. People rarely change.

That kind of hurt led me down a dark road that came close to taking my life on more than one occasion.

"Shit, I look like hell." I stare at my reflection in the mirror, my grip on the sink becoming tighter as I examine the dark circles under my eyes from the lack of sleep.

Not even a half bottle of whiskey after we got back from the bar last night had the strength to numb my thoughts enough to get some rest last night.

All I kept thinking about was how I'd see Alana soon. That thought kept me tense and on edge with what might happen over the next six days.

She's good at getting what she wants, and she *almost* had me last year when I gave in to her and allowed her to kiss me. One kiss led to her sleeping in my bed. The memories that brought on led to me making love to her and almost forgetting about the hell she put me through.

Luckily, Jake talked some damn sense into me before I had the opportunity of asking her to come on the road with me.

Finally over feeling sorry for myself, I push away from the sink and gather my things into a pile by the front door.

My brother and Natalie were already gone by the time I rolled off the couch this morning, so I can only assume that means she's not going to budge on her answer even after what happened last night.

My plan was to try one more time to talk her into it when she showed up at Logan's last night, but as soon as that message from Alana came through my head was so screwed up that I didn't have the fight inside me to convince her to come. Not even what I said at the bar was giving her my all like I should have.

It's just like Alana to have the best timing when it comes to ruining me.

Logan and I said our goodbyes last night before he went to bed, so I lock up and begin loading my truck with my fishing gear, acoustic guitar, and my suitcase full of clothes.

I hop into my truck and am just about to pull away from the house when Natalie's little white car pulls into the driveway.

I sit here for a minute, watching as she steps out onto the blacktop and eyes my truck over as if she's debating on what to do next.

Keeping my eyes on her, I shift my truck into park and step out onto the road, before walking around to lean against the hood. "Logan is still at work."

I can't help but notice how cute she looks as she nervously runs her hand over her long hair, pulling the mahogany braid forward to hang over her right shoulder.

"Yeah. I heard. I just left the diner he failed to meet me at since he apparently couldn't find time for me."

"Okay..." I cross my arms over my chest and wait for her to tell me what she's doing here. I should be on the road already, but if there's even the slightest chance that she's changed her mind I'll stand here all night just to hear her say those words.

"Your brother gave me your number. I tried calling but you didn't pick up."

I cock a brow and try to keep a straight face. "Yeah, my phone sort of quit working on me. Looks like I'll be getting a new one once I get back..." I pull out a smoke and place it between my lips, lighting it up. "If you were calling to say bye you could've just said that this morning before you crept out the door. I was awake."

"That's not why I called." She walks around her car and pulls a suitcase from the backseat, setting it down beside her feet. "I decided I could use that vacation after all. My boss is pushing me to use my days before I lose them. I figured it'd be a waste not to go."

Her words say one thing while her eyes say another. She knows just as well as I do that she feels sorry for me after witnessing my little breakdown last night. And it probably didn't help that Logan stood her up for probably the millionth time since they've been dating.

I nod. "Let me get that for you." I walk over and attempt to take it from her, but she places her hand on my chest to stop me.

"I'm not useless. I managed to get it into my car without you, so back up, rock star."

A small smirk crosses my face as I toss my smoke aside and watch her throw her suitcase into the back of my truck.

I'm so relieved she changed her mind that I find myself scooping her up just under her ass and roughly kissing her cheek. I need to remember to thank Carla next time I see her.

She slaps at my bicep until I finally drop her back down to her feet. "Do that again and I'll twist a nipple until it pops off."

I open the truck door for her with a playful grin to lighten the mood. "Watch it. I may be into that sort of thing."

She narrows her eyes at me and pushes my chest, before hopping into my truck. "Just drive before I come to my senses and change my mind."

"Whatever you say, *babe*. It turns me on when a woman gives me orders." I wink and jog to the other side of the truck, hopping in myself. Then I turn to her and shift into drive. "That's something you might need to know about me since we're going to be spending so much time together. Just a warning. So do us both a favor and keep it to a minimum."

She looks a little surprised. Her eyes linger on my crotch, before she quickly turns away and looks out the window. "Noted. Thanks for the warning."

The first two hours of the drive goes by fast with little to no conversation at all. To be honest, I'm trying to figure out how this will all work without us having sex and keeping kissing to a PG rating.

There's no way Alana is going to believe we're a real couple unless we're kissing and touching each other a majority of the trip. Back when Alana and I dated, I couldn't keep my hands to myself, and she sure as hell couldn't either.

But this is my brother's girlfriend, not mine. I need to make this work while still being respectful of their relationship.

"I should've eaten when I was at the diner. I'm so hungry right now."

"Check the glove compartment."

I can't help but to laugh when she opens it and a stash of jerky falls out. "Please tell me these haven't been here the whole time your truck has been chilling at your brother's while on tour."

She begins picking them up, gathering them into a pile on her lap. "Not all of them. Be sure to check the date before shoving one into your mouth."

"That's a joke, right?"

"Sadly, no." I smile while turning down the road we need to travel for the next hour or so.

My chest is aching just knowing we'll be there soon, and I suddenly realize that we haven't even discussed the details of 'how we met and started dating'.

"Okay... so we met eight months ago when RISK played at a venue in California. We've casually kept in touch ever since, settling for FaceTime sessions every night before bed, because with my busy schedule and you managing a hotel we've only been able to spend every other weekend together. Oh, and no one knows about us because we've kept our relationship away from the prying eyes of the media."

When I look over, she's carefully checking the dates on the jerky, before deciding which one to eat. "Do you really think they're going to believe we FaceTime every night? That seems a bit much for someone with your lifestyle."

I grip the steering wheel and think back to mine and Alana's relationship. I wasn't exactly famous back then, but I was still on the road playing at different bars and other small-time gigs that would schedule us to play. "Yes. They'll believe it. I did it with Alana."

She gives me a surprised look, as if she wasn't expecting that response. I wasn't joking either. When I'm in a relationship, I'm committed one hundred percent on making it work.

"Every night?" she questions.

"Except for the nights Alana didn't answer, yes."

She looks down at her phone as if she's been waiting for a message or call.

"You're about to lose reception in about fifteen minutes. If there's a call or a text you need to send, then you should do it now. It might be a while before you get it again."

She shakes her head and powers down her phone. "Was waiting on your brother to text me back, but I guess he's too busy with work still. Nothing new."

The disappointment in her voice has me wanting to get her mind on something else, so I turn up the radio and begin singing along to *Arizona* by Highly Suspect.

She may not realize that I can see her watching me, but I do. She seems to be focused on my lips every time I glance her way.

"You listen to Highly Suspect?" I raise a brow and wait for her reply.

"I love them. They're one of my favorite bands, actually."

"That's awesome. Ever been to a concert?"

She laughs. "Is this the whole 'getting to know each other' as a fake couple thing?"

I shake my head, because it's not. "I'm just curious about your likes and dislikes. This has nothing to do with putting on a show for anyone else. It's okay for us to be friends in real life, you know."

"I've been to a few." She smiles. "Johnny is pretty cute. Not gonna lie."

Now I'm the one laughing. "You do realize that Johnny's looks are the complete opposite of Logan's, right? Sounds like you're dating the wrong Parker Brother."

It's silent for a moment, until RISK playing on the radio has me singing at the top of my lungs.

"You've buried me once, but I dug my way out. Not even the devil can hold me down now. Bury me with this bottle I clutch in my hand. The tighter I hold, the lighter it gets. Fuck the demons that scream at me now..."

"Is this your new song?" She turns the radio up and I can't help but to watch her face as she listens. She seems to be really into it.

I'm surprised that she knew RISK's new song just by hearing my voice on the radio. Clearly, she's a bigger fan than I realized, but I won't bring that up and ruin this good feeling.

"It's really good."

"Thank you. I wrote the song a long time ago, but we just recorded it a few months back and decided to put it on the new album."

"Will you be singing it on this year's tour?"

I nod and take a deep breath, not wanting to think too hard about the fact that I wrote this song about Alana. It's the only thing that almost kept me from recording it. It's bad enough that *Without You* makes me think about how she screwed me over every time we perform it.

My heart sinks, realizing the cabin is just a few miles out now. Natalie must notice my sudden onset of tension, because she's silent as she turns to watch the road.

"There's a little gas station about twenty-five minutes out of the way. We'll stop there to fill up on gas and get some snacks first. Think of anything you might need for the weekend and we'll grab it." We don't really need any snacks, because the cabin is full of anything we'll want and need, but truthfully, I just need an excuse to put off getting there for longer.

I'm pretty sure she can tell too, because all she does is nod and go with it.

When we pull up at the gas station, there are more people than expected. I figure there might be a person or two who might recognize me, so the moment I get out of the car, I walk over to Natalie's side and grab her hand, lacing my fingers through hers.

"Why are we—"

"In case someone recognizes me. Come."

"So pictures of us holding hands might end up on social media?" She shakes her head and attempts to free her hand from mine. "I don't think so. That's too much for me."

"It needs to look real. We're taking our "relationship" public now." I raise our hands higher. "And *this* will do that. I don't hold girls' hands in public and you know that, Nat. *Please* work with me here."

"Fine." She looks around us as if hoping no one notices me. And no one does until I pay for our things and grab her hand to walk outside.

"Dude! You're the lead singer of RISK." Some teenaged kid says after snapping a few pictures of me and Natalie on the way out. "Can I get a selfie?"

I release Natalie's hand—more like she practically yanks it away—and I grab the phone from the kid to take a few pictures of us.

"Your music changed my life, man." The kid smiles down at his phone while saving the picture he just snapped of us. "Gave me something to look forward to when I was lost. I stumbled upon *Without You* a few months back on *Youtube* when my girlfriend dumped me, and it helped me get over her. I never thought I would. But I've been better off without her." He winks at me, while backing away. "Thank you, man. Can't wait to show my friends I just met you. I'll probably get my ass kicked when I get back to town because they missed out, but it'll be worth it."

"I hope so, kid. Hang on a minute." I reach into my truck and pull out a spare CD that's been sitting around for a minute. "Got a marker?"

"Shit. No!" He grabs his hair anxiously. "I can go ask for one inside. Hold up a minute. Don't leave!" The kid rushes off inside in search of a marker as if he thinks I'll take off if he doesn't hurry back. I'm not going anywhere.

"That's nice of you." Natalie is smiling now as if seeing me interact with my fan has made her forget all about us being seen together holding hands. "You're going to make this kid's entire life from this moment."

"I hope so," I say honestly, reaching for the pump handle. "It's people like him who make the stress worthwhile."

"Here!" The kid hands me the marker and I scribble my name across the front of the disc, before handing it to him.

"There's my number, kid. Text me and I'll hook you up with tickets next time we perform in the area."

"Hell yeah! I will. I'll text you now so you have my number."

"Give me a few days. I won't receive your text because my phone is broken. Text me on Tuesday. Think you can remember that?"

He nods overly anxious. "Tuesday it is, Madden. Hell yeah! This is the raddest shit that's ever happened to me. You're the man. I'll never forget this."

Once the kid walks away and we're inside my truck, I can feel Natalie staring at me so I look over. "You gave a fan your number. Do you do that often?"

I shake my head and start my truck. "Nah. There was something about him though. Reminded me of myself back when I was sixteen, I guess."

We both jump when a knock sounds on the window seconds later. I laugh and roll down the window when I look over to see one of the posters that Chance had printed out smashed up against it. "Where did you get that?"

"Can you make it out to Deacon?" He shrugs and holds it out for me to sign. "I don't know. My mom had it in her bedroom and I took it. It's been in my backseat for weeks. How lucky is that?"

"Pretty lucky." I smile and hand the marker back to him. "Take it easy, Deacon."

"I'll try, dude." He barely steps away from my truck before he's on the phone calling someone.

"Nice poster," Natalie says with an amused smile. "Needed a reminder of one of the many times you've been arrested?"

"Apparently my cousin thought so," I mutter, pulling out of the parking lot.

In less than thirty minutes we're pulling into the mile-long driveway and parking next to the other vehicles.

We've been sitting here for a good five minutes when Natalie finally breaks the silence. "Are you okay? You look like you're about to break something."

"Yeah." I run my hands through my hair, before pulling out a smoke and stepping out of the truck. "I just need a second to gather my thoughts."

I can see the flames from the bonfire lighting up the night sky from behind the cabin, and the blaring music and familiar voices shouting already have me feeling at home, reminding me of why I refuse to give these trips up.

I pull my eyes away when Natalie leans against my truck beside me. "How many people are here?"

"At least seven of us are always here; unless someone couldn't make it this year. There could be more. I'm not sure." I take a long drag and slowly release it, being sure to blow the smoke away from Natalie's direction. "There are three bedrooms and two couches in the living room for sleeping. We play games, drink and dance, go swimming, and just kick back and relax without the stress of the outside world. It's one of the things I look forward to the most, minus Alana."

"You do or used to?"

I grind my jaw and lean my head back, looking up into the night sky. "I don't know anymore. I still do, but it's been hard the last few years. Alana and I broke up at this very place three years ago after I confronted her about cheating." I take one more drag off my cigarette before tossing it and running my shaky hands through my hair. "She told me she wasn't sure who she cared about more and then walked away from me, ripping my heart straight from my chest as if the last seven years we'd been together meant nothing to her."

I can feel her looking at me, so I turn to face her and

lower my gaze to meet hers. "What happened with the other guy? I mean... she obviously wants you back, so I'm guessing things didn't work out. But did you know the guy?"

I shake my head. The only thing stopping me from turning around and punching my truck is the fact that I don't want to scare Natalie. "I never found out who he was. That's one of the reasons I refused to give her a second chance when she begged me to take her back. She told me I'd hate her if I ever learned the truth and she wasn't willing to take that chance."

"She sounds like a bitch. I want to kick her ass now, to be honest. She doesn't deserve you."

My lips twist up into a smile when I see that she's serious. "You're not going to stun her, are you?"

She lifts a brow as if she's thinking about it.

I laugh and nod toward the driveway. Everyone is out back drinking, so they probably have no idea we've arrived yet, unless they happened to see the headlights. "Let's go introduce you to everyone. I'll come back later and grab our bags."

Before she can say anything, I reach down and grab her hand, lacing my fingers with hers. She stiffens at first, just like at the gas station, but then falls into step beside me as I head through the gravel.

"We could've waited until there were actual people in sight before holding hands, you know," she mumbles from beside me.

I have a feeling her feisty side will be coming out a lot here soon, and I need it to. She really has no idea what being my girlfriend entails.

"You're gonna have to relax and go with the flow if we want this to look real. If you *were* my girlfriend, you'd be much closer than you are right now. In fact, you'd be tangled up with my body, unable to keep your hands and mouth off me. Trust me." Smiling, I pull her closer to me. "This will have to do for now, though."

"For now?"

"That's what I said." I stop walking and look down when I almost twist my ankle on a big rock. This is the worst excuse for a driveway I've ever seen. "Come here."

Without giving her time to react, I scoop her up and throw her over my shoulder, causing a surprised gasp to leave her lips.

"Madden! What are you doing? Put me the hell down." She places her hands on my back and pushes up so she can most likely see where we're walking. "Put me down. Now."

Ignoring her demand, I keep on walking, trying to avoid the uneven gravel. "I'm not gonna let you twist your ankle on these rocks. I've gotta protect *my* girl." I smile, because I know she wants to strangle me right now.

But hey... if she's going to pretend to be my girlfriend, then she's getting the same treatment a real girlfriend of mine would get.

"You're just loving this, aren't you?" she asks once I set her down with a carefree smile when we reach the side of the cabin. "I think I could've handled walking on rocks, Madden."

I shrug and grip her waist, pulling her against my side. I've got to make sure everyone here knows we're together. Especially Alana. "You can never be too careful, babe." I give her hip a small squeeze and lean in to whisper in her ear. "Relax, Nat."

She takes a few deep breaths, before nodding her head and wrapping her arm around my waist, under my leather jacket. "It's kind of hard to relax when you're making me nervous," she bites out.

I squeeze her hip again and she stiffens up. "This is making you nervous?"

She nods and moves my hand higher up her waist and away from the top of her ass. "When you're squeezing one of the areas I love to be grabbed at... yeah... it's making me nervous. Your brother's hand is the only one that's been there over the last twenty-three months."

I stop in place, causing her to stop beside me. I'm not sure why, but that little detail slightly excites me. "It turns you on to be grabbed there by a man?"

She huffs and pulls me to start walking again. "Just forget I said anything. We're not going to discuss what turns me on. Not happening."

Her hand slightly grips my waist tighter as if she's preparing for our introduction once we're standing just feet away from the bonfire.

Nerves kick in even stronger, and as I look around, I can't help but to notice that Alana isn't one of the bodies around the fire.

"Oh, hell yeah!" Jake throws his arms up once he notices Natalie and me approaching. "You really did make it today like you said. I'm impressed, Parker." He quickly gives me a one-armed hug, causing me to release Natalie's waist.

"I told you I'd be here on Thursday. I meant it. Nothing could keep me away."

Once he pulls away, I turn his attention toward Natalie, and he slowly eyes her over in approval. I don't blame him. She looks great in those ripped up jeans and snug little leather jacket. "This is Natalie... my girlfriend."

Even though Jake knows Natalie isn't really my girlfriend, I don't want to say the truth out loud now that I'm here with her. Not even to him. It needs to feel as real as possible for both of us for this to work.

He nods and reaches out to take her hand, pulling her in for a hug. "Nice to meet you." Backing away from her, he makes her do a little spin, while whistling, which gets everyone's attention. "Madden is one lucky dude. Come meet Natalie, everyone. Our boy Madden didn't come alone."

Natalie doesn't even have time to react before Jess is rushing over and wrapping her arm around her shoulder with excitement. "Madden Parker brought a girl. This makes me so happy." She motions to all the guys surrounding them. "It's sort of a dickfest here in case you haven't noticed. It's nice to add another girl to the mix."

Natalie laughs as she takes everyone in. "I've noticed."

I shake my head and point around at the guys as they come in closer. "Natalie... this is Jake, Jess, Walker, Seth, and Riley. We've all basically known each other since we were in diapers."

With everyone jumping up to welcome us, Natalie ends up getting pulled away, everyone wanting their turn to talk to her and drill her with questions of how we met.

I'm standing here with a huge smile on my face as she loosens up and laughs, making herself comfortable with all of my friends. I like that a whole lot.

In fact, I'm so into watching her interact with everyone that I don't even notice Alana until she's jumping into my arms and hugging me.

My heart leaps out of my chest when she wraps her hands in my hair and places her forehead to mine just like old times. "I've missed you so much, Madden. You have no idea how much I've been dying to see you again."

She leans in to kiss me, but I'm quick enough to turn my face away that she misses. I drop her back down to her feet before I make that huge mistake again like last year. "You aren't going to do this shit this time. Were the ignored texts not obvious enough? There won't be any more kissing me, Alana. Don't try that again."

"Why not?" She sounds surprised and refuses to release my neck, forcing me to pull at her hands. "Don't do this,

Madden. Please. You have no idea how much it hurts that you won't talk to me. Just give me another chance to prove myself." Her grip on me tightens, but I pull until she finally releases my neck and takes a step back. "What's your problem? Why even bother pushing me away when you know you miss me too?"

She looks past me and notices Natalie. At least, I'm guessing it's her she's looking at, because her face is slowly turning from confusion to anger. "Are you serious?" She pushes at my chest with wide eyes. "Did you seriously bring a girl with you? How could you, Madden? This is *our* place. You can't just bring some one-night stand to piss me off and get back at me. That's not fair."

I stand here and let her push me a few more times, letting her anger out before I speak. "No, Alana. This isn't *our* place. It's Jake's, and if we're going to be coming here every year we need to learn to move on and deal with seeing each other with someone new. And she's not a fucking one-night stand. We're together."

"You're a bad fucking liar. We both know no other woman will ever be more to you than a one-night stand. You've proven that multiple times. Let's not pretend otherwise." She gives me one last shove and gets up in my face. "I told you I wanted us to work things out and you do *this* to me."

"Really," I growl out. "You fucking *cheated* on me. There are no 'working things out'."

"Whoa... break it up over here." Jake slips between us, and that's when I look over to see that everyone, including Natalie, is staring at us, and they probably have been this whole time.

She looks pissed, which is good, because that means she's playing her part well. It almost looks as if she wants to come over here and give Alana a piece of her mind, but she's holding back.

"I apologized for my mistake more times than I can even count, Madden. How long will you make me to pay for it?"

"Getting caught cheating on a test is a mistake, not cheating on your boyfriend."

Alana gives me a hurt look and walks past me. "I need another drink if I'm going to deal with this."

Well, fuck me. *Looks like I'll be needing quite a few of those tonight too...*

CHAPTER SEVEN

NATALIE

When I looked over and saw some beautiful blonde chick in Madden's arms, hugging him, it had my heart racing and my blood pumping with anger.

Seeing her legs wrapped around his body as if she owned him made me want to go over there and rip her back by her hair. She doesn't even deserve to see him, let alone *touch* him after the way she broke his heart. The fact that she doesn't see that only pisses me off. She had her chance with him and she ruined it. She needs to back off and stop playing with his heart. She's already hurt him enough, and I don't plan on letting her rip his heart out again. Not if I can do anything to stop it.

I'm trying my hardest not to walk over there and blow up in her face for the simple fact that I don't want to upset Madden and give him a reason to break down right here in front of us all. He hasn't seen his ex in a year, and I can't even begin to understand what he might be feeling right now. I need to play this cool and let him react first.

All eyes are on Madden as he stands there with his jaw tense, watching as Alana walks away and disappears into the cabin.

He waits until she's completely out of sight before he stalks over to me and places his lips against my cheek for show—his way of publicly apologizing for the scene I just witnessed—before he takes off into the woods.

"I think we could all use a drink right about now. I'll get you started while Madden takes a breather." Jess sounds nervous as she wraps her arm around mine and begins pulling me away from everyone toward the cabin.

I try my best not to focus on Madden as he disappears beyond the tree line, but I can't seem to take my eyes away from where he just disappeared. It reminds me of his little breakdown back at Logan's the other night. I *hated* the way it made me feel—useless. I feel like I should be helping him right now or something. "I should go talk to him."

"I don't think that's a good idea. I know it must be hard to watch, but trust me, it's best to just give him a few minutes to adjust." She pauses to exhale. "I hope this doesn't scare you off. They have a long, complicated history, but I'm sure you've heard *all* about it. He has a right to be angry with her. I'm sure a little air will do him some good."

"Yeah... you're probably right." I step into the cabin and look around as Jess goes straight for the kitchen, hoping that Alana isn't anywhere in sight. She isn't, which relaxes me a bit.

"Please don't be pissed over this. Alana really had no idea you two were together, and as far as she believes..." She turns to face me while pouring a couple of mixed drinks. "Madden will *never* be over her. She's used to seeing him with random girls on social media all the time, but he's never brought another girl here before. This is all new for both of them. I can't imagine being in your shoes, but I hope you understand

and give this place a real chance, because you must be really special for Madden to bring you here. I'd love to get to know you. I'm sure all of us would."

"Understandable. I get it." I reach for the drink when she hands me one of the cups. I immediately take a sip, feeling as if I *need* one now. My emotions are all over the place, and I seriously don't know how to act. "I'm not going anywhere. I'm looking forward to getting to know you all. As far as I've been told, you're all very important to Madden."

Jess eyes me over the rim of her cup. She can sense my awkwardness as I eye the closed door in front of us that Alana most likely disappeared behind. "She's here, but things will calm down. I promise. I hate to say it, because Alana is my friend, but she needs to see that you two are serious or she won't back off. I hate how she hurt Madden in the past and I want more than anything for him to be with someone who won't hurt him that way. Madden is a good guy. I'd like to see him happy. Ever since Alana decided they're not over, she makes it hard for him to move on. Maybe this year will be different. With you here, I'd say we're off to a good start, so please don't pay any attention to her when she's rude." She smiles. "Let's go join the others, shall we? I'm sure Madden will be back soon."

"Wait." I take a sip of my drink, keeping my eyes on Alana's room. "Which room is ours?"

She offers an apologetic smile and nods toward the door right next to the room I want to be *far* away from. "Sorry, sweets. Jake refuses to give up the master, so unfortunately, you'll be right next door to Alana. But don't worry. Things will be fine. Come on."

When we walk outside the first thing my eyes land on is Madden carrying the suitcases with his guitar case draped over his shoulder. His face is void of any emotion as he walks past us and into the cabin.

Not knowing what to say or do, I follow Jess back to the fire, feeling uneasy. Even though everyone is trying to make conversation with me, I can't keep my eyes from looking at the cabin, waiting for Madden to walk out.

It's only been five minutes, but I'm feeling a little over-protective of him at the moment, worried that Alana is getting to him.

"...here he comes!" His friend Jake throws his arms up as Madden steps outside. "Hurry up, dude! The party doesn't start without you and you know it."

A small smile forms on Madden's lips as he slips his arm around my waist and brushes his lips against my neck. The gesture causes my heart to do a little jump inside my chest. "Hope you're ready," he whispers. "It's going to be a long six days."

"Awe. Aren't you just so fucking sweet, rock star. Stop making me look bad, dick."

He laughs into my ear and grips my waist tighter as Jake teases him. His grip on my waist has me tilting back my drink, needing some liquid courage to get through this night. "I see Jess got you a drink," he whispers next to my ear. "What is it?"

Before I'm able to answer him, he wraps his hand around mine and pulls the cup to his mouth to take a drink.

The fact that he makes sure to place his lips right where mine just were causes my heart to speed up for some strange reason.

He clearly did that on purpose for his friends, yet it still excites me. Maybe it's because I'm so used to his brother being a germaphobe and never sharing anything like that with me, which makes no sense.

"Want me to get you one?" I ask, my heart racing as he leans in to take another drink. The way he's looking at me over the cup has me swallowing to moisten my dry mouth. "We don't have to share. I'm sure it's weird for you..."

"It isn't," he says immediately. "I don't have a problem sharing, or placing my lips where yours have been. I'm not my brother, Nat."

His comment has me clearing my throat and taking a step back. It suddenly feels as if we're standing too close and I need some space to breathe.

He's not his brother.

He's nothing like him.

Being here is going to show me just how different they truly are, which makes me nervous. I don't know why that is, but it does.

I can feel Madden stiffen beside me at the sight of Alana making her way over to join us by the fire pit. Everyone quietens down as she pulls up a chair, takes a seat, and brings her cup to her lips. "Let's not all stare at once," she mumbles. "Someone pass me the marshmallows."

Seth grabs the large bag and tosses it to Alana. "Roast one for me too, babe, will ya?"

"Yup, might as well." She's speaking to Seth, but her gaze is clearly set on Madden. "Anyone else want one? We all know how much you love S'mores and how I make them for you."

"Nope, but I think I'll make one for Natalie," Madden says stiffly. "Jake, toss me the other bag." He holds his hand up and catches the bag that Jake throws our way.

He keeps his eyes on me the whole time he's preparing the stick for the fire. It's as if he's trying his hardest not to pay attention to his ex's reaction.

Before I know what's happening, I'm pulled down into Madden's lap and he wraps his free arm around my waist, pulling me flush against him. The feel of the natural bulge in his jeans pressing against my bottom sends my heart into overdrive.

This is not the lap I'm supposed to be sitting in.

I push back the urge to jump out of his lap, even though I want nothing more than to elbow him in the ribs for the unwanted surprise he just gave me.

"Sorry, but I have to do this," he whispers into my ear, handing me the S'more he just made. "She's set on proving you're nothing but a one-night stand I brought here to piss her off. I need to show her otherwise." I suck in a small breath as his lips lightly brush across my neck. *They're so close. Too close.* "Please, save kicking my ass for later."

"I don't know if I can. You're too damn close. I can feel your *dick* pressed against my ass, Madden. Not cool. Not cool at all."

My words trail off when he tosses the stick aside and his lips press against my neck. The kiss is gentle, yet it's so sexual the way he moves across my skin that I find myself squeezing his thigh when he does it for a second and third time. As if that's not enough, him slightly hardening beneath me has me gripping his thigh even tighter, unsure of how to react right now.

His breath hitting my skin has goose bumps forming across my entire body as he moves up to whisper into my ear again. "She *knows* how I treat my women, Nat. I fucking *worship* them. I'm gentle *outside* the bedroom, but wild and rough *in* it. You're going to have to fake that at some point."

"What!?" I shake my head and get ready to push out of his lap, but he cups my face, forcing me to look at him. I can *feel* Alana's harsh glare on us, but I'm too caught up in the fact that he expects me to fake having sex with him before this trip is over to care. "What the hell, Madden?" I whisper-yell. "I never agreed to that. No. Absolutely not."

"All you have to do is scream a little... okay a lot, and maybe knock a few things off the dresser and tables." He laughs in my ear, most likely to calm my angry breathing even though I'm trying my best to hide my need to *strangle him* from his friends. "Relax, Nat. I won't touch you. I'll even let you slap me a few times if it makes you feel better. It'll be fun. I promise."

"And it'll also be fun to use my stun gun on you," I say stiffly, forcing a smile for show. "And yes, I brought it."

"Turn the music up!" Jake yells as one of RISK's songs comes on. "I still can't believe this shit. I don't think I'll ever get used to hearing you on the radio."

Madden stiffens from below me as his friends begin belting out the lyrics to *Without You*. I take the opportunity to scoot down his lap a little so that I'm no longer sitting on his dick.

With each lyric Alana's face turns redder with anger. I just now realize the song must've been written about her. It's about a girl cheating on him and then dumping him for some guy that she doesn't even end up with. He's torn up inside, drinking his nights away, until he tells himself that he's better off without her.

I've heard this song a hundred times but never once thought about the possibility of it being about him and his ex. I hate how bad she wronged him.

"I'm better off without you..." Seth is in the middle of singing but stops to slap the flaming marshmallow off of his shoulder that Alana flings at him. "What the hell? Did you *not* see that shit was still on fire?"

"No, I saw." She gives him the middle finger and tilts her cup back until there's nothing left. "I'm just sick of you assholes singing that song every time it comes on the radio, when clearly the entire world knows it's about *me*. I made a mistake, now can we all just move the hell on from it?"

"Oh, come on, Alana," his friend Riley says after turning the music down with a small remote. "You laughed the last time we sang it. Stop being so pissy all of a sudden."

89

She stands up and tosses her cup into the fire. Her gaze lands on me, and the way she's looking me over as if I'm not good enough to replace her has me wanting to bitch slap her. "Last year Madden didn't bring some random chick to try and piss me off either, when clearly *we* still belong together, so excuse me for being a little pissy. I didn't expect anyone else to suddenly join in on our annual trip at the last minute."

"Dammit, Alana. Stop calling her that shit," Madden says, his voice taut. "Nat and I are together, and if you can't fucking handle it then that's too bad. I don't feel sorry for you. I haven't responded to *any* of your texts or given you *a single* reason to believe we're getting back together this year. If you can't deal with her being here, then leave. Either way, stop being a bitch to her."

"I'm good," she says, finally pulling her eyes from me. "I've known you long enough to know when you're faking it. I've got six days—well, five since this shitty one is almost over —to figure you out, Madden." She pulls her hair up into a ponytail before speaking again. "I'm going to sleep, but tomorrow is a new day; just remember that."

Everyone watches as she stomps toward the cabin. "Sorry, guys. I'll be back." Jess stands up and follows Alana.

"I need a drink," Madden says, before lifting me out of his lap. "Want another one?"

I nod and tilt back the rest of what's left in my cup before handing it to him. "Make it a double."

I don't know why her words have me so worked up, but they do. Who is she to say I'm just some random chick? I may not actually be dating the brother I'm here with, but a random chick is something I've never been. And who is she to give Madden a hard time when she's the one who screwed him over?

It takes a good ten minutes for Madden to return with our drinks, and when he does, he's extremely tense, as if fighting hard to hide his emotions. I don't know if his ex said something to him inside, but I do know that if anyone pays attention to Madden right now, he's going to give away that he's not over her, and if we want this to work everyone needs to believe that he is.

Standing, I grab my drink from him and nod toward the side of the cabin. "I think I left a few things in your truck. Mind walking with me?"

His jaw tightens as he tilts his drink back, before nodding and following me. Once we're alone, he opens the tailgate of his truck and hops up, then reaches for my hand to help me up. "Fuck," he breathes. "It's so much harder to act like I don't give a shit in person. As much as I hate what she did to me, I can't erase everything else. I need this shit to work, Nat. I can't leave here until it does."

I shift so that I'm facing him. I hate seeing him in pain. We're only a couple hours in and I'm already wondering just how he's going to make it through the rest of the trip. "You need to try. At least for the weekend." I take a sip of my drink, eyeing him over the rim as he watches me. "I know it's not going to be easy, so let's do this for a while to clear your head. We're not even here."

"Do what?" he questions with a small smile. "Sit here, drink, and pretend we're not here?"

"Yeah." I hold up my drink. "I mean, we'll have to sip them if we want them to last, but I don't mind just hanging here for a bit."

"All right. I can handle that." He eyes me, taking a drink from his cup. "You still going to kick my ass for pulling you into my lap?" he questions moments later. "I have to warn you that I might like it."

I laugh and push his arm, the mood feeling lighter already now that we're alone. "That *wouldn't* surprise me."

"How about my brother?"

"What about him?" He turns to face me as if waiting for an answer.

"Does my brother like it when you're rough?"

"That's none of your business." I shake my head, not liking where this conversation is going. I brought him to his truck to help him relax, *not* to make me uncomfortable.

"Oh, come on." He jumps down to his feet and crosses his arms. The way he's looking at me is making my pulse race just a little faster. "At least tell me if *you* like it rough. I should know these things."

"*No*, you shouldn't." I drop down to my feet, drink in hand and head toward the side of the cabin—the opposite side we came from. "A hot tub? Really?"

"What's wrong with a hot tub?" he says from beside me, almost scaring me. I hadn't even noticed he was following so closely.

I shrug and dip my fingers into the steaming water. It's been years since I've been in one and the water feels incredible. "I've just never been to a cabin with a hot tub. Or a pool for that matter. This is different than I expected."

"Yeah, it didn't always have these things." He moves in behind me and splashes his fingers in the water. "Jake had the pool put in a few years ago and added the hot tub last year."

"That pool looks really expensive." I point out.

"It was." He backs away, the night air suddenly feeling cooler now that he's no longer pressed against me. "But Jake has done a lot for me over the years, so I wanted to do something nice for him. Plus, this place is like home."

Madden's generosity has me tilting back my drink. I've only ever seen him as the reckless rock star either screwing some groupie or getting arrested for fighting. Being here with him is going to show me a whole new side of him. One I'm not sure I'll expect.

"Want to get in?" He reaches for his jacket and slips it off, before going for his shirt.

Before he can get too far, I grab his arm, stopping him. "What? Are you going to strip down to your underwear and get in? I'm not doing that."

"That was the plan."

"I'm good." I yank his shirt down so that it's covering his tight abs—I hate how hard they are—before grabbing his cup and holding it out to him. "How about we don't and say we did."

"Where's the fun in that?"

"In what?" Jake—at least I think it's Jake—comes from the shadows, a drink in hand. "You two going to join us or make out by the hot tub all night? Just let me know so Jess will stop asking for Natalie."

I clear my throat, my face growing hot over the idea of them thinking we're making out. "We were just on our way back."

"Cool. Cool." He slaps Madden's back. "Let's get this party started then."

The rest of the night has gone by smoothly since we've rejoined the gang, and I'm thankful that Alana hasn't joined us again. I seriously don't know how much more of her I could've taken tonight, or Madden for that matter. I'm not usually one to bite my tongue, but for Madden I held back with it being the first night here, because I'm still not sure what he expects from me when it comes to her.

I don't like her—not even a tiny bit—and after meeting her, I want him to stay away from her even more.

She seems like a woman who's used to getting what she wants, ruining whoever else in the process, but it's not going to be Madden.

Not again.

She's right about one thing, though... tomorrow is a new

day. I'll be refreshed and ready to play my part. At least, I hope.

Everyone is laughing and having a good time, telling funny stories about prior trips to the cabin, and to be honest, I'm having a great time with everyone—Madden included.

It does suck that I didn't come here with Logan, but at the same time, I'm happy to be here with his friends, getting to know the people that are important to him.

"All right." Madden stands up and grabs my hand, pulling me up to my feet. "I think we're going to call it a night."

"What?" His friend Walker looks down at his watch. "It's only ten past two. I'm sure you have later nights after a concert. You can handle a few more hours."

Jess and Jake went to the cabin over twenty minutes ago, and I think Madden can sense that I'm ready to call it a night. The only time I'm up this late is when I have to pull a double at the hotel.

"It's okay," I say, pulling my hand free from Madden's. "I can find my way to bed. Stay and have fun."

He shakes his head and grabs my hand again. "Nah, I'm not letting you go to bed alone on your first night here. I'm ready for bed if you are."

"That's so fucking cute, and lame," Seth says, tossing his empty cup into the fire. "But I get it. If I had a girl, I'd be taking her to bed too, man."

"See you guys in the morning."

"Good night, everyone," I say, as Madden begins pulling me away.

Seth and Walker nod and Riley smiles and winks, before they turn the music back up and jump back into joking around with each other.

My heart speeds up the moment we walk into the quietness of the cabin. Alana's bedroom door is closed, but the fact that Madden and I are about to sleep in the same room feels extremely... wrong.

I didn't for one second think I'd be sharing a room with my boyfriend's brother—his famous, manwhore of a brother, to make it even worse.

"Your friends seem really great," I say once we step into the small room and he closes the door behind us. "It just seems weird meeting them with you, instead of your brother."

"I'm sorry about Alana's behavior earlier." He looks up from making a bed on the floor, his jaw flexing. "I didn't really think of the shit you'd have to deal with from her by me bringing you here. I should've apologized earlier when we were alone, but my head was too messed up. That'll happen a lot here."

I toss him the extra pillow, before taking a seat on the bed. "Turn your head for a minute." I peel my jeans off and hurriedly slip under the blanket as he turns away. "Okay, you can look now."

"So, I'm sorry. I promise I'll make this trip up to you once it's over. Anything you ask for is yours."

"The only thing I want is for you *not* to get back with her. I knew how much she hurt you, but actually seeing her and being around her makes it much more real. I can handle her, trust me."

Without any warning, he yanks his shirt over his head and tosses it, before going for his jeans and stripping out of them.

"Whoa." I quickly turn away just as he's kicking his jeans aside and adjusting himself in his black boxer briefs. "A little warning before you strip next time would be nice."

He laughs. "Don't act like you haven't seen me in my underwear before, Nat. In fact..." I turn around to see he's now lying on the floor, placing his hands behind his head. "You were under the same blanket as me *while* I was in my underwear. I don't recall you minding then."

I toss a decorative pillow at him and grunt. "That was an accident. Now go to sleep."

"If you say so."

"It was. Now shut up."

"Alrighty, then."

As much as I want to keep reminding him that it was in fact an accident, I'm so tired that I can barely keep my eyes open.

I need some quiet time to think about what I'm going to do over the coming days to prove to his cheating ex that he's finally unavailable.

All I know is that I need to somehow do that *without* letting things go too far, but I have a feeling that she's going to make that harder than I'd like.

CHAPTER EIGHT

MADDEN

Once Natalie fell asleep, I spent most of the night staring up at the ceiling trying not to think of the years Alana and I spent in this very room back when we were together.

I'm almost positive she chose the room next door instead of our old room on purpose, just to make me think about *us* and the good times we've spent here. It pisses me off because it worked.

Things between us were flawless for so long. I believed she was the woman of my dreams; the one I would get down on one knee for when the time was right.

The fact that she screwed that all up over some worthless dick still messes me up more than she'll ever know. I can't even count the number of cigarettes I smoked due to her before finally falling asleep early this morning.

Not only that, but I'm almost positive I heard Alana creeping outside the door a few times, probably trying to decide whether or not she should brave poking her head inside to check on us.

She knows damn well that none of these doors have locks on them. Jake's dad removed them back when he and his sisters were kids and locked them one too many times, because he didn't want them hiding out in the bedrooms instead of spending *family time* together.

He still refuses to add locks, which is one of the reasons every single person here has accidentally seen each other naked at one time or another. Apparently, no one remembers to knock.

If Alana decides to start snooping around, she's going to discover the truth about Natalie and I not really being together, and then I'll be screwed.

She knows more than anyone how I like to sleep at night, and that's naked and tangled up around my girl with her head on my chest.

Sighing, I sit up and look over to see that Natalie is still sleeping, so I grab my pillow and blanket and place them back on the bed as quietly as possible.

The last thing I need is for someone to open the door to see if we're awake, only to find that my ass slept on the floor and not in the bed with my "girlfriend".

"Hey," Natalie whispers as I'm in the middle of slipping into my jeans. "What time is it?"

"Ten past eleven." I turn around, and even though Natalie tries her best to hide it, I don't miss her gaze roaming over my naked chest before she swallows and looks up to meet my eyes. My brother isn't quite as cut as I am; not like he used to be when they first met, so it's not surprising that she seems impressed with what she sees. "I like to wake up before everyone else and take a walk in the woods to relax."

"When will everyone be awake?" She sits up and stretches, before reaching to pull her hair into the messiest bun I've ever seen. She looks cute with the loose hair falling around her face. "I've been forcing sleep for the past two hours. I'm not used to sleeping in since Logan always has to be up early for work."

"Probably not for another hour. I'm always the first one up. I don't sleep much." I reach into my bag for a long-sleeved shirt and throw it on. "Come with me. We'll be back by the time everyone should be waking up."

"An hour?" She shakes her head. "That's a long time to be alone with you. I'm still feeling stabby from last night."

"Why is that?"

She offers me a sarcastic smile. "Because I'm still trying to figure out if I should hurt you or not for placing your dirty lips all over my neck without a warning first."

"Oh yeah?" I laugh and cock a brow. "What makes my lips dirty?"

"Oh, come on, Madden. The fact that you've used them on about a hundred women."

"Not true," I correct her. "Alana was the first girl I kissed, and since our breakup, I've kissed *one* girl on stage and zero girls in the bedroom. I don't like kissing unless it means something to me. That kiss on stage was to piss off some girl's boyfriend for treating her like shit right in front of me. I regret doing it too."

She swallows and pauses for a moment, as if to think of a way to change the subject. "How well do you know your way around these woods? Are you going to get us lost?"

I laugh and toss her jeans on the bed beside her. "Hey, look on the bright side. If we *do* get lost, I can entertain you with my sexy voice." I smirk as she rolls her eyes. "Besides, do you know how many women would jump at the opportunity to get lost in the woods with a hot rock star like myself?"

"Okay, no. I'm definitely staying now." She plops back down and covers her face with her pillow.

She says something that's muffled by the fabric, so I pull it away from her face and yank the blanket down to her feet to get her up and moving. "Let's go, babe."

"Madden! I'm not dressed!" She tugs her small shirt down in an attempt to hide her blue panties, and as much as I know I should look away, it's a struggle.

Her body is fucking perfection.

I grab my baseball cap and put it on, looking away to give her a minute to get dressed. "I thought we were both past that part, Nat. I've seen you in your underwear and you've seen and *felt* me in mine. We're both adults. We know what parts each other has. Now come on."

"I really want to punch you right now," she says out of breath, hopping around behind me to pull her tight jeans up. "Is it too late to change my mind and go back to your brother? The *less* cocky one."

"Yup!" I reach into my bag and grab my leather jacket. "Here." I toss it to her. "It's a little chilly in the woods this early."

She looks down at it in her hand, before tossing it back to me. "The only jacket I wear other than my own is your brother's. It's weird to wear another guy's jacket. Besides, I have my own."

"Does *he* offer you his jacket, Nat?"

She turns away for a quick moment, as if to hide her embarrassment. "That's not the point. I have my own, and like you said, no one is awake right now anyway. Mine will work just fine."

I step up to her and grab her arm to stop her from reaching for her own jacket. "When you're *my* girl, you wear *my* jacket," I whisper against her ear. "And you're *mine* for the next six days. Let me treat you how I would if this were real."

"Fine," she says while I slip it on her, not giving her a choice. "You're much—"

"*Different* than you expected me to be with women?" I interrupt. "Or much different than my brother?"

She nods and adjusts my jacket. "Yeah... I mean... to both. Let's just go."

"Yeah, well, I've known since a young age what the most important thing in my life would be, and that's to find a good woman to love and take care of. Logan was always more consumed with finding a great career and putting it first. That's the difference between us. I'm not truly happy unless I have someone to love."

I tense my jaw and turn away, pretending I'm not letting my emotions get the best of me at the moment, but even the thought of *love* and what it *used* to feel like has me wanting to punch something.

"I'll wait outside so you can brush your teeth." I walk out of the room and past Alana's door, not giving it a second glance.

If I had any cell service here, I have no doubt that my phone would've been blowing up last night with messages from her, and I hate myself for even wondering what those messages would've said.

I hope she's hurting; not because I take pleasure in her pain, but because I know that hurting her is the only true way of getting her to move on and cut me out of her life. What she did is something I can't get past. The trust I had in her is gone.

She did this. Not me.

As long as I keep reminding myself of this, I should be able to make it through the rest of the trip pretending that Natalie is mine.

Once stepping outside, I pull out a smoke and place it between my lips, lighting it up. It's too early to drink right now, and if I break down and get drunk before everyone wakes up, then Alana is going to know that I'm still not over her.

I can't have that again.

I'll smoke cigarette after cigarette if I have to, but I need to stay away from the whiskey for as long as I can. At least until someone else has a cup in their hand first. I'm counting on that being before one.

"I'm ready."

I look up at the sound of Natalie's voice, and I can't help but to swallow due to my suddenly dry mouth at the sight of her in my jacket. I hadn't gotten a good look of her inside, but holy shit, she makes that jacket look good. Much better than *I've* ever made it look.

I kick away from the cabin and toss my half-smoked cigarette at the ground, trying my best not to gawk at my brother's girl. "Let's get out of here before someone wakes up. I don't want anyone joining us."

I nod at her to walk first, before I place my hand on the small of her back and guide her toward my favorite path. I'm the only one who walks this one since it splits off into three trails and easily confuses everyone.

We used to get lost out here almost every year as kids, but I've taken it so many times now that I know it just by looking at the trees. "What do you and my brother do for fun?" I ask, breaking the silence.

She looks up from her feet for the first time in minutes. "I don't know."

"Okay..." I say on a laugh. "You don't know, or you don't want to tell me?"

She's silent for a few minutes, as if thinking. "I'm starting with the easy questions here. Is it really that hard to think of one thing you guys do for fun?"

"What if it is?" she asks quietly. "Your brother is busy a lot and our schedules don't give us much time for *fun*. We barely get to spend more than three hours a day together."

I stop walking, not liking her answer. "You don't need *time* to have fun, Nat. I could plan a fun activity for us that lasts only thirty minutes if I wanted to. You take what *time* you do have and use it to make your partner happy. That's part of being in a relationship. My brother really needs to take lessons from me in the relationship department, because he's clearly lacking there."

"Okay." She stops walking when I start, so I stop to look back at her. "What kind of activities would you plan for *us* if we were a real couple? I suppose I should know these as your "girlfriend"."

"Axe throwing. I do that sometimes when I'm in California to let off some steam. Doesn't take long. I bet if you imagined my face as the target, you'd be pretty good."

"All right." She laughs and begins walking again. "I have wanted to try that out for a while now. What else?"

"Darts. Again, my face could be the target, which I'm sure it was the other night." I smirk when her lips curve up into an amused smile. I'm trying to loosen her up and it seems to be working. "You're imagining it again, aren't you?"

She ducks under a branch as I hold it up for her. "No, but I find it funny that you think I hate you that much. I don't. You just drive me crazy most of the time." She squeezes my left cheek and laughs. "Besides, we both know that your face is too pretty to be a target. I'm sure millions of women would hunt me down and hurt me if I ever messed it up. What else?"

I should have a smartass remark over her finally admitting that she finds me attractive, but instead, all I can think of is the most inappropriate activity of them all. "I'd take you for a ride on my motorcycle and find a nice, quiet spot to take care of your body. That's my favorite one." I turn my baseball cap backward, before turning around and looking straight ahead as I walk.

She doesn't say anything more, and I wonder if maybe, just maybe, I've taken things too far with the last one.

It's not like I was telling her what I'd like to do to *her*. She asked which activities I'd plan if we were a couple and that's most definitely something I'd plan for my woman.

It's quiet between us for a while, both of us enjoying the peace and quiet of the trail, until Natalie walks over and takes a seat on a fallen tree.

I take this as my opportunity for a smoke break and pull out another cigarette to help calm my nerves. I can feel Natalie watching me. "When did you learn to play the guitar?"

I smile at the memory. "When I was eight. My uncle used to be in a band, and I wanted to be *cool* like him." I snuff out the rest of my cigarette and take a seat next to her. "Don't get me wrong, the band was horrible. I might've been young, but I remember that much. That didn't matter to me, though. I thought it was so cool to watch him play, and I wanted people to look at me and feel the same awe that I felt while watching him. I begged him for weeks to teach me how to play before he finally gave in."

When I look over at Natalie, she's watching me with a smile. "I can picture a miniature you, holding a guitar way too big for your size, while drowning in that leather jacket of yours."

"Cute, right?" I nudge her side and she nods.

"Don't like this too much, but yes. I bet you were *adorable*."

I flash her my best 'adorable' smile, and with the way her lips curve into a smile, I know I've got her. "Were? I still am."

"Adorable with a side of annoying."

I shrug. "I'll take it."

She's quiet for a moment, her lips still curved into a small smile as she looks around the woods, looking peaceful and at ease. "It's nice to have easy conversation in the morning. It helps to start the day out right. Your brother *hates* talking when he first wakes up. It puts him in a bad mood."

"Still?" I ask on a laugh. "I haven't risked trying since that one time when we were kids and he threw his G.I. Joe at my head for asking him if he wanted to go swimming."

She looks at me and laughs. "Ouch. That sounds painful."

"It left a huge welt on my forehead that lasted for almost two weeks. It looked like I had a horn attempting to grow between my eyes. They called me uni-boy for months after."

She bursts out into laughter, so I keep to myself that I made that last part up. I like seeing her enjoying herself like this, and I want to keep it this way for as long as I can.

I grab her hand and pull her back to her feet, before I take off walking again. It's silent, except for the sound of branches and leaves crunching beneath our feet.

"Does your brother have an ex that he used to bring here?" I look over at her, noticing that her expression is uneasy now, all playfulness gone. "Is that why he hasn't mentioned me to your friends? Please be honest. I can take it."

I shake my head, feeling like crap that Logan is such a douche sometimes. "No. He's never brought a girl on this trip. I'm not really sure why. Although, he really only had a girlfriend one year during the trip."

She looks confused. "What do you mean? You guys have been coming here for years."

"His relationships have never lasted long. He was always single come trip time, except for the trip from three years ago and he didn't invite her along. You're his longest relationship, Nat. The others have never lasted longer than three or four months." I let out a sarcastic laugh, thinking back to

Logan's dating life before Natalie came along. "I can't even count the number of girlfriends he's had. The women have always loved my brother."

The way her mouth drops tells me she's probably hearing this for the first time. It also tells me that I probably should've kept my mouth closed, but I expected her to know these things since they've been together for almost two years. "He's had that many? I can't picture Logan being the type of guy who hops from one relationship to another. He's never told me about the numerous women he's been with. I need some air." She takes off walking faster, as if she needs to get away.

"Shit." I hurry to catch up with her, grabbing her waist to stop her from walking. "Nat, wait."

She sucks in a breath at the same time I give her waist a slight squeeze, so I quickly remove my hand, not wanting to upset her more. "I'm sorry. I assumed Logan had talked to you about his past. I didn't mean to upset you." I walk around to face her. "Alana and I knew everything about each other. Apparently, my brother isn't as open as I am. But it was in the past. He's a good man and he's dedicated to you, Nat. No need to worry or be upset. It's clear that he loves you and he's changed."

"I'm not worried, Madden. I'm just pissed off that he lied to me about his past. He told me that he didn't date much before we met, then I have to hear from you that he's had too many women in his life to count. I don't like liars, and I expected him to be truthful with me. I've never given him a reason to lie to me. I've been honest with him about everything, even the bad things I'd rather not repeat."

"That makes two of us." An ache hits me straight in the chest, and I find myself gripping the closest tree, digging my fingers in as I try to keep my cool. "Let's not think about liars. It's not good for either of us right now. We have almost a week to get through. Fuck the negative shit. We don't need it. Let's make the best of this, yeah?" I push away from the tree and turn to face Natalie. "Come on."

She nods and falls into step beside me as I take us farther into the woods. "How do your parents feel about seeing you all over social media and hearing your voice on the radio?"

"My father loves it while my mother complains I cuss and drink too much. She's not wrong."

"Definitely not," Natalie says with a hint of humor. "I've seen plenty of videos and interviews, and I'm not sure any of them were profanity free."

I stop and smile, causing her to bump into me. "Have you been stalking me online?"

She clears her throat and pushes my shoulder, before walking past me. "Absolutely not, rock star. Keep walking."

"You don't have to be ashamed, Nat. Most females are obsessed with me. I'm used to it. My brother never has to kn—"

She elbows me in the side, cutting my words off. "You're a moron, Madden. I am *not* obsessed with you like ninety percent of the female population is. I enjoy your music. RISK is one of my favorite bands. There, I admit it. Are you happy?"

"Hell yes I am, *babe*."

"Must you really call me that in private?"

"The more I call you it, the more natural it will feel and sound to others, so yes."

She rolls her eyes and heads back the direction we came from. I let her lead the way, knowing she'll most likely get lost like everyone else does. The truth is, I'm enjoying being alone with her and away from Alana. I want to make it last a bit longer, so I continue to follow her even after she takes a wrong turn.

"I don't think any of this looks familiar," she finally says after a while. "What the hell, Madden?" She turns to face me, her expression annoyed. "I've been going the wrong way this entire time, haven't I?"

I nod and risk a smile, knowing there's a chance she may physically hurt me. There's also a chance I may like it.

"See..." She turns to walk back the direction we just came from, bumping my shoulder in the process. "Annoying."

"With a side of adorable," I point out as I pass her to lead the way. "Don't forget that part."

She rolls her eyes, but I notice a hint of a smile that she attempts to hide as she falls into step beside me. She may never admit it out loud, but she's having fun being alone with me.

"How long have we been out here?" she questions once the cabin comes into view.

"I don't know. Why?"

"Just wondering if anyone is awake yet."

"We've been gone long enough, so I wouldn't be surprised if someone wakes up soon."

"I think I'm going to jump in the shower now so I'm not in anyone's way when they do."

I nod and roll my sleeves up. "I'm gonna stay out here and get some air. There's soap and shampoo in the small compartment of my suitcase in case you need some."

She makes an 'oh crap' face and shakes her head. "I knew I was forgetting something when I packed. Are you sure it's cool if I grab them myself?"

I wouldn't be surprised if she's asking because my brother doesn't like her going through his things. He's always been extremely private, even when it comes to his only brother.

"I don't have anything in my suitcase to hide, except maybe my underwear, but you've already seen them anyway. Considering I gave a pair to a complete stranger once, I guess you could say they're not secret."

She rolls her eyes and begins walking backward. "I won't be going anywhere near your underwear, so we're good there."

After she disappears inside, I walk to the picnic table that's setup right outside the trails and light up a smoke. It feels good to be out here alone, taking in the trees and morning air.

No cellphone.

No social media.

No screaming fans.

No manager barking orders at me.

And most of all, no pressure.

"What the hell, Madden!"

At least, I thought.

My stomach twists into knots the moment I hear Alana's pissed-off voice coming toward me, but I refuse to show her the affect she still has on me. "How can I help you on this beautiful fucking morning, Alana?"

She makes it a point to walk around the table so that we're facing each other. I was looking forward to keeping my back toward her for this shit.

Her angry eyes meet mine as her hands go to her hips. "Your favorite jacket? You let *her* wear it? I thought it was special to you. You told me you'd never let anyone else but me wear it. You lied."

I flick my cigarette at the ground and look up to meet her harsh glare. "You also told me you'd never *fuck* anyone else but me, and you lied about that too. It doesn't feel good, does it?"

"It was a mistake!" she yells, coming at me to push me back down when I go to stand up. "I didn't do it to hurt you, but you *did* let her wear your favorite jacket to hurt me. That's so messed up, Madden."

"Did I?" I pull out another cigarette and light it, keeping my eyes locked on hers as I take a drag and quickly exhale. "Who said I was even thinking about you when I let Natalie wear it? Despite what you seem to think, I haven't thought about you in a long time. Have you ever stopped to consider that? Maybe I forced myself to stop because it was killing me. Now back off."

"No." She moves in close enough to wrap her arms around my neck, her lips lightly brushing mine when she speaks. "I *need* you Madden, and I know you need me. Stop trying to hurt me on purpose. Send her home, because we both know she's nothing more than some random girl that means nothing to you."

Hearing Alana refer to Natalie as a random girl that means shit to me has me yanking her arms off me and jumping to my feet. "Fuck off, and I don't *ever* want to hear you call my girl random again. We're together whether you like it or not, and you're going to see that you're wrong. You *can* be replaced, Alana. In fact, you already have."

Before she can work me up even more than she already has, I walk away. I can't let her get to me. I can't let her work her way under my skin again.

My focus needs to be on Natalie.

My hands, my lips, and my fucking body needs to be on her if this is going to work.

I'm going to have to push the boundaries a bit with my brother's girl, and I have no doubt that she's going to kill me before this trip is over, but I'd rather die from her bare hands squeezing my throat than Alana's squeezing my fucking heart until it bleeds out.

Either way, I may not make it out of this trip alive.

CHAPTER NINE

NATALIE

THE LOOK OF HURT AND ANGER ON ALANA'S FACE AS I passed her in the hall moments ago tells me she most likely wasn't expecting to see me in Madden's jacket. She kept looking me over in it as if she wanted to rip it from my body. I could tell she wanted to say something to me, but instead, she stormed outside to most likely find Madden and take it out on him instead.

I wonder what she's saying to him, and *that* has me tense and wanting to get through this shower as quickly as possible. I'm not sure why I feel the *need* to protect him from her, but I do. Doesn't she know that she's already done enough damage? Does she even care?

My mind should be on Logan right now and what I learned about him in the woods, yet here I am, worried about his damn brother instead. It doesn't feel right. This whole situation is fucked up.

"What am I doing here?" I lean against the wall of the shower and run my hands over my face, feeling lost. It's only the second day and I'm already confused on how to feel and what to do. "You don't belong here, Natalie. This is stupid."

I stand here motionless for a few moments, lost in my head, before I shake off my thoughts and reach for the body wash that I borrowed from Madden's suitcase.

Less than a week. Then Madden is on his own and I'm back to the Parker brother I belong with. I can do this until then. I can handle it.

At least I tell myself that, until I squeeze the soap into the palm of my hand and get hit with a scent that *isn't* Logan's. It smells incredible and I *hate* Madden right now for it. "Ugh!"

Madden's scent assaulting me while naked in the shower is the last thing I want since I'm stuck here in the middle of nowhere with him. Especially after knowing what his rock-hard abs feel like under my fingertips. I haven't forgotten the fact that my hand almost went to the *last* place I want it to ever go. At least he had the decency to wake me up, but I'll admit, it has me wondering just how long he was awake before he decided to stop me from making a fool of myself.

The cocky jerk was probably awake the entire time, enjoying me mistaking him for the wrong Parker Brother. As much as that thought should disturb me, it does the complete opposite.

Exhaling, I quickly rinse his soap from my body, needing to wash away his scent, along with all thoughts of him. I need to ask Jess if I can borrow her shampoo and body wash next time. Using Madden's was a stupid idea. I should've just waited for Jess to wake up.

That thought runs through my mind the entire time I'm stepping out of the shower and getting dressed. How would Logan feel knowing that I smell like his brother right now? Not sure why it's on my mind, considering he agreed to me coming here in the first place.

Pushing that thought aside before I get angry over it

again, I step out of the bathroom. The first thing my eyes land on when closing the door behind me is Madden leaned against the counter in the kitchen, dressed in a snug black T-shirt. His dark eyes are on me, his jaw tense as he looks me over in his jacket that I slipped back into.

My heart pounds from the intensity of his stare. I hardly even noticed Alana, Jess, and Jake in the kitchen at first, because his eyes have me frozen in place for a moment, unable to turn away.

"I'll be back," he mutters to the others, coming at me with purpose, my heart rate speeding up the closer he gets.

I get lost in his eyes as he holds our gaze and grips me by the waist, yanking me to him. The little unexpected squeeze that he does has me releasing a sound that instantly embarrasses me.

Without breaking eye contact, he gives my hip another squeeze, his jaw flexing as he watches for my reaction. He doesn't say anything, making this moment even more intense. His body moves in closer and presses into me, a heavy breath escaping me, before he drags me into the bedroom and slams the door behind us.

Once alone, he snatches my clothes from my arms and presses me against the door, being sure to make as much noise as possible. "What are you doing?" I ask breathlessly, my heart close to pounding out of my chest.

"What I have to for this to work," he growls into my ear, pressing me harder against the door with his body. It's so firm I can barely breathe. "You may hate me after today, but I'm not leaving here without Alana believing we're an actual couple, and so far, that's not the case."

I press my hands against his chest to put some space between us. I *need* some space. "And what?" I give him a hard shove. "Backing me against a door in private is going to show her that? This is extremely unnecessary."

"Yes," he says firmly, pressing his hand against the door right beside my head. "I'm aggressive in the bedroom, Nat. I thought we've already established that." He leans in so that his lips are brushing my ear. "When I *want* someone, everyone knows it. And right now, I want *you*." He whispers the last part, causing me to swallow. "At least, that's what they need to think."

Fighting to catch my breath, I give him one last shove, forcing some space between us. "Let me breathe, Madden. How do you expect me to breathe with your body so close?"

His lips turn up into a cocky smirk as he looks me over. "What? My body making it hard to breathe, Nat?"

"No," I say quickly. "That's not... never mind. I don't need to explain it to you. Just don't do that shit again without a warning first or I will rip your balls off. I mean it."

"You're right, I'm sorry." He gets serious again, his expression changing. I can tell he's struggling with how to act right now. This is an adjustment for both of us. "The moment Alana saw you in my jacket she began questioning me. I saw you step out of the bathroom all wet and looking cute in my jacket and I did what I would've done if we'd been a real couple. What she *knew* I would've done if we were a real couple. I'm going to have to do things to you, Nat." He runs a hand through his hair and takes another step back. "But I'll try my best to warn you next time. It's not a damn promise, though. Sometimes my body reacts before my head can figure out what the hell it's doing. That will happen a lot here this weekend. Can you handle that?"

"I guess I have no choice," I whisper, barely able to force the words out. "I'm stuck here now, aren't I?" When he doesn't say anything, I add, "I need to put my clothes away and brush my hair. I need a minute to get my shit together to deal with the rest of the day. So... just stay away for a few minutes and let me breathe."

He nods and takes a seat on the bed, pulling his suitcase to him. "Reasonable enough. Might want to get your bathing suit out while you're in there. It's about time to take a dip in the pool."

"This should be interesting," I mutter to myself, while gathering my scattered clothes and heading to my suitcase. I'm in the middle of going through my things when I get a whiff of Madden's body wash again. The more I move, the more powerful the scent becomes.

"It smells better on you." Madden's voice surprises me, reminding me that he's still in the room with me.

"Wait, what?" I look up to see Madden now leaning against the door, his arms crossed over his chest. "What smells better on me?"

He smiles. "The body wash you're sniffing. It's okay, I won't tell my brother you're in love with my scent."

"What!?" I drop my arm once I realize I've been holding it to my nose. "I'm not in love with it. I like it. I recognize a good fragrance when I smell one, that's all. It's... nice. Now stop smiling at me like that. It's really starting to piss me off."

"Why?" He lifts a brow. "Because I know you're lying?" He pushes away from the door and walks over to stand in front of me. "Hey. Quit getting snippy. No judgment from me. My brother's taste in body wash and cologne has always been shitty if you ask me. He smells older than his age. Get used to my scent, babe. Take it all in, because it's the only body wash you'll be smelling for the next five days. Just don't get too attached," he adds with a small grin.

"Yeah... that won't be a problem." I slap his chest. "By the time we leave here I'll never want to smell your body wash again. In fact, I'm sure of it."

"Are you positive?" he questions beside my ear.

I swallow and take a step back, trying my best not to sniff

the jerk. He's wrong. I'm positive it smells better on him. "A hundred and ten percent."

"If you say so." He opens the door and grips the door-frame while looking down at my suitcase. "Everyone is waking up. Change into your bathing suit and meet me in the kitchen. Unless you need to borrow a pair of my underwear."

"Yeah, no. I'm good. I'd swim naked before wearing your underwear." I snatch my bikini out of my suitcase and push him out of the room. "Stop looking at me like that. I have one, so it's not happening. Now leave so I can change."

I exhale the moment he walks away, finally feeling as if I can breathe again, but the moment I inhale, I get hit with his scent again, and it has me wishing I could smack Madden for being so cocky.

Less than ten minutes later, everyone is headed outside with one cooler filled with drinks and another filled with food for the grill.

Madden tugs the end of the leather jacket I'm still wearing. "Nice touch."

"I only kept it on because it's a little cloudy right now. Don't worry, I plan to take it off the moment the clouds disappear."

He flashes me a grin and reaches for my hand, lacing his fingers through mine. Leaning in, he whispers, "Sure. We'll go with that."

"What is that supposed to mean?" I ask, coming to a stop.

"It's okay if you *like* wearing my jacket, Nat. No need to make up excuses."

"Excuses?" I grab the end of the worn-out jacket, causing him to look down at it. "To wear this old thing that smells like your partying habits? Ha! Very funny."

He leans in, his eyes focused on mine as he sniffs close to my neck. "Smells like my body spray to me. But I forget that you like the way I smell." He sniffs me again, his closeness causing goose bumps to form. "With a hint of Victoria's Secret *Bombshell.* It's a damn good mix if you ask me. It's *hot.*"

I make sure no one is watching us before palming his face and pushing it out of my space. I don't even want to know how he knows the name of my fragrance. "Knock it off, Madden," I growl through clenched teeth. "Nothing about the two of us together is *hot.* It's annoying. That's what it is. Now, do you want me to play along with your little game?" He nods. "Then stop pushing my buttons just to get a rise out of me."

"I'm only doing what I have to, Nat." He grabs the back of my head, forcing our eyes to meet. "I need you to loosen up and stop acting so stiff around me. The thought of me close to you makes you nervous... I get it, but we need to change that and fast."

"It doesn't make me nervous." I lie.

He grins and moves in closer now that we have an audience. "So, if I kissed you right now, you wouldn't be nervous?" I swallow and peek over his shoulder to see Alana staring extra hard. "I *know* she's watching us right now. I also know she's probably expecting me to kiss you, but I won't. Not yet."

Not yet is a phrase that has me feeling weak in the knees as he takes a step back and grabs my hand again, not releasing it until we've reached the lounging area.

Why the hell did my body react that way to the idea of him kissing me? I knew from the very beginning there'd have to be a kiss at some point. I even mentally prepared myself for it before showing up at Logan's the other day ready to jump into his truck.

But now that we're here and things are real, I'm not sure I'm ready for Madden to kiss me. Even if it is only for show.

"Hey, babe! Join us over here." Jess motions for me to join her and Alana over by the pool, so I free my hand from

Madden's, glad to get away. "Us girls usually just hang out and relax while the boys man the grill. It's a little cloudy right now, but it'll warm up by the time we get done eating."

"Sounds good." I take a seat on the other side of Jess, glad to not be too close to Alana, who hasn't stopped staring at me since the moment we all got out here."

"A little warm for a *jacket*, isn't it?" Alana mutters, before sitting back and slipping her sunglasses on. "Someone just wake me up when the food is done."

Jess rolls her eyes and gives me an apologetic smile. "How did you sleep last night?"

"Like a baby." I lie. I couldn't sleep for crap last night. I woke up every couple of hours, looking down at Madden, reminding myself that my boyfriend—his brother—is at home where I should've been. "I always do in Madden's arms." I add loud enough for Alana to hear.

"Good to hear. It's sometimes hard to sleep the first night with everyone being excited to see each other and being away from home, but I've seen how Madden sleeps, so I can see why you slept like a baby. I wish Jake would cuddle me like that at night. Must be nice."

"It is. It's one of the things I love about him." *That's not a lie.* I got a small taste of how that felt that night on the couch.

"Good. I'm glad he brought you." She lays back and closes her eyes. "I'm going to rest my eyes for a bit too. Feel free to do the same and relax. The boys will get us when it's time to eat."

I nod and close my eyes, feeling anything *but* relaxed. The best I can do is pretend. It's not like I can call *Logan* and ask him to get me out of this situation. I'm here and I need to do what's needed of me.

WE'VE BEEN OUT HERE for close to an hour now and I couldn't help but notice that Madden was quick to pour himself a drink the moment Seth cracked open a fresh bottle a bit ago.

He looked anxious, as if he'd been waiting all morning for someone to start drinking so he could too. Now that we're around everyone else, he doesn't seem as laidback and relaxed. He's not the fun, carefree Madden I saw in the woods earlier, and I'm not sure how I feel about that. I liked that side of him, whether I want to admit it or not.

I didn't think seeing him upset over his ex would bother me so much, but it does. I hate that she has the power to hurt him to the point he feels the need to drown himself in alcohol just to function around her and his friends. It's unhealthy.

Seeing him like this makes me want to do something to change that, but I know I can't. I'm not the right girl to be here right now. What Madden needs is someone who can truly get him over her. He needs someone who can show him it's okay to move on, and that not every girl is going to hurt him the way she did.

He put all his trust and heart into Alana, and she crushed him. I can see why he hasn't had anything deeper than a sexual relationship with anyone else since. I know more than anyone what it's like to be lied to by someone you trust. It's not easy to recover once that happens.

I look away from Jess talking and take a moment to watch Madden interacting with the guys at the picnic table next to the one us girls are eating at. Jess suggested I eat with the girls so we could chat and get to know each other. It's been awkward, since Alana hasn't spoken one word the entire time I've been sitting down. If looks could kill I would've been dead over twenty minutes ago.

"I don't know about you ladies, but I'm ready to swim and

work off this greasy burger. You done with that?" Jess is talking to me, but my focus is on Madden as he tilts back his drink again.

"Yeah. I'm done."

Jess smiles and turns her attention toward the guys' picnic table once she notices where I'm looking. Her smile widens when Madden looks at me and winks just like he has every time our gazes have locked.

"I'm surprised you haven't melted from that wink yet, Natalie. Don't tell Jake, but our famous rock star has the hottest wink I've ever seen. He must really adore you too, because every time I've looked over there, he's looking right at you."

"And I'm sure he's also making sure I'm comfortable," I say nervously while gathering my dirty plate and napkins. "Since it's my first time meeting everyone and all."

"And your last time," Alana whispers into her cup, but I ignore her, not wanting to give her the attention she's seeking.

"Maybe so, but it's still cute." Jess stands and gathers her trash before yelling over to the boys. "You boys done chit chatting like girls so we can swim?"

"Hell yes," Seth yells back, before standing and yanking his shirt over his head. "We've been waiting on you girls to ask. You take forever to eat."

"Yeah, but it won't take me very long to kick your ass," Jess jokes back.

Madden stands to throw his trash away, and when he walks toward me, without thinking, I meet him in the middle and wrap my arms around his neck for show. "Your ex has been stabbing me in her mind this entire time. I think I even *felt* it break skin once."

"Ouch. Want me to grab your stun gun?" he teases. "We'll see which one hurts the most."

I laugh, before removing my arms from his neck. "Don't even try to be adorable right now, because I'm still considering using it on *you*."

He raises a brow, before taking a step back, and slowly pulls his shirt over his head. His eyes lower to his chest once he realizes where mine are focused. Not that I meant to. It happened naturally, and I hate myself for it. "Told you I'm bigger than my brother."

I growl under my breath, but before I can give him a piece of my mind he winks and backs away to join the guys by the pool.

When I turn back around Alana is down to a little black bikini. She's eyeing me up and down as if waiting to see if I can top her.

The bitchy look on her face has me wanting to rip her throat out, but instead, I force a smile and strip down to my bikini—the same exact one that she's wearing. Was not expecting this scenario.

Her nostrils flare out as she looks me over angrily, like she's imagining drowning me in the pool. "Nice bikini," she says stiffly. "Trying extra hard to replace me, I see. This is just great." She walks away, eyeing Madden up and down in his gray and black swim trunks.

He barely looks at her before his eyes land on me, visibly widening as he takes me in. His Adam's apple moves as he swallows. "Holy fuck, Nat. Does my..." He stops before slipping up. "You look entirely too sexy in that bikini. Is that the only one you brought?"

His compliment causes my heart to jump with unwanted excitement. "He didn't care, and neither should you. Besides, your ex is wearing the same one. I don't see you complaining."

He turns behind him to where Alana is standing with her hands on her hips, watching us. His eyes harden when they land on me again. "Yeah... but she's not the one making me *hard*. Answer my question."

"Yes, it's the only one I brought." My pulse races as my gaze roams over his hard body, stopping on the thick bulge beneath the thin fabric of his trunks. He does nothing to hide it, which immediately has me forcing myself to look anywhere else but there. "Next time maybe I will just swim in my clothes."

I walk away before either of us can say something stupid. It's natural for a guy to get aroused from seeing any decent looking girl in a bikini for the first time, right? That *has* to be it. He's seen Alana naked hundreds of times in the past. That explains why he's not excited by her right now. It's the only explanation.

"Did I miss the memo on what bikini to wear?" Jess asks, looking down at her white and pink top. "I'm totally ordering that the second this trip is over. We can all bring them next year and match."

Alana rolls her eyes. "This is bullshit. Why can't anyone else see he only brought her here to hurt me? If you all can't see it then clearly you don't know him as well as I do."

"Be cool, Alana. It's not nice to make assumptions. She's here with him. She *came* with him, and she's our guest." Jess gives her a hard look, before turning back to me. "Please don't take it personally."

"It's cool." I shrug it off. "She's set on believing what she wants to be true." I bring my attention to Alana. "Doesn't mean it is."

"Ladies, is everything good over here?" Madden wraps his arm around my waist and rests his chin on my shoulder.

"Yeah," Alana mutters. "Fucking peachy."

"Good." Madden's lips brush my neck, causing goose bumps to form. "Let's swim then."

I release a surprised yelp when he picks me up and slaps me hard on the ass. "Ouch! Why did you do that?"

"Because everyone is watching us, Nat," he says the moment we're at a safe distance from the girls. "Don't act like you didn't like it when we both know you did."

"What? I didn—"

"If you say so."

"I didn't. Now put me... Don't you dare throw me—"

Before I can finish our argument, he jumps into the water with me in his arms. I scream out as we hit the cold water and sink below the surface, his arms still wrapped around me when we come back up for air.

"I should kick your ass." I laugh when he pretends to push me back under the water. "Keep it up and I just might."

"Do it then," he pushes. With a small growl, he yanks me to him and grabs my right leg, wrapping it around his waist, before reaching for the left. "I bet you *really* want to now... being this close to me and all."

"How did you guess?" I mutter, pushing his chest hard enough for him to release me. I go to swim away, but he grabs my leg and bites it under water. "Did you just bite me?" I scream when he comes back up.

"What if I did? What are you going to do about it, Nat?" He pulls me back to him so that he can speak in my ear. "Bite me back?"

I laugh and place both of my hands on the top of his head. "Nope!" I shove him underwater, my laugh turning into a screech when he yanks me under with him, our bodies tangling together as he holds onto me.

Without realizing it, I wrap my legs around his waist again, my heartbeat skyrocketing when his semi-hard dick presses between my legs.

"Dammit, Madden," I mutter quietly. "Let me go."

"Why?" he questions, holding onto me tighter. "Don't be embarrassed, Nat. You know how they work. It's natural."

"To get an erection with your brother's girlfriend? I don't think so."

"Relax, okay." He grabs the back of my head and brings his lips to my ear. "Everyone is watching us. Just ignore my dick pressed up against you for five damn seconds. It doesn't take much to make it hard. It's not going to hurt you."

"It's impossible to ignore it," I growl, moving in closer so no one can hear us. "I need a drink."

"Probably a good idea. You're going to need to loosen up." With a crooked grin, he releases me, and I swim off in a hurry in need of some alcohol.

This is not what I signed up for.

And me being turned on by the situation is definitely not what his brother agreed to.

CHAPTER TEN

MADDEN

THE FACT THAT I'M ENJOYING NATALIE'S REACTION TO MY body is fucked up on many levels, since she's my brother's girlfriend. I know it, yet I can't help but like it. My brother would kill me if he knew how many times Natalie has made me *hard* since we've been here, but the fact that I'm in the same place as Alana and it's *someone else* keeping me distracted at the moment is a miracle. It's what I need to make it through this trip, so I don't fuck things up again like I almost did last year and the year before.

I need to finally make Alana a thing of the past, and I have a feeling Natalie is the girl to make that happen. Last night might've started out rocky, but I'm feeling more confident now that I know what needs to be done. I feel like an ass for what I'm about to put her through the remainder of this trip, but I also have to remember the reason she's here to begin with. And that is to make my ex believe that I've moved on.

I'm willing to go to extreme measures to make that a reality, and all I can do is hope that Natalie will forgive me by the end of the trip. Her *and* my brother...

I keep my eyes on Natalie as she pours a drink, before making her way back to the pool and sitting down to dangle her legs in the water. Right as she brings the cup to her lips to take a drink, I take it from her and tilt the cup back, emptying half of it. "I was about to drink that."

"I saw. You still can."

"We don't have to share this time, Madden. You've already proven to everyone that we're serious enough to drink after each other."

"Who says it's for show? Maybe I like sharing." I tilt the cup back, taking a small swig this time, before handing it back to her. "*Or* maybe I like the taste of your Chapstick. I haven't figured it out yet."

"It's Cake Batter," she mumbles over the cup. "If it's the taste of my Chapstick that you like then I'll just give you an extra one. Problem solved."

"Where's the fun in that?" I tease, loving the way she looks when she's all worked up over me. The blush across her cheeks has my smile widening.

"Here." She pushes the cup to my chest with a playful grin. "Your "girlfriend" likes to play Water Volleyball, and it looks like a game is starting. See you in there?"

With a smile, I bring the cup to my lips and watch as she dives into the pool with confidence.

Standing on the same side of the net as Alana, she peeks over her shoulder at me, waiting to see if I'm going to join. The fact that she took the last spot on Alana's team tells me she did it to keep Alana away from me.

And the look on my ex's face makes it clear just how pissed off she is. We have *always* played on the same team. *Not this time.* I'm grateful. I'll have to remember to thank

Natalie later, because I know being on the same team as Alana can't be comfortable for her.

Setting the cup down, I swim to the other side of the pool to join Jake's team. I can practically *feel* Alana's stare burning a hole into me, but I ignore it, keeping my focus on Natalie as she reaches behind her to tighten her bikini top.

Fuck me... She's the perfect distraction. I've barely even looked at my ex since Natalie stripped down to her bikini. The same exact one that *she's* wearing. Also, the same one I told Alana I loved on her last year.

"...ready?" Alana clears her throat louder than necessary, before nodding at the ball when I look her way. With a scowl, Alana serves the ball in my direction.

Just to make a point of ignoring her, I let Jake go after the ball. She's working too hard to get my attention. Even though a part of me still wants to give it to her, I'm fighting like hell this weekend to change that.

Jake hits it over and Alana and Natalie go after it at the same time, Natalie getting to it right as my ex swings out to hit it. The fact that Natalie got it instead of her has Alana giving the side of her head an evil glare.

"Nice hit, babe!" I clap my hands once, before hitting the ball when it flies in between myself and Seth.

"Nice, man!" Seth slaps my back, before returning his attention to the ball.

Walker and Riley both dive for it, Walker hitting just high enough to keep it above water so that Alana can tap it over to Jess, who hits it back over.

We volley for a while, the tension between the girls thick, before Jake finally misses it.

"Shit! That was a good one, everyone." He claps. "Let's keep it up. Drink anyone?"

"Me," Alana says stiffly. "Make it a double."

"I got ya, babe." He points around. "Anyone else? Madden?"

"No, I'm good, man."

"Natalie?"

She shakes her head. "No, thanks. We have one."

This earns a hard glare from Alana, but Natalie ignores her and swims to the net to chat with Jess while waiting on Jake to get back.

"Dude. Is Natalie a pro or some shit?" Walker says from beside me. "I haven't seen anyone that competitive in volleyball with Alana in like... well, ever."

I nod. "She played Volleyball in High School for four years." I know this because I heard her tell my brother about one of her old games last year when I stayed with him for a weekend. "She was the Speaking Captain."

"Impressive."

"Really, Walker?" Alana mutters from her spot. "Being able to hit a ball over a net isn't *that* impressive. I never played in High School and I'm just as good as she is."

"Drinks!" Jake yells from outside the pool. "Swim your asses over here and get them. I'm setting them down away from the game so they don't get wet."

Alana rolls her eyes, before swimming to her cup.

"Whatever, man. Ignore her. You know she's just pissed that you brought another girl. She'll eventually get over it." He slaps my back. "She'll have to. Especially since you'll be bringing her here from now on, right?"

"Yeah," I say softly, watching as Natalie laughs at something Jess says. *I'm sure my brother would love that.*

"Good. Let's play!"

Thanks to Natalie and Alana being on the same team, we lose our asses off twice. It's usually a close game even though Alana's team always manages to win each year, but this time, with two powerhouses on their side, it wasn't even a competition.

"Everything good?" Jake swims up beside me and leans against the edge of the pool. "How is Natalie handling things, and where the hell did you find someone so perfect for the part?"

"Good." I take a sip of my drink, my attention focused on Natalie and the girls. "She's my brother's girl," I force out.

"Fuck!" He runs his hands over his face in a hurry. "You're kidding, right?"

"Nope."

"Shit, Madden. You do realize that you and Natalie will have to get pretty damn cozy, and real soon if you want Alana to believe this shit, right?"

"Yeah."

"And your brother doesn't care? Did you tell him you'd be kissing and touching all over her this weekend? That your lips —the ones that all girls crave to kiss—will be on hers?"

I nod and take a swig of my drink. "He knows and he's fine with it. No tongue was his rule."

He laughs. "No tongue? And you think that shit's going to fly with Alana? She's been watching you two like a hawk since the moment you showed up with her."

I shake my head. "Nope. That's why I'm going to have to break his little rule."

"You do realize he's going to kick the shit out of you once this trip is over, right? I've seen that fucker pissed off and it's not a good thing to witness."

"What the fuck else can I do, Jake?" I pull my attention from Natalie to face him. "I *need* this to end. I can't do it anymore. I won't."

"Damn, man," he whispers. "Just don't take things too far. Don't do anything you'll regret later."

"Thanks for the tip. Can we stop having girl talk now?"

"All right. I'm done." He nods to Jess when she calls him over with her finger. "We'll talk later."

Releasing a frustrated breath, I set my drink down and swim my way over to Natalie, who is floating around on a flamingo with her eyes closed.

She sits up and opens her eyes when I grab the flamingo and pull her to me. "Crap, you scared me."

"How are things going with Jess? You two seem to be getting along well."

"I like her a lot." She smiles. "It's been a while since I've been able to talk to someone so easily other than Kayla and Carla. I wish your broth..." Her words trails off. "It would've been nice to come here and meet everyone sooner. Except your ex who is staring right as us. Is that ever going to stop?"

"Nope. I'm afraid not." I grab her arm and pull her into the water with me, moving in close until our bodies are touching. "She'll be watching every move we make, Nat."

"I kind of figured that," she mutters. "I was hoping she'd give up by now."

"That won't happen, because she's still *in love* with me. Like you're *supposed* to be." I grab the back of her head and move my lips along her ear. "Do you know what girls do when they're in love with me, Nat?" I grip her hip and breathe into her ear. "They *touch* and *kiss* me every chance they get. They can't keep their hands off me. *You* can. And she sees that."

"I think I'm going to need another drink first. Maybe even two if I'm going to pull *that* off. This isn't as easy for me as you expected. But I'm here and I'll do what I can."

She places her hands on my chest and pushes off so she can swim away to make another drink. I'm still watching her when I hear someone swim up beside me. I immediately stiffen up at the familiar scent of Alana.

"Did you do that on purpose too?"

I clamp my teeth together when I feel Alana's breath hit the back of my neck. "Do what?" I grind out.

"Have her buy the same bikini that you told me you loved so much on me last year. That's really low."

"What the fuck, Alana." I turn around to face her, my eyes meeting her hurt ones. I hate that it has me feeling bad. She's the one who did this. It's because of *her* that I have to lie. "I'm not that much of an asshole. That was just a coincidence. Whether you choose to believe it or not is on you."

She shakes her head, before focusing her attention over my shoulder. "You haven't done shit to prove to me that you're in love with her. You haven't even kissed her, and I know what that means... Kissing *means* something to you, and don't think I didn't do my research about your little kiss on stage the other night, which apparently Natalie has "forgiven" you for. I saw the video of you sticking up for that girl. I also saw the look of regret on your face after you kissed her." She pauses for a moment, and I'm thankful for it to stop. "I'm not giving you up so easily, Madden. You might've brought a girl with you this year in hopes of hurting me—and it did—but my plans haven't changed. You *will* realize how much you still miss me before this trip is over." She moves in closer until her mouth brushes my ear, sprouting goose bumps across my skin. I hate that my body reacts to her. "That's a promise."

Her words leave me on edge and my muscles tight as she swims away to join the others. *Fuck!* I run my hands down my face, before settling my attention on Natalie, who is in the middle of pouring a mixed drink. She just had to bring up that kiss on stage. I should've known it.

I don't think too hard about what I'm about to do next. It's something I *need* to do. Climbing out of the pool, I walk toward Natalie with purpose before I can change my mind.

"What's up? Everything—"

"No, it's not." Grabbing the back of her head, I crush my

lips to hers, causing a small moan to escape her as I grip her hip with my free hand. That moan is exactly what I needed right now, so I take that as a win. "Now it is," I say against her lips after breaking the kiss.

She swallows, her heated eyes locked on mine, and I can't tell if she's planning my death or if she somewhat enjoyed it. I have to admit, it wasn't terrible. Definitely far from it. It might just be the best tongue-less kiss I've ever had.

"That couldn't have waited until *after* I'd had at least two drinks?" she mutters quietly, pulling her eyes from mine before clearing her throat. "You can release my damn hip now before I kick your ass."

I release my grip and move in close to speak into her ear. "I need you to step up your game, Nat. This *won't* be the last kiss. In fact, it's the first of many to come. Even my brother knows that, and he still allowed me to *borrow* you. Think about *that* for a minute."

Before she can say anything or argue with me, I walk away and disappear into the cabin, needing a moment alone.

For one split second, I allowed Alana to get to me. And one second is too goddamn long when it comes to her. It was probably an asshole move to leave Natalie standing there alone after surprising her with a kiss and that dickhead remark, but the truth is, I'm not sure I'm ready to look at Alana after kissing another girl in front of her for the first time.

I can't risk letting her see how fucking nervous I am. She knows more than anyone what kissing means to me. It's a huge deal. "Shit!" I grip the kitchen island and take a few deep breaths to calm my nerves.

"Do you know how much of an ass—" Natalie pauses once noticing my tight grip. "Are you okay?"

I loosen my hold on the island and look up to see her standing in the doorway with two drinks in hand. "Here." She holds one out for me and I grab it. "Looks like we could both use a drink right now. Might as well drink them together, right? It's not like we're going to get away from each other anytime soon."

"Thanks." I empty half the drink in one gulp, before setting it down and turning to face Natalie again. "I'm sorry for leaving you out there alone. I just needed a minute."

"I get it." She takes a sip of her drink, leaning beside me against the island. "Alana looked like she was about to die when you kissed me. Not sure if that's what you need to hear right now."

"Good," I force out, my chest tight. "That means she's starting to believe you're not just some random girl I brought."

"But aren't I?" she asks, looking down into her cup.

"No." I pick her up and set her on the island, before stepping in between her legs. "You're anything *but* random, Nat. You may not like me much, but I've always enjoyed your company. Even though most of it has consisted of you insulting me over the years."

She laughs. "It's not that I don't like you, it's that..." She turns away for a second, as if to think of how to word it. "I just don't agree with your lifestyle when it comes to women. I get it, Madden. You're a hot rock star that all the women go crazy over. You're practically God's gift to women, but that doesn't mean you need to sleep with them all, does it?"

"Who says I sleep with them all?"

"Oh, I don't know... the world. The internet. Your fans. You've been spotted leaving hotel rooms with numerous women over the years. Are you trying to tell me you guys were playing a nice game of Scrabble?"

"Not at all." I meet her eyes so she can see the truth in them. I know a lot of people think I'm just some reckless rock star that fucks up all the time and bangs every girl I can get, but they don't know why. "You're right. I did fuck most of them. It was either that or drown myself in liquor until I forget who I am and how much I hurt. My brother knows just how good at that I am. And to tell you the truth, I've only fucked *one* girl while sober and none of them were it."

Her eyes soften, and I can't tell if it's because she pities me or understands. "Do you drink every day, Madden?"

I nod. "Yeah. You could say that."

"Can we make a deal then?"

"What kind of deal?"

"I'll push your *brother* out of my head and give you my *all* if you can promise me that you'll stay sober for two weeks after this trip is over. Just two weeks, Madden. Anyone can handle that." She releases a breath, her eyes locked on mine. "Will you do that for me? Please."

I nod and reach for the drink she made me. The way she mentioned my brother gives away that what I said outside about him worked, and she's pissed off at him. Unfortunately, I have a feeling that's the only way this thing between us is going to work this weekend. Call me fucked up and I won't deny it. I guess it's just part of my *reckless* nature. I'll make up for it later.

"If you can get me through this week, I'll do anything you fucking ask, Nat. Even *that*. I may hate the idea of it, but I'll do it. But I have to ask. Why *that?* You could ask for anything you want. I've already told you that."

"Because I care about you. Despite what you think you know about me and how I feel about you, I do wonder about your wellbeing when seeing all this crap on social media about you."

"So that's why you stalk me online." I flash her a crooked grin to lighten the mood. "I always thought it was because of my good looks. Like you said... I am sort of God's gift t—"

"Don't even say it or I'll change my mind." She jumps

down from the island, a small smile playing on her lips as she walks away. "You coming, *babe*?"

"Shit." I smirk and fall into step beside her. "I don't think you want me to come."

She stops and slaps at me a few times, before taking a quick drink from her cup to most likely calm her nerves. "Don't make me regret this, Madden."

I'm not sure there's much I can do to make her *not* regret this deal after this week is over. She said she's all in. Now she's about to see what it's like to belong to the *other* Parker Brother.

The moment we step outside and close the door behind us, I back her against it and wrap my hands into the back of her hair.

"*What* are you doing?" She stiffens when I move in, closing the distance between our bodies.

"What does it look like I'm doing?" I whisper against her ear, before running my lips along her jaw. The closer I get to her lips, the stiffer she becomes. "*Loosen* up, Nat. Remember our little conversation inside?" I tangle my hand into her hair, giving it a slight tug until our lips are an inch apart. "My brother doesn't exist right now, remember?"

"He doesn't," she whispers. "Is this you *testing* me?"

"What do you think, Nat?"

She stands up straight and wraps her arms around my neck, showing me she's finally ready to play. "Well, I don't fail tests. Never have, never will."

"*Good* to know," I whisper.

"Now, if you need me..." She releases my neck and takes a step back. "I'll be over by Jess getting some sun."

A small smirk plays on my lips as I watch her walk away with a newfound confidence she didn't have just moments ago. "This is either going to be fun or really fucked up." I hold my cup to my lips, about to take a drink, when Walker whistles from behind me.

"She's got to be the hottest chick I've ever seen, man."

His choice of words has me flexing my jaw in annoyance.

"If things don't work out between the two of you, I might have to ask for her number." He slaps my back and I bring my cup to my lips before I can say anything I'll regret. "Where did you meet this one?"

"At a concert."

"Shit. Guess I need to start going to more of your concerts then. I'd give my left nut to find a woman as beautiful as Natalie."

"Yeah. I guess so, man."

I walk away to refill my drink, my attention going to Natalie, who's now sunbathing beside Jess with her eyes closed. The way her breasts burst from the sides of her bikini top has me wanting to go over there and cover her up.

I don't understand why my idiot brother isn't here right now, wanting to protect her from all of us guys. Surely, the dick knows just how damn beautiful she is, right? He's not blind.

I'm not sure what the fuck Walker thinks is going to happen, but moments later, he takes a seat in the lounge chair beside Natalie's. That dickhead doesn't sunbathe and everyone knows it.

Taking one last drink of my whiskey, I squeeze the cup in my hand, before tossing it into the trash and making my way to Natalie. She jumps once she feels me in her space. "Shit, Madden. You scared me."

"Get up," I say stiffly.

"Why?" She sits up, confused, as I grab her hand and pull her from the chair.

Without answering her question, I sit down and pull her

into my lap, wrapping my arms around her. "Doesn't matter. Just close your eyes and relax."

"Awe! Aren't you two just adorable." Jess pushes her sunglasses up to get a better view of us. "I love it."

Alana standing up has my attention moving to the other side of the pool, where she was sunbathing with a pair of oversized glasses. Without a word, she grabs her towel and walks away, disappearing into the cabin.

Apparently, my kiss with Natalie has shaken her up a bit. She may be keeping her distance now since it's still fresh, but I give it a few hours before she's back on our asses.

"Yeah," Walker mutters. No one else may pick up on the disappointment in his voice, but I sure as hell do. "Super adorable."

"What can I say..." I smile against Natalie's neck, knowing she's going to kick my ass after this. "I had a hot little stalker at a few concerts, so I finally asked her out on a date. It was only fair after all that hard work she put into it. We've been a couple ever since."

"What?" She goes to sit up, but I hold onto her tighter, not giving her a chance.

"No shame in that game. That stalking paid off, girl. Own it." Jess pulls her glasses back down and sits back. "If Jake doesn't step up his game, I may have to do a little stalking myself. RISK is *full* of sexy men."

"I agree with you there," Natalie says, most likely to get me back for my little stalking comment. "Especially—" Grabbing the back of her head, I pull her in and bite her bottom lip, cutting her off before she can finish. "Ouch!"

"Funny," I mutter against her lips. "Who were you going to name?"

"If you're going to bite me again, I'd rather not say."

"Good." I smile against her lips, before kissing the bottom one for show. "Better finish that for the others."

She forces a smile and turns away to face Jess. "Madden. He's the one I had my eye on from the first time I saw RISK play. Him in that leather jacket of his, with those full lips and light eyes... He's absolutely gorgeous. No girl could deny it."

"Hey. I've known him for almost twenty years and I don't deny it. Even Jake has to hear about how hot Madden is from time to time. I'm not ashamed to admit that my friend is attractive. Doesn't mean I'm attracted to him like *that*. Just means I have eyes."

"Unfortunately, so do I," she says under her breath, like I can't hear her. She's dead wrong. She *meant* what she just told Jess about me. At least about my looks. The part about her wanting me... I doubt that. *That* was just for show.

But damn if she didn't do a good job convincing the others. If I didn't know how much she hated me, I'd almost believe it myself. *Almost.*

Fortunately, it's not me she needs to convince.

CHAPTER ELEVEN

NATALIE

IT'S BEEN A FEW HOURS SINCE MADDEN KISSED ME FOR show. My thoughts are still flip-flopping back and forth between being pissed at the reminder that his brother gave him permission in the first place and being angry at myself for enjoying the way his lips felt on mine for even just the slightest moment.

His kiss was soft, yet powerful in a way I can't explain. If *that* was just for show, what would it feel like if it wasn't? What would it be like to kiss Madden Parker for real? The type of kiss he's apparently only given to one woman.

Luckily, I won't have to find out. A girl could easily be ruined for life after experiencing just a small portion of what his mouth can do. It won't affect me, though. I know this is pretend. I won't fall for America's hottest rock star, no matter just how pissed I currently am at his brother—*my boyfriend* —who is *supposed* to want me all for himself.

I need to stop thinking, because the more I do, the

angrier at Logan I become. I can't be angry at him right now; not when I'm stuck here with his brother.

Pushing those thoughts from my mind, I open the bedroom door, my mouth instantly dropping when I get a glimpse of Madden's firm and very naked ass on display. "I'm sorry! I didn't—"

Without a word, he turns around completely naked and stalks across the room, slamming the door shut behind me. My eyes take in every inch of his hard, muscular body; its tattooed perfection now etched into my brain forever. "Don't fucking apologize, Nat. *Never* apologize for seeing me naked. Do you want Alana to hear that shit? She's already on my ass."

I swallow and back up against the door, needing to put some space between us. He makes no move to cover his naked body. In fact, it's as if he's completely unashamed by it. "How do you expect me to react when walking in on my boyfriend's *naked* brother?" I put my hand up to shield my eyes. "*Please* put some clothes on."

"Why?" he pushes.

"Because your nakedness makes me uncomfortable. I can never un-see your junk, Madden."

"Do you even want to, Nat?" I stiffen up when I feel him move in closer. He's not quite close enough for me to feel him against me, but close enough that I can feel the warmth of his naked body. "Because your eyes were quick to veer south the moment I turned around. Now you don't have to search for nude photos of me online. You're welcome."

"Excuse me!" I open my eyes moments after I feel him move away, catching him right as he's pulling his jeans up. "I've never searched for nude images of you online, and the fact that your ego is big enough to assume that I have only makes you that much more annoying."

"My ego or my dick?"

The slight tug of his lips lights a fire inside. I move in to give him a shove, but he catches my arms before I can and pulls me into him. "Let. Go."

"Nat, lighten up. You're making too big of a deal over seeing me naked. I was just trying to see how worked up you were, and apparently, that's pretty fucking worked up."

"I'm not worked up." I lie. "And I didn't see anything other than your ass." Another lie. I definitely got an eyeful of his very sizeable asset, along with the perfect V of muscles leading down to it. The bad part is, it wasn't even hard and I can already tell it's bigger than his brother's. "I just wasn't expecting to see you without clothes. Did you forget that we share this bedroom? You could've given me a heads up."

He shrugs and reaches for a plain white T-shirt. "You were busy talking with Jess. Not my fault you followed me to the bedroom."

"Followed you?" I grit out. "I did not *follow* you."

"If you say so. Doesn't bother me. I'll walk around naked twenty-four-seven if that's what you like. We both know my brother won't do that shit."

"How do you know what your brother does and doesn't do for me?" He's annoying me more with each word that leaves his lips.

"I've known my brother his whole life. We're the complete opposite. I guarantee he only gets naked long enough to fuck and shower. Don't tell me I'm wrong either."

"Whatever. Just leave the room so I can change. Jess is waiting on me."

"Which is exactly why I'm *not* going to leave the room while you change. What kind of boyfriend does that?" He crosses his arms over his chest and laughs. "They all know I sure as hell don't."

"Fine. Then turn around and close your eyes or I'll pluck them from your head." He grins and shakes his head, before turning to face the wall. "And don't peek."

"Don't worry. I won't look at you naked until you ask."

"Ha!" I toss my bikini top at the back of his head. "You're delusional if you think I'll *ever* ask for that." I quickly pull on a pair of panties, before slipping on some jeans. I go to reach for my bra next, but quickly cover my breasts when Madden turns around, holding my bikini up by the strap. "I'm not done yet. Turn back around." He balls up my bikini top in his hand and turns back around. "And give that back." Without a word, he tosses it over his head and I catch it, quickly stuffing it into my suitcase before pulling on a loose T-shirt. "You can turn around now."

Turning around, he places a cigarette between his lips, keeping his eyes on me as he lights it. *Why do I find that so hot?*

"Are we good now? Did you get your anger and frustration out from me kissing you earlier?" He walks over to open both bedroom windows. "I know you've been holding it in since earlier. That's why I pushed you to let it out."

"Really, Madden?" I throw my messy hair up and walk over to snatch the cigarette from his lips. "I already told you I was ready to play this little game. I don't need any more push-ing. Let's get this night started so we can get it over with. The sooner we can go to bed, the better."

Before he can say anything, I put his cigarette out on the window ledge and toss it to him, walking away.

The moment I'm free from Madden, I press my back against the door and place my hand over my racing heart, mentally begging it to slow down. I don't know why he has the ability to work me up so much or why I'm allowing him to do it.

"...whatever, Jess. Just stop..." Alana's voice coming from the kitchen has me standing up straight and moving closer to hear better. "...I'm getting Madden back before this weekend is over. I saw the look on *her* face when he kissed her. She looked just as surprised as I was. It's bullshit, Jess. He's fucking with me. Trust me. He's not in love with her."

Jess says something that I can't make out, before Alana comes back with a "Screw that" and storms outside, slamming the door shut behind her.

I wait a few seconds before pushing away from the door and making my way down the hall to join Jess in the kitchen.

"Hey, babe!" Jess holds a cup out to me the moment she sees me coming. "Made you my specialty drink. Hope you like it."

"Thanks." I nod and grab the cup from her. "What was that about?"

She shakes her head while sipping from her cup. "Nothing to worry over. Just Alana being Alana."

She's wrong. It is something to worry about and I need to change that.

"Let's join the others outside. The boys are gathering wood for the bonfire and I'm sure Madden is tuning up his guitar to play for us."

"To play for us?"

"Yup!" She loops her arm through mine and begins walking me outside. "Madden always plays for us on Friday nights. It's been his thing for as long as I can remember. If you think he's *hot* on stage, just wait until you see him in the light of the fire playing his acoustic. If you're not completely in love with him yet, you will be."

Yeah, cause that's what I need. Another reason to be attracted to my boyfriend's brother.

The memory of the night I caught him playing his guitar in his brother's living room creeps in, reminding me of how badly I wanted to stick around and watch that intimate moment. It was stupid, and luckily is was ruined by a text from Alana. At least, lucky for me... him, not so much.

I still remember the look in his eyes when she ruined him for probably the millionth time since she first broke his heart.

And that look—the one etched into my brain—is going to get me through this night as his girlfriend. *Fuck Alana*. She broke him. This—me playing pretend with mister cocky rock star—is all her fault to begin with.

Once outside, Jess unloops her arm from mine and motions for me to take a seat in the chair beside her. Alana is across the fire pit once again—no surprise there—in the perfect place to keep her eyes on me. *Good. Hope you like what you see.*

"Does Madden play for you outside of concerts often?"

"Not often enough," I admit.

"Seems he likes to save his private concerts for himself or here around the bonfire. I'm not even sure his brother has heard him play many times outside of being here." The mention of Logan has me almost choking on my drink. "Have you met him yet?"

I nod. "A few times."

"He's cute, right?" Her smile widens, as if remembering something. "We *almost* hooked up once before I got with Jake. A bit of a player, he is."

"A player?" I nearly choke on my tongue, fighting back asking a million questions that I know would catch me and Madden up.

She nods and points across the fire pit to where Alana is still watching us. "Yeah. Supposedly he even hit on Alana a few times when her and Madden were dating. I mean... he was drunk, but it still counts. Plus, he's practically hooked up with every girl he grew up with."

The more I hear, the sicker I become with anger and disgust.

"What did Madden do about him hitting on Alana?"

She shrugs. "Not much. I guess he just brushed it off as

Logan being Logan. He knew nothing would ever happen between them. That's a line Logan wouldn't cross. Didn't matter how drunk he was."

My stomach hurts just thinking about the side of Logan that he's apparently kept hidden from me. The bastard is lucky there's no service here, because I can think of a lot of questions I'd like to ask him right now.

I'm so wrapped up in what I just learned about Logan that I didn't even notice Madden was outside until he drapes his jacket over my shoulders and moves in close to my ear. "You forgot this," he whispers.

My eyes follow him as he walks over to a tree away from the rest of us and leans against it, setting his guitar down beside him. Once again, I'm drawn to the way he places a cigarette between his lips and lights it. Taking a drag, he leans his head back and slowly exhales, the smoke surrounding him.

I'm still watching Madden, unaware of anyone else, when his eyes finally meet mine. Instead of turning away, he brings the cigarette to his lips again and takes a long drag, before tossing it and stomping it out with his foot.

Without a word, he grabs his guitar and walks over to a stool, pulling it out so that he's sitting directly in front of me, facing my way. My heart rate speeds up from the anticipation of him playing so close to me.

"Right on, man." Jake takes a seat on the other side of Jess and wraps his arm around her. "What are you going to play for us first?"

Madden smiles, his attention focusing back on me, but instead of answering the question, he begins playing *Send Me An Angel* by Highly Suspect.

An instant smile takes over at his choice of band. The moment he begins singing, my breathing picks up, my chest quickly rising and falling as I listen to the passion in his voice. It's so goddamn beautiful that it's taking my breath away.

And *this* is the exact reason I've only seen RISK in concert once. It was just months after I started dating Logan. In fact, I hadn't even met Madden yet. The first song he played had me forgetting about all the stuff on social media in regard to the reckless, playboy rock star. I felt him creeping into my soul that night, and that's when I decided it was best to *hate* him... to believe all the shit put out there about him online.

I squeeze my cup in my hand, before bringing it to my lips desperately, needing it at the moment. Good thing Jess's specialty drink is good, because I'll be needing the whole thing before this song is over.

After taking a long drink, I chance a glance at Alana to see her expression has turned to anger. I can't tell if she's pissed at Madden or pissed at herself for breaking his heart in the first place. If I were her, I'd be pissed at myself. In fact, I'm pretty sure this moment would make me *hate* myself—seeing the man I love play for another woman.

When I turn my attention back to Madden, his eyes are on me. His gaze is so penetrating, and mixed with the intensity of his voice, I nearly forget to swallow the drink I've just taken. How the hell am I supposed to breathe right now with him looking at me like that?

"You've got goose bumps," Jess says in my ear with a slight laugh. "Told you."

Pulling my eyes away from Madden, I slip my arms into his jacket to hide the goose bumps that have apparently formed on them. I can't even blame the night breeze, because the fire is so hot that my face feels like it's on fire.

Once the song ends, someone whistles loudly, which has Madden smiling at me while he prepares for the next song.

I return his smile, unable to stop myself. I *hate* that smile. It's incredibly adorable, which means he's doing it on purpose to get a rise out of me.

The next song he plays has me dying even more inside as I listen to the lyrics. His voice in this song holds so much pain, but in a good way. Too damn painful.

"Who is this?" I ask Jess.

"Imminence," she whispers. "*A Mark On My Soul.* Love this song."

Well, looks like I do too now. I just wish he would stop looking at me while singing it. I seriously don't know how many more songs I can sit through with those damn eyes of his on me. He's doing *this* on purpose—pushing me—and I'm starting to believe he loves getting a reaction out of me. It's working more than it should.

Luckily, after the song ends, he sets his guitar down beside him, giving me a moment to catch my breath. Surely, he's not done yet, though.

Walking over to me, he kneels down in front of me and grabs the back of my head. "You okay over here?" he asks with a slight smile. "*Breathe*, Nat."

"I am," I say quickly. "Who said I'm not?"

"No one has to say it. I can tell you're not." He moves in close, his lips brushing over mine. "*See*... not breathing."

"You're wrong," I whisper. "But I would appreciate it if you'd *stop* looking at me while you sing."

His grip on the back of my head tightens as he smiles against my lips. "Kiss me, Nat. Everyone's watching. Or are you too afraid after being lost in me for the last ten minutes?"

"There's *nothing* to be afraid of. Your lips don't affect me in the slightest."

"Then prove it," he breathes out. "Kiss me."

Before I can talk myself out of it, I grab his face in both hands and press my lips against his, kissing him harder than I meant to. The brush of his tongue over my sealed lips almost has me opening up, but I pull back before I can make that mistake. It was almost too natural.

"Madden," I mutter so only he can hear. "You know the rules."

"Rules are meant to be broken, Nat. I'm the reckless rock star, remember?"

With that, he walks away and grabs his guitar. I keep my angry gaze on him as he begins playing again. This time it's one of his songs, and just like before, he makes a point to look at me while he sings.

My thoughts are bouncing back and forth between wanting to murder him and wanting to get lost in him again. No one has ever been able to work me up this way before. Not even Logan on his worst days.

Shit, this was a bad idea. A very bad idea.

"I'll be back," I mutter to no one in particular, before standing up and walking away, my heart racing so hard it feels like it's going to burst from my chest. I need to get away.

Once I make it to the cabin, I finish what's left of my drink and quickly make another one, being sure not to make it too strong. As much as I wish I could be drunk right now, being drunk is probably a bad idea. Not that I'm saying I'd do anything *inappropriate* with Madden, just that it's best to be in my right mindset while playing this little game with him. I've gotta make sure things don't go too far.

"Pass the Vodka if you're done with it." Walker's voice has me turning to face him. "The bottle..."

"Oh, right. Sorry." I pass him the bottle and watch as he pours himself an extra strong drink.

He catches me watching and flashes me a playful smile. "Nice game today. You were looking good out there."

"Thanks. I played in High school."

"I know. Madden mentioned that earlier."

"He did?" The question comes out before I can stop it. I don't remember telling Madden about my volleyball days on the way here. Apparently, he's done his research.

"Yeah." He brings his cup to his lips and takes a small drink. "You looked a little flustered out there when Madden started singing. Your first time hearing him sing outside of a live concert?"

I shake my head. *Yes.* "No. He's played for me a few times. I just needed another drink, that's all."

"You must really be into him if you needed another drink. He have you feeling a certain way you weren't expecting? I can do that too."

Before I can question what he meant by that, the door opens to Madden stepping inside. He takes one look at how close Walker is to me and grabs my hand. "Let's go, Nat."

"Okay..." I say when he pulls me along beside him as if in a hurry to get me away from Walker. "What's the deal?" I ask the moment we get outside.

"Nothing," he says rigidly. "Everyone's waiting on you to come back out. Knowing Walker, he'll keep you to himself for as long as the fucker can."

"What's wrong with Walker?" I laugh. "He seems nice."

"Yeah, a little too fucking nice. Trust me."

"Calm down, Madden." I take off walking toward the bonfire. "You're acting like he's going to make a move on me."

"He might," he grits out, falling into step beside me. "You let me know if he does and I'll lay the dickhead out. I mean it, Nat."

I swallow, not used to someone being so protective over me. "Okay, I will."

"Good. That's all I ask."

Once back with everyone else, Madden keeps his eyes on the cabin, as if he's waiting for Walker to come out. Jake and Seth are talking to him about something, yet he isn't paying much attention to them.

I can't believe how worked up he is over Walker getting me alone. I deal with assholes all the time at the hotel who hit on me and try to pick me up, and all Logan does is shake his head and say, "It's a good thing you have that stun gun then," as if he isn't worried about someone getting to me in the slightest.

Just *once* I'd like to see him care enough to get worked up like his brother is right now. He might be playing *pretend* this weekend, but his reaction in the cabin was anything *but*.

I shouldn't like it, but I do. Maybe I don't have to be drunk to do something inappropriate. And that scares me.

CHAPTER TWELVE

MADDEN

I'M PROTECTIVE OVER NATALIE IN A WAY I'VE NEVER BEEN with Alana. Hell, my own brother used to hit on her and I brushed it off, knowing nothing would ever happen between them. I know for a fact nothing would *ever* happen between Natalie and Walker, yet I still want to keep him away from her.

I've known Walker my entire life—he's one of my best friends—but when it comes to keeping Natalie safe I'll fuck him up if it comes down to it. *I* brought her here, which makes her *my* responsibility, and the way he was eyeing her over earlier like a piece of ass he wants to conquer, he will now be in my sights at all times.

"Who's got the speaker?" Riley questions from behind me somewhere. "I'll hook it up to my phone."

"It's right here," Alana mutters. "And *no* you won't. I'll hook it up to mine. I'm done listening to that song from RISK. I've got something better to play."

Seconds later, Alana's playlist begins playing over the

portable speaker. Her song choice has my eyes meeting hers as the lyrics to *Alone* by I Prevail surrounds us. It's the song I played for her after she walked away from me and broke my heart. I was desperate to get her back. Apparently, she wants me to remember this song and what it meant that night.

Well... it's working. That familiar ache hits my chest as I get lost in her stare; the one that used to take my breath away. I'm lost in Alana—lost in that moment of our past—when a hand grabs my cheek and I'm face to face with Natalie.

"Dance with me," she whispers in my ear, wrapping her arms around my neck as she moves in close; so fucking close. "Come on."

Pissed that I allowed Alana to get to me, I wrap my arms around Natalie and move my body against hers to the song that's haunted me for years; the lyrics that break me and remind me of how Alana left me bleeding each time I hear it. "You sure you want this with me? I can't be held liable for what I do right now."

"Not sure I have much of a choice," she says quietly. "You were about to lose it, Madden. *Everyone* was watching you."

"Including you?" I question above her lips.

"It was hard not to. You only stood there for a solid minute staring at your ex. The girl you're trying to prove to that you've *moved on* from."

"This song fucks with me, Nat. It gets in my head and makes me think about what I lost. In case you haven't noticed, music talks to me and fucks with me in the worst ways. She *knows* this."

"Then show her how much this song *doesn't* affect you anymore. It's what I'm here for, right? *Use* me."

My gaze lowers to hers, and without a second thought, I bring my lips to hers, growling against them when she kisses me back. She's less hesitant this time, which has me swiping my tongue out like an asshole. The slight brush of her tongue on mine before she pulls it back has my dick hardening.

"Fuck," I whisper, before biting her bottom lip and tangling my hand into the bottom of her hair. I'm completely lost in this moment with Natalie—and so damn turned on— that I don't even realize I'm grinding my dick against her until she moans against my mouth and presses her hands against my chest.

"Stop, Madden," she breathes out. "Don't... move..."

"Why?" I push, continuing to move my body against hers. I'm taking my anger out on her even though I know I shouldn't. I need to feel anything but what I was feeling before we started dancing. "I asked you if you really wanted to do this. You wanted to dance, so..."

"I need you to *stop* now," she growls against my lips. "Your dick—"

"What?" I move my free hand down to grip her ass, pulling her closer to me. The feel of her ass in my hand causes my dick to jerk against her. "Feels *good* against you? It's okay to admit..."

"Fuck you. I'm done helping you." She bites my lip hard enough for me to release her. "Good luck on your own."

I stand here, hands in my hair as she heads toward the cabin. I can feel eyes on me, but I'm too focused on what I need to do to make up with Natalie to care.

"Everything okay?" Jess questions. "Need me to go talk to her?"

"No. She's good, Jess. She just had a drink too many and needs a moment to cool off." When I turn away from Jess, Alana's gaze is on me. I can't tell if she's hurt by me kissing Natalie or happy about her stomping away. "I think we're going to call it a night and wind down in the hot tub."

The mention of the hot tub has Alana's eyes narrowing in

anger, but before she can say anything, I walk away in search of Natalie.

I find her in the bedroom with her phone in her hand. She doesn't look up when she hears me enter the room. Instead, she continues to type furiously. "What do you want?"

"What are you doing? There's no service here."

"Oh, nothing. Just sending out a long, detailed message to your brother and how I want to kick his ass for being a liar. *And* for agreeing to let me come here this weekend. I want to get it all out before I forget any details."

"Are you drunk?"

She holds up her empty cup before flicking it my way. "That's none of your business. Now go away. I'm done with you for the night. I've played your game all day."

"What exactly are you saying to my brother about me? That I'm a better kisser?" I tease her, hoping to get her attention long enough so she'll stop typing. "Because he already knows. You're not the first girl that we've both kissed."

"What?" She finally sets her phone down and looks at me. "Is that true?"

I shrug. "I don't know. Maybe."

She rolls her eyes at me. "What do you want, Madden? I'm not feeling up to playing any games right now. Especially after what you just pulled out there. I told you to stop and you kept dancing."

"I'm sorry. I shouldn't have said what I did. But I'm not sorry about making you *feel* good, Nat. You deserve more attention than you get."

"How do you know what kind of attention I do and don't get?" she asks angrily. "Your brother isn't as neglectful with me as you might think."

"Come on. I've never seen my brother touch you. Does he even grab your ass like I did out there? Because it's a beautiful fucking ass and deserves to be grabbed and bit and whatever else you want done to it." I shouldn't have said what I just did, but I can't help myself right now. Maybe I had a few too many drinks too, because more unwanted words spill out. "My hands would be all over it twenty-four-seven if you were mine. Probably my *tongue* too."

She swallows nervously and clears her throat. "He touches my ass plenty." It's a lie and even she knows it. Her nervous expression gives her away. "Your brother knows what he's doing with me. In fact, sex with him is the best sex I've ever had."

Not sure why that last part annoys me, but it does. "Because you haven't had me," I say with confidence. "But enough about my brother for tonight. We're both a little tipsy and need some downtime. I already told the others we're going to spend some time alone in the hot tub. We can talk for a while. About anything you want."

With my eyes on hers, I yank my shirt over my head and toss it aside with a smirk. "Undress."

"Undress?" she questions. "You mean change?"

I laugh as I kick my jeans aside and adjust my boxer briefs. "Your underwear is fine. I've already seen you in them. Besides, your bathing suit is more revealing."

"I'm wearing a thong," she mutters. "It's definitely more revealing than my bathing suit."

"Do you feel like changing back into your bathing suit?"

She shakes her head. "Not really."

"Then wear your underwear. No one's going to see you but me." I cover my eyes. "Here. I'll even cover my eyes while you strip if you want."

"Fine. Throw me that clean towel over there."

I smile and throw her the towel she asked for. "Let me know when I can look."

"You can look," she says a few moments later.

I remove my hand to see her wrapped in the fluffy white

towel. "Looks good on you," I joke. "Sexiest towel I've ever seen."

She cracks a smile. "Shut your face before I change my mind and go to bed instead."

"I'll behave the rest of the night. I promise."

She hesitates for a moment, before following me through the cabin and out the side door that leads to the hot tub. There's a small deck around it which gives us some much-needed privacy.

I know it's been a long day of pretending for Natalie, and I need to do my best not to wear her out or piss her off too much before this trip is over. Plus, I need some time away from Alana anyway. I don't think I can take her eyes on me any more tonight.

"So what do you want to talk about?" I ask after we're both settled on opposite sides of the hot tub. "The hotel? My brother? I'm all ears."

"I pretty much hate my job, so I'd rather *not* talk about that right now."

"Fair enough." I place my locked hands behind my head and get comfortable. "So my brother it is. How did you meet?"

"He never told you?"

I shake my head. "We don't usually talk about things like that."

"We met at *Beggie's*—the diner he was *supposed* to meet me for lunch at yesterday. He was taking a lunch break from the office that day and I had just gotten done with my shift at the hotel. I overheard him cussing at someone on the phone and laughed at his seriousness."

"And then he came over to give you a piece of his mind?"

"Yup. Told me to mind my own business. When I told him to fuck off, he took a seat instead and apologized for his confrontation."

"Sounds like him. Always with that stick up his ass."

She tries not to laugh at the last part, but I catch her up before she wipes her smile away and crosses her arms. "What next?"

"How many times have you seen me in concert?"

"What makes you think I've seen you in concert?"

"You have at least once." I smile at the way her cheeks flush. "Did you really think I didn't notice you in the crowd? A few months after you started dating my brother—we hadn't met yet actually—you showed up at that concert we put on in LA. It was a smaller venue than usual, and you caught my eye in the front of the crowd. I didn't know who you were at the time, but I recognized you the moment my brother introduced us for the first time."

"You noticed me that night?" she asks softly. "How? There had to be close to three hundred people there that night."

"And none of them stood out but you," I admit. "The girl with the mahogany hair that disappeared rather quickly. I looked for you for like two songs before I finally realized you probably left. Was I right?"

She hesitates before nodding.

"Why did you leave?"

"The truth?"

"The truth..."

"I couldn't stop staring at my boyfriend's brother and it made me feel guilty. That mixed with the emotions you possessed while you sang was too intense for me and I had to get out of there."

"Kind of like tonight?" I say, pushing more boundaries. "I saw the look in your eyes before you walked away, Nat." I add when she doesn't respond quick enough. "It's okay to feel that way. Most girls do, and that's not me being cocky. Music is supposed to make you feel that way. It's supposed to make you *feel* something. That's why I love doing it."

"Why does it make me feel guilty then? Like I'm doing something wrong?"

"Do you *want* to do something wrong?"

Her mouth opens as if she's about to speak, but the side door opening has me pulling her across the hot tub and into my lap.

"Hey, guys." Jess pops her head around the privacy wall so she can see us. "Just wanted to make sure you're feeling better, Natalie. Madden said you needed to cool off because you had a little too much to drink. Sorry if I made yours too strong."

"I'm fine," Natalie confirms. "Just needed a few minutes to calm down and gather my thoughts."

"Nothing wrong with that, hon. Especially when you have, well... you know who to deal with. You don't know any of us very well and I'm sure it's not easy being here." She pauses for a second to smile when I kiss Natalie's neck to comfort her. "But I'm glad you came. Even *if* Alana is freaking out on me every chance she gets. I'm not going to pretend I don't like you just because she doesn't. So just know that I do and so does everyone else, Alana excluded, of course. But that can't be helped."

"Thanks for checking on her." I should've known she would, because that's how Jess is. "And thanks for being supportive, Jess."

"Always. We just brought out some blankets to lay around the fire and hang out. No one is really drinking or talking much anymore. I grabbed an extra blanket in case you want to join us after the hot tub."

"Thanks, Jess. That was nice of you," Natalie says from my lap, where my arms are tightly wrapped around her waist. "Sounds like a good idea."

"Okay, good!" Jess offers a friendly smile before turning around when Alana calls her name from inside. "I better go before Alana comes out here looking for me. I know she's dying for an excuse to come spy on the two of you."

"Are you wanting to join them?" I ask once we're alone. "All it'll require is me cuddling you on the blanket. You can pretend I'm my brother if it helps. We don't even have to talk."

She looks as if she wants to say something, but instead, she just nods and moves out of my lap. "Yeah. Cuddling by the fire sounds nice."

That's something we both can agree on.

CHAPTER THIRTEEN

NATALIE

I haven't been able to stop thinking about mine and Madden's conversation in the hot tub since we climbed out and changed into dry clothes. The fact that he noticed me *before* his brother introduced us has been on my mind since the moment he admitted it.

Out of all the women at the concert that night, I stood out to him. He noticed me and even looked for me when I disappeared. That's going to screw with my head for a long time after this trip is over. I hate it, but it will.

Madden is first to take a seat on the empty blanket, before he grabs my hand to pull me down to him. I'm not surprised when he immediately guides me between his legs and wraps me up in his arms. What I am surprised by is how good it feels to be held by him. If I'm being honest, I don't think his brother has ever held me like this before.

His arms and legs wrapped around me make me feel so warm and protected. A fire isn't needed right now; just *him*.

"You comfortable?" he asks quietly.

I nod. "Very, actually."

He smiles against my cheek, before whispering, "I've always been good at cuddling. You can *borrow* me anytime after this trip is over, as long as it's in bed."

I pinch his arm playfully. "Ha. Ha. Always with the jokes. Do they ever get old?"

"Not really. You should know this by now."

I sort of do. He's always been the playful type. Just in a *different* way than this weekend.

"Is it bad that I'm already tired?" Jess yawns from her place in Jake's arms. "It feels like it's close to two a.m. already. I think I'm getting old."

"It's barely nine," Walker points out. "It's probably from playing volleyball. Plus, we all stayed up late as shit last night." He rolls over on his back and locks his fingers behind his head. His eyes land on me. "I could go all night long. I don't get tired."

"That's a fucking lie," Seth says on a laugh. "That's not what Nicole said last Summer."

"Fuck off," Walker mutters in response to Seth, pulling his eyes from me suddenly. I wonder if it's because of Madden. Whatever the reason, I'm thankful. "I was so drunk I could barely walk. She's lucky she got the ten pumps she did before I passed out on top of her. I guarantee they were the *best* ten pumps of her life."

"Fuck that noise," Riley adds. "She ended up in my bed two weeks later, and unlike you, I lasted more than ten pumps, brother."

"Sounds like a lucky girl," Alana mumbles. "I bet neither one of you losers made love to her all night, or made sure her needs were met first. Men like you two don't put women first in the bedroom. You're too fixated on pleasing yourselves and just expect her to come before you." Her attention turns to Madden and my cheeks burn hot from realizing that she's most likely comparing them to him. "I've only met one man who could completely satisfy me in the bedroom. I don't expect anyone to ever compare."

I feel Madden's arms tighten around me, and that's enough to turn my attention away from Alana before she catches me staring at her. My face feels tight, so I'm guessing the look on my face right now isn't a good one. I wear my emotions more times than not.

"Soooo..." Jess clears her throat to change the subject. "Are you staying with your brother for a bit before you go back to being a famous rock star or what?"

My heart pounds with anticipation as I wait for Madden's response. A part of me hopes he says yes, while the other part knows I should hope he says no.

"Nah, not with my brother. I'm going to stay with Nat at her place for a few days before heading back to the wild life. I want some alone time to take care of her before I leave again..." He squeezes my hip, making my heart flutter. "I have a lot to make up for from being gone so much. After this, she's *mine* for a few days. Just the two of us, alone, with no distractions."

Why do I like the sound of that?

I swallow, my mouth suddenly feeling dry.

"Lucky you!" Jess grins at me. "You're dating probably the most loyal and loving rock star to walk this earth. You're a lucky woman. I hope you know that."

"I do." I smile and rest my head on Madden's chest. When he grabs my throat and pulls my head back so his lips hover over mine, I stop breathing for a moment.

"Say that again," he whispers against my lips. "Tell me you're lucky to be *mine*."

"I'm lucky to be yours, Madden." My eyes meet his, and for a second, I almost believe my own lie.

"Good. Because I'm keeping you."

"Turn that up," Alana mutters to Riley who is holding the remote for the music. She's sitting on the same blanket as him, so when he doesn't move fast enough for her, she grabs the remote and does it herself. "There... much better." She shoots Madden a hateful look before leaning against Riley's shoulder to keep warm.

Everyone's quiet for a while after, just sitting around enjoying the warmth of the fire, few words spoken here and there. I have to admit that I'm enjoying the simplicity of the night. I expected every night to be nothing but a party, but it's not like that with this group of friends and I'm thankful. *This* is exactly what I'd like to have with Logan and our friends back home. I crave it.

"You warm enough?" Madden whispers against my ear. Without giving me a chance to answer, his entire body is wrapped around mine, holding me closer than before. I couldn't move away if I wanted to. "There... much better."

"I was fine," I say quietly. "If you hold me any tighter, you're going to suffocate me." But I like it. He just doesn't need to know that.

"Then I'll just have to resuscitate you. I'm good at mouth to mouth." There's slight humor in his voice, mixed with a bit of seriousness. I swallow, wondering if that's his way of letting me know he wants to kiss me again.

We've already done too much kissing and there's still a few days to get through. Avoiding kissing him as much as possible for the remainder of the trip is what I need to be doing. Kissing him gets more confusing for me each time it happens.

"I'll take my chances."

"Is that right?" He flips us over so that his body is pinning me to the blanket. "And why is that? My mouth getting to you, Nat?"

I suck in a breath when his hard body lowers to lay in between my legs. I don't have to look to know that eyes are on us, which also means that Madden is most likely going to take this position to his advantage. "Like I said before... *no*."

He positions his weight on one elbow, moving his free hand to caress my cheek as he lowers his mouth to just right above mine. "I think we need to test that out." When I shake my head, he whispers. "Everyone's watching us. Let me treat you like *my* girl."

"You said cuddling," I point out. "Not making out."

"Plans change." I close my eyes when his finger moves to brush a strand of hair behind my ear. "It's all for show, Nat. If you can't handle that then clearly you lied about my mouth having no effect on you."

I can't let him believe that, so I wrap my arm around his neck and yank him to me, my lips instantly parting for his. The softness of them mixed with the little growl he releases has me pulling him closer and playing my part. Although, at this point, I can't tell if it's just for show or partially due to the liquor I've consumed tonight. If it was just for show, then why do I feel slightly guilty? Logan agreed to this, I remind myself.

That reminder has me holding onto him even after his tongue dips into my mouth, causing my heart to jumpstart. He tastes of whiskey, cigarettes, and everything I crave right now.

"Holy fuck, Nat," he breathes when finally breaking the kiss. "Either you're really good at acting or you're beginning to enjoy my mouth on yours. Which is it?"

"Stop talking and get off of me," I say quietly.

He rolls off me and immediately pulls me back into his

arms, his warm, hard body surrounding every inch of me. He's giving me something I've craved from his brother since we started dating, and for that, I'm angry at him. Angry that this is pretend and angry that when I get back home, I'll go back to not having this.

CHAPTER FOURTEEN

MADDEN

EVERYONE'S BEEN LOST IN THE MUSIC, JUST DRINKING AND relaxing for the last hour, and here I am still thinking about the way Natalie tasted. I expected her to reject my tongue, but instead, her kiss became needy as if she wanted it just as much as I did.

It's been fucking with my head since the moment I pulled away. I wanted to keep going and I almost did, but then I had to remind myself that Natalie isn't my girl. She's Logan's. I knew I'd have to twist the rules a little, but when I first told myself that, I didn't realize just how much I'd like it.

"Anyone need anything from inside?" Jess says, breaking the silence as she stands up.

"No, I'm good," Alana says from Riley's arms where she's been trying to make me jealous and failing. "I think I'm about to call it a night and watch some TV." Her attention is on me when she stands, and the fact that I don't react to her pointing out she's about to be alone has her expression falling. "I'll be inside if anyone needs me."

"Anyone else?" Jess questions.

"Nah." I stand and reach for Natalie's hand, pulling her to her feet. "We're going to take a walk."

"We are?" she asks once we're alone, headed for the woods. "In the dark?"

"What's wrong with the dark?" I smile and pull her to me when she hesitates. "I'll keep you safe if that's what you're worried about."

"I'm not worried about that," she says quickly. "I'm worried about us getting lost. We've both been drinking, and I can barely see ten feet in front of me."

"I do this all the time," I point out, guiding her down a different path than this morning. "I've only gotten lost twice and both times I was wasted."

"How close to trashed are you?"

I laugh and lift a branch for her. "Not even close. You won't ever see me wasted. I wouldn't do that to you. No one wants to see me that way. Trust me."

"When was the last time you got that way?" she asks after a few minutes.

"After my last concert," I admit. "I got so fucked up that I blacked out. But I don't want to talk about that. I'm feeling good right now. I don't want to ruin it."

Once we're a good mile into the woods, I stop at my favorite spot and turn on the two spotlights I hung up in the trees a few years ago. Natalie looks surprised when she notices the thick sheet of plywood painted with a target hanging in front of us. "Remember when I said I like to axe throw in California sometimes?"

"Yes." She grins when I hand her the axe. "I didn't realize you meant here. What do I do? Just throw it?"

"Just aim and throw, Nat. The point is to have fun. If you miss, you miss. No pressure. This isn't a competition."

"Where should I hold it?" She looks down when I grab

her right hand and move it down to the end of the handle. "Like this?" She holds it over her right shoulder and does a fake swing to test it out.

I nod and pull out a cigarette. "Perfect. Now throw it."

She laughs when the flying axe hits the bottom of the plywood and falls to the ground.

"Harder," I say, walking over to grab it for her. "Put some strength behind it. Don't be afraid to let loose. Just fucking do it."

She swallows when I stop talking, breaking a peaceful silence, before throwing it again, putting some force behind it this time. My heart beats excitedly when it sticks just below the target this time.

"Hell yeah. Feels good, doesn't it?"

"Really good." The grin spread on her face when I hand it to her makes me happy I brought her out here. I usually do this alone. "Again?" she questions. "What about you?"

"You first. Always. That's how I work."

She looks at me for a few seconds longer than normal, before turning away and throwing the axe at the plywood again. "Oh, my God!" she shouts. "Did you see that?"

"I did." I smile and take one last drag off my cigarette before putting it out. "You looked great doing it too." She walks over to grab the axe from the middle of the bullseye, but I get there first, tossing the axe aside before pulling her into my arms. "Are you having fun?"

She nods, looking up at me.

"Want to stay out here for a while? We can do anything you want. We don't have to go back and put on a show any more tonight. I just want you to enjoy yourself for as long as possible."

"I want to stay," she says. "It's been a while since I've had this much fun. Buuuuttt..." She maneuvers her way out of my arms to grab the axe off the ground. "I'd have more fun if you joined me."

"I can do that." The way she watches me as I adjust the axe to get a comfortable grip has me feeling nervous for some strange reason. She's never looked at me this way before, and I can't tell if it's because we're having fun or because she might be slightly drunk, which has me off my game, missing the bullseye.

"Better luck next time, rock star." She laughs and attempts to grab the axe from the plywood, but it's buried so deep that she's struggling.

"Here," I say over her shoulder, smiling against her ear as I give her a hand. "That was just my warm-up throw. Honestly, I've done this so many times I could probably hit the target without even looking."

"Show me then. I want to see." She gives my chest a slight push, putting some space between us. "I want you to look at me while you throw it."

"Okay." I grin and get back into position, my attention on her off to the side, watching me with eager eyes. "Ready?"

"Why are you asking me?" she questions. "You're the one..."

Her words trail off at the sound of the axe splitting the wood. Instead of looking to see if I hit my target, I watch the huge smile that crosses her face instead.

"Impressive. *But*, I bet you can't do it again."

Smiling, I yank the axe out and walk over to stand right in front of her. Keeping my eyes on hers, I grab the back of her neck with my left hand and tangle my fingers in her hair. We're staring at each other in the silence of the night lost in each other as I throw the axe for the third time.

"Did I hit it?" I ask after a few seconds.

She clears her throat and finally turns toward the target. "There's no way."

I release my hold on her and turn to see what she's looking at. The axe is stuck directly in the center of the bulls-eye. "My best shot yet."

She steps away and looks around us. "Maybe we should head back. I'm getting kind of tired."

"Anything you want, Nat." I walk over and turn off the first light. "We should probably shower and get ready for bed."

"Yeah," she says quickly, her face disappearing when I turn off the second light. "I'll let you shower first."

I grab her hand and begin guiding her through the darkness, lifting branches and kicking stuff out of her path. "There are no taking turns, babe. If people are awake, they're going to expect us to shower together. Showering separately doesn't make any sense."

"Are you serious?" She stops walking.

I laugh and tug her back to me. "Don't worry, you can wear your bikini. No one has to know."

"And you?"

I grin, even though she can't see it. "What about me?"

"Are you going to wear your trunks?"

"Why would I do that?"

"So you won't be *naked. That's* why."

I plan on wearing them, but she doesn't need to know until then. "Nah. Why does it matter when you've already seen me naked? I've got nothing to hide."

"Oh, it definitely matters. Your bro—"

"My brother isn't here, is he?"

"Dammit, Madden." She yanks her hand from mine and shoves me away from her. "I'll skip a shower then."

"Wait a second." I hurry and wrap my arms around her from behind before she gets too far ahead of me. "We can't have them thinking we're fighting. I was joking. Okay?"

"Okay, well stop," she says firmly. "Let's get this over with then."

I have to admit, the thought of taking a shower with Natalie has me slightly excited even though we're both going to be partially covered.

My brother might be a little pissed about our shower time, but he should've known this would happen from all the times he's been here. He's just lucky I won't be naked.

CHAPTER FIFTEEN

NATALIE

WHEN WE GET BACK TO THE CABIN, JAKE AND RILEY ARE the only two left outside. It gives me hope that everyone else has called it a night; until we walk inside to see the others hanging out in the living room watching TV.

Alana looks over the back of the couch the moment she hears the door open, her attention settling on our hands as Madden's grip on mine tightens. "We're taking a shower and calling it a night," he points out. "We'll see you guys in the morning."

"Okay," Jess yells back. "Just don't use up all the hot water, because none of us have showered yet. You know how quickly it runs out."

"We'll make it quick," I say, my pulse racing as Madden leads me to the bedroom to grab our things. Even though we won't be naked, just the idea of being in the bathroom while each other showers feels so... dirty. "Quick," I repeat once we're alone. "I don't want to be stuck in the bathroom with you forever. You'll get in and then I'll jump in once you're done."

"Here." He flashes me a sexy grin and tosses me a pair of his boxers and one of his T-shirts.

I look down at the worn-out RISK shirt in my hand and then down at his underwear. "What? The rock star needs me to carry his change of clothing for him?" I toss the T-shirt at his face. "You can handle it just fine, I'm sure."

"No." He tosses the shirt back to me. "They're your pajamas."

"I have my own," I clarify.

"Yeah, but you're *wearing* mine." He leans over me and begins digging through my suitcase for my bikini, stuffing into his back pocket. "Can't let anyone see you bring this into the shower with us."

"I need underwear and a bra," I say when he pulls me to my feet and kicks my suitcase closed.

"No, the fuck you don't, Nat. You're going to sleep. You should be comfortable. A T-shirt and boxers are all you need."

Too tired to argue with him, I let him pull me into the bathroom and lock the door behind us. I stand back, nerves kicking in as he turns the shower water on. "This is so weird."

"What?" He reaches for his shirt and strips it over his head, before going for his jeans. "Are you going to stare at me the whole time or get changed?"

Embarrassment creeps in once I realize I've been watching him undress. "I'm waiting on you to turn around so I can change. So..."

He flashes me a cocky grin before kicking his jeans aside and turning away. My attention immediately lands on his firm ass in those tight boxer briefs he's wearing. I swear under my breath and avert my eyes toward the wall as I quickly change, scared he'll peek if I don't move fast.

Once I'm in my bikini, I wait for him to get in, but he

motions for me to instead. Figuring he's just letting me go first, I step into the small shower, swallowing when Madden steps in behind me. We're so close I can feel his chest against my back. "Some space would be nice."

"There isn't much to give, babe." He reaches over my shoulder for the body wash, his lips dangerously close to my cheek. "Don't worry... I'll make it quick."

I suck in a breath when I feel his hands moving behind me. I can't tell which part of his body he's touching, but what I can tell is that the thoughts running through my head are extremely inappropriate right now. "You just touched my ass," I point out.

"If I touched your ass, you'd know it, Nat. Or did you forget already?"

No, definitely haven't forgotten the way he touched me. "Maybe. Or maybe I'm trying to."

He laughs. "Good luck."

Annoyed, I turn around to face him, pushing him against the back of the shower. "Do you ever stop with the cockiness? We just had a nice night together. Let's not ruin it. You could've waited until I was done to get in."

Without a word, he reaches over my shoulder for the soap again, except this time he squeezes it over my chest. "Can't use all the hot water, remember?" He runs his hand over my body, his gaze focused on mine as he cleans me. Even though he skips my breasts, his hand moving along my stomach causes butterflies.

"I can do that myself," I finally manage to say once he moves down to my thighs. I push his hand away and he spins me around and goes right for my back.

"Really? Looked to me like you were just going to stand here all night while I took care of *myself.*"

My eyes close, my heart racing faster the longer he touches me, and when his hand skims my left ass cheek causing skin to skin contact, I decide I've had enough and step out of the shower. "You finish yourself off and then I'll take a shower. How about that?"

It's what we should've done in the first place. Getting into the shower with Madden to save hot water was a stupid idea I should've never even entertained. The moment he got in I should've got out.

"All right. Your loss, babe." He winks and closes the shower curtain.

It feels like forever has passed when he finally opens the shower curtain again. My eyes practically pop out of my head at the sight of him stepping out, naked, with his hands covering his junk. "A towel would be nice."

I turn away so fast that I almost give myself whiplash. "Again, with nakedness, Madden." I throw the towel at his face and pretend I'm not the slightest bit turned on by his nudity, when we both know I am. I can see it in his eyes. "Now hurry so I can wash my hair."

He steps out of the way, and without waiting for the shower curtain to close behind me, he releases his junk to run both hands through his wet hair. Luckily, I'm quick enough to turn away before I can get another eyeful of his sizeable package.

"What do you want to do tomorrow?"

"I don't know," I say, trying my best to focus on washing my hair and not the fact that I'm showering with my boyfriend's brother right outside the curtain. "Whatever everyone else is doing."

"I want you to choose. Anything you want, we'll do. Just the two of us."

My stomach does little flips at that idea. "What about your friends?

"They'll be fine without us for a bit."

"Okay." I shut the water off and reach for the towel he already has ready for me. "What is there to do around here?"

"Anything we fucking want, Nat. We can take a walk in the woods or hang out at the bar next to that gas station we stopped at on the way here. Think about it tonight."

"Okay."

"Here." He smiles and grabs the towel from me to help me dry off. I should probably ask him to stop, but admittedly, it feels nice having someone want to take care of me for a change. Not that I *need* someone to, but it feels good on occasion. Everyone can admit that.

"Thank you." I smile and toss the towel over his head. "No peeking while I change into pajamas."

I'm not sure why, but I feel oddly comfortable in Madden's clothes, and the way he's looking at me from seeing me in them is almost one of admiration. It gives me the feeling he likes seeing me in them. Why do I like that so much?

"You two done in there?" Jess yells through the door. "Jake and I are next."

It takes Madden a few seconds, but he finally turns away from me and opens the door. "Yeah. It's all yours."

Alana is still on the couch when we exit the bathroom. Her face falls when she sees Madden's clothes on me. I'm not sure if she's finally starting to believe we're together or not, but she genuinely looks hurt.

Madden must see it too, because he grips my hip and kisses my neck, moving me down the hall with his body, making a show of it. "She's starting to doubt herself," he says, tossing our wet towels and clothes onto the dresser. "We just need to keep doing what we're doing, Nat. Can you handle that?"

"If it's going to get her to move on, then yeah," I say, climbing into bed. "I can handle it."

"Good." He scoots me to the side of the bed and climbs in beside me, his body practically taking up all the space. "Because our sleeping arrangement has to change. I'm not chancing anyone walking in to see us sleeping separately. Remember, no locks."

"You're not serious, are you?" My heart slams against my ribcage, waiting for his response. "Are you?" I ask again.

"Relax, Nat. I'm not going to touch you inappropriately. It's late. We'll both probably be asleep in the next five minutes." He wraps his arm around me and pulls me down to his chest. "Don't fight me on this, please; not when there's a chance it's working."

I exhale and place my arm over his chest. "Fine. But just know I'm *only* doing this because I want this to work just as much as you do. I still find it weird and uncomfortable."

"Sure, you do," he says quietly, running his fingers through my hair. "You seem pretty comfortable to me."

"I'm not," I mutter. "Your chest is rock-solid."

"So is the rest of my body. I've never had any complaints about it. Just because my brother's chest is soft like a pillow..."

I roll my eyes and laugh. "Stop talking and go to sleep."

"Is it true you left the concert that night because you felt guilty for not being able to take your eyes off me?"

"Yeah," I admit, remembering that night. "Is it true that you looked for me for two songs?"

"No." It's quiet for a moment before he adds, "I looked for you the rest of the night. Up until I got piss drunk and the boys dragged me to my hotel room. It was a rough night."

My heart sinks. "What were you going to do if you found me?"

"Shit, I don't know. Buy you a drink and get to know you maybe. There was something about you... The way you looked at me was different than what I was used to. Like you saw the real me and not what the rest of the women around me always see—a famous rock star they want to be fucked by. You sang every single lyric to every song and you were so lost in the feel of it all. I liked that. Not to mention you were sexy as fuck."

My pulse speeds up from hearing him call me sexy. But more than that, he just admitted that he wanted to get to know me that night. Hearing this now, I know without a doubt that if I weren't dating his brother already I would've let him buy me that drink. I would've spent all night talking to him if he wanted to. I was lost so deep in my emotions that night after hearing him perform.

"I don't even remember how I looked that night. I was probably wearing—"

"A pair of faded blue jeans and a white tank top. Your hair was braided to the side just like it was the other day and you kept playing with it until you finally took the braid out and shook your hair out. I couldn't stop watching you run your fingers through it."

His own fingers still running through my hair feels so much different now than it did just a few seconds ago. More intimate somehow, which makes me nervous, yet I don't want him to stop. "Did you recognize me when your brother intro-duced us?"

"Fuck yeah, Nat. Why do you think I was awkward as shit? I couldn't stop thinking about the fact that you were the girl I was going to go for at my concert and my brother had you in his bed all along. Then I kept wondering if we would've ended up in a hotel room together with me between your legs and my brother hurt had you stayed."

"I never would've cheated on your brother."

"I know that now," he says. "I know you, Nat. Back then I didn't know shit about you other than I had wanted you that night."

"I never would've thought you'd give me a second look," I admit. "I didn't even think I stood out. There were hundreds of women there that night."

"You always stand out," he says into the top of my hair. "My brother is one lucky guy. Don't ever let him make you think otherwise. You're too fucking hot and sassy for him. You're more my style."

"So, I'm not too hot and sassy for you?" I joke.

"I never said that. But I'd be able to handle you in a way I know he can't. Everywhere. In and out of bed."

Oh. My. God.

Suddenly feeling hot, I roll over on my side of the bed and kick the sheet from my legs.

"You overheating?"

"No," I say defensively. "Just a little warm. Maybe we should turn the ceiling fan up. You give off a shit ton of body heat."

"I'm not the only one." He laughs and sits up to pull the string above us. "There. Better?"

I nod and exhale, finally feeling as if I can breathe again. "Yes, much better."

"Good." He rolls over and pulls me into him until I'm snuggled into his body. "Now go to sleep and stop thinking sexual things about me. It's not cool and my brother wouldn't like it."

"What?!" I try bucking him off me, but the only result me moving against him does is him pulling me even tighter than I already was.

"Do that again and you're going to feel a surprise against your ass. If you don't want me hard, stop fighting me and go to sleep."

I try my best to not think about him hard against my ass, but I can't help it, and all it does is make me hot and sweaty again, so I do as he says and chill out.

He doesn't say anything else once I stop resisting, and I'm thankful for that, because too much has already been said tonight. Things I wasn't expecting came from him and it has me feeling emotions I shouldn't. *None* of the feelings I've felt since getting into his truck with him I should be feeling. It's only night two and my head is already playing tricks on me.

CHAPTER SIXTEEN

MADDEN

Sitting up, I run both hands over my face, before looking beside me where Natalie is still asleep. I probably shouldn't be enjoying the way she looks in my clothes right now, and I know my brother would kick my ass if he knew I had her wearing them, but I couldn't resist last night.

I wanted her in my clothes to make it feel more real. And it worked. Looking at her now, it almost feels as if she's really mine. Talk about fucked up.

Cussing under my breath, I slide out of bed and slip into a pair of jeans and a hoodie. My thoughts are scrambled. I need a cigarette to get my head on straight.

I open the door to step out of the room and freeze when I spot Alana sitting in the hallway between the two bedroom doors. "Shit, Alana. What are you doing out here?"

She looks up from her spot on the floor, her eyes red from lack of sleep. "Couldn't sleep. All I could think about was you and how it should be us in that bedroom right now. Not you and *her*. It should've been me you were holding all night."

"What's done is done, Alana. You did this, not me. All we can do now is move on. Both of us."

"I don't want to, Madden. I don't want to fucking move on. Can't you see that? Can't you see how much I hate myself for hurting you? I've been a bitch this entire trip because of it. You know that's not who I am. *You* pushed me to be bitter and question everything I thought I knew."

"I didn't push you to do anything. Don't even fucking go there. I'm not going to pity you. Maybe you should have thought about all this when you did what you did. And stop questioning shit. Clearly, you poked your head inside to spy on us and got your answer. I've moved on, Alana. You need to do the same." I flex my jaw, unable to deal with these emotions right now. I really need that cigarette. "I'm going outside to smoke. I suggest you go to bed and get some sleep."

"Madden, wait..."

Ignoring Alana's plea, I hurry out back and light up a smoke, my nerves causing my hands to shake. As much as she deserves it, I don't feel good hurting her. She was an important part of my life for a long time. She fucking *killed* me, and yet I feel bad. Isn't that fucking great.

"Madden, please."

"Dammit, Alana." I walk around the side of the cabin in hopes of getting away from her, but I hear her footsteps behind me, not willing to give up. I stop walking and turn around to face her. "Go back—"

My words are cut off by her mouth slamming hard against mine. Her kiss is needy and desperate, her hands tangled in my hair, pulling me into her.

It takes a good few seconds for me to come to my senses and push her away. When I do, my eyes land on Natalie, who just came around the corner.

"Nat—"

"I don't want to fucking hear it, Madden." Her angry eyes land on Alana, and I can't help but notice just how good she's playing her part as the jealous girlfriend. It's almost believable. "Hope you enjoyed that, because it'll be the last time your lips touch his again. That's a fucking promise." With that, she walks away.

My heart races as I watch her disappear into the woods, because her performance was so good I wonder if maybe she's really pissed at me for kissing my ex.

"Let her go, Madden."

I toss my cigarette, eyes still focused on where Natalie disappeared just seconds ago. "We're through, Alana. Take a hint and get over it. Oh, and stay the fuck away from us for the rest of the trip."

"You're not in love with her!" she yells at my back as I walk away to go after Natalie. "If you were, you wouldn't have kissed me back for even a second. Stop fooling yourself, Madden."

I don't even allow myself to question what Alana is saying, because truthfully, I'm worried about Natalie right now. I'm not even sure why. Surely, she can't really be pissed. It's not like she has feelings for me. Her reaction had to be for show.

It takes me a few minutes, but I finally catch up with Natalie, grabbing her arm to stop her from walking. "Hey, wait up. Are you okay?"

She stops and exhales but doesn't turn to face me. "Why wouldn't I be okay?" She starts walking again and I do too, letting her lead the way. "Gotta play my part, right?"

"Right," I say, but mostly to myself. "Well, you played it really fucking well just so you know. Almost had me believing you were actually mad about her kissing me."

"If she kissed you then why did you kiss her back?" She turns around to face me. "I thought the whole point of me coming here was to prove to her that you've moved on, yet you just kissed her."

"That wasn't a kiss, Nat. Trust me. It was barely a peck that lasted all of five seconds. If I had truly kissed her back, you'd know." I run a hand through my hair, feeling guilty all of a sudden. "*Are* you mad about it?"

"Of course not. I have no reason to be other than it makes me look like a fool." She takes off walking again, taking the same trail we took the other morning.

"I'm sorry, Nat. I never meant to make you look like a fool. She caught me off guard and I didn't act fast enough. That's all that was."

"No need to explain. Clearly, you still have feelings for her. Nothing I can do about that so let's just walk in silence."

I don't know what to say to that so I just follow her lead.

"Do you miss my brother yet?" I ask moments later, changing the subject.

She shrugs. "I don't know. I'm used to us going a few days apart on occasion. Sometimes we're too tired to see each other, so it seems easier to wait until one of us has a day off work."

"Are you serious?"

"Yeah, why?"

I lift a branch for her and grab her hand to help her over a heap of fallen limbs. "You two live like ten minutes apart and work twenty minutes apart. That makes no fucking sense to me. Even if I was just coming to your house to hold you while you slept, I'd be there at the end of the day."

"Your brother sleeps better when he has space. He sweats easily."

"Then turn the fucking air up. A lot of shit he does has never made sense to me. I'm surprised he's kept you this long."

"Why is that?" She laughs and pushes a branch out of the way. "He's a good guy."

"Sometimes being a good guy isn't enough. Not when you're with a girl that deserves so much more than what you can give."

She suddenly stops and looks back at me as if she wasn't expecting what I just said. "What makes you so sure I deserve more?"

"Because being around you makes me want to *give* you more. Whenever I learn that my brother isn't giving you something, I think of all the ways I could if you were mine. You deserve a man who'll make you his top priority, not put you in line behind his job and himself."

Instead of responding to me, we walk in silence for a while longer just enjoying the scenery and peacefulness of our morning walk.

The more time I spend with Natalie and get to know her, the more protective over her I feel, which has me questioning even more why my brother would agree to her coming on this trip with me. It makes no fucking sense, because if the roles were reversed, I never would've let her leave with him. Not a chance in Hell.

"How would you feel about getting away for a little bit tonight? Just the two of us. We could go to that bar we passed by the gas station and just be ourselves for a while with no pressure from everyone else."

"Really? Are you sure you're okay with that?"

I nod and brush her hair behind her ear. "Yeah. My friends will be fine without us for a few hours. I think we both need a few hours to just breathe and be ourselves. Don't you agree?"

"Yeah. I'd really like that."

"Then, yeah. I'm okay with it. After the show you just put on, you deserve it."

AFTER MY LITTLE confession in the woods earlier that Natalie deserves someone better than my brother, I knew time away from *pretending* would probably be good for both of us.

Too much pretend can start to feel real. I learned that this morning when Alana kissed me and I felt guilty for kissing her back. What the fuck does that even mean? I haven't been able to figure it out and it's been bugging me.

"You two heading out for a while?" Jake asks from across the picnic table.

I nod and finish off my beer. "Yeah. Figured it'd be good to give her some time away from playing the rock star's girl-friend. There's still a few days left of this shit, and if we're going to pull it off, she needs some time to breathe."

"I'd say so," Jake mumbles into his cup.

"What is that supposed to mean?"

"It means you two definitely need some breathing room. It's beginning to seem a little too real for even me, and I know the truth. You sure you can pull this off without falling for your brother's girl, or vice versa?"

I avert my attention over to the pool where Natalie is hanging out with Jess, Riley, and Walker. Seeing how close Walker is sitting to Natalie, I become tense, just like every time I've noticed him practically on top of her.

"You're flexing your jaw, man. I'm not sure that's a good sign."

"Stop worrying for nothing, Jake." I stand and toss my beer bottle into the trash. "She's my brother's girl. I'm supposed to be protective of her; especially since my brother isn't here to do it."

"You sure it's only for your brother's benefit? I'm only

asking, because I'm friends with both of you and I'd hate to see some shit go down that ruins your relationship."

"I'm sure." I say the words, not fully believing them myself. "We'll be back in a couple of hours. We'll grab something to eat at the bar, so don't worry about cooking for us."

"Gotcha, man." He stands himself, eyeing me over. "Take some time to breathe and have fun. Alana is already starting to believe you and Natalie are real. That's why she's inside instead of out here with us."

"I'm not so sure about that."

"What does that mean?" He studies me hard. "I don't like that look."

"She kissed me this morning and I kissed her back."

"Why the fuck would you do that? You trying to screw this all up?"

"It was only for a split second and then I pushed her away. It's no biggie. Tomorrow is a fresh day for Nat and me. After spending some time away tonight, we'll be refreshed and ready to play tomorrow."

"I hope so. The next two days are important. If you want to leave here a free man, without Alana hounding you every single day, you gotta sell it hard. Just be careful."

I nod at Natalie when she looks at me. She says something to the crew before standing from her chair and heading my way.

"See ya later, man."

"We going?" she asks, still smiling from whatever her and the others were talking about.

I grab her waist and pull her to me, before moving to speak into her ear. "You okay?"

"Yeah," she whispers. "Why?"

I press my lips against her neck and set my eyes on Walker, who is watching us. "Just checking. Let's go."

"What was that about?" she asks the moment we're in my truck.

"Nothing. I just noticed Walker kept leaning in on occasion to talk to you. I wanted to make sure he wasn't making you uncomfortable."

"Not really. He was a little flirty, but nothing I can't handle. You really have no idea how many drunk guys I fight off at the hotel when I work night shifts. Why do you think I have a stun gun?"

"That's why you bought that thing? To keep guys from making moves on you?"

"Yeah. And it works too. Trust me, I can handle myself. When a guy gets handsy I pull it out and it sobers him up quick."

Anger rises and the need to protect her has me squeezing the steering wheel to keep from going off. "Does my brother know?"

"He's heard a few stories."

"And?"

"And what?"

"What does he do about it?"

She exhales as if this subject is frustrating her. Well, it's frustrating me too. "Can we stop talking about work and your brother for a while? I just want to have a night of fun and a few drinks with you. No heavy shit tonight, please."

"Fine. I'll drop it." *For now.*

The bar is pretty quiet, so as long as we're out of here before dark we shouldn't run into too many people who might recognize me.

"Two beers and two orders of barbecue wings."

"Make that three orders of barbecue wings. Extra ranch."

"Someone a little hungry?" she asks teasingly.

I shrug and thank the bartender when he drops off our drinks. "I'm always hungry. I'm down to eat whenever, wherever. I even bring snacks with me on stage sometimes and sneak in bites between songs."

"Seriously?" She looks amused as she takes a drink of her beer. "What kind of snacks?"

"I had a bucket of fried chicken sitting on a stool next to Landon once. He gave me a weird look every time I'd sneak a chicken leg, but I just gave him the middle finger and kept eating."

"Sounds messy. How did that work out for you?"

"It was really fucking messy and I smelled like grease the rest of the night, but I was satisfied and full. It was the best chicken of my life, so no regrets."

"Do you miss being on stage?"

"What? Right now?"

"Yeah. Since we've been here."

"No," I say truthfully. "I love it, but everyone needs a break to just be themselves once in a while; to be normal. I miss my old life more than I thought I would at times. *This* is what I love to do; hang with my friends and chill away from all the fame and people recognizing me everywhere I go."

"Oh, there are definitely a few people who recognize you here. Like the girl at the table behind us for one. She keeps looking your way every few seconds," she points out with a smile. "She keeps holding her phone this way as if she's trying to not so discreetly take a picture of you. I've counted at least five different times so far."

"Does she look like she's about to freak out?"

She laughs. "Oh yeah. Totally on the verge of a freak out."

I set my beer down and stand. When I look the direction the girl is sitting, her eyes widen, and her mouth falls open in shock.

"Then I should go say hi. What do you think?"

"From the looks of it, she'll probably faint if you do, so you might want to be prepared to catch her if she falls."

"Good advice."

As soon as the girl realizes I'm walking her way, she sets her drink down and takes a few deep breaths as if to calm herself. "Wow," she says when I take a seat at her table. "I can't believe this is happening right now. Would it be rude to ask for an autograph? I've wanted one forever and it'd totally make my night."

"Hell no. Ask away."

"Oh, my God. I'm freaking out inside right now. You have no idea." She places her hand on her chest. "My heart is about to beat out of my chest. You have no idea how crazy this is. I'm so embarrassed that I'm acting like a fangirl, but I can't help it."

"It's okay. No need to be embarrassed." I laugh and grab her phone from her because her hand is shaking so hard the screen keeps blurring. "I've got it."

"I can take it for you." Natalie holds her hand out for me to give her the phone. I can't help but notice how happy she looks for the girl as she snaps a few pictures of us. "I took a few so you have options."

"Oh, my God. Thank you so much." The girl gives me a hug, before walking over and giving Natalie one too. "You're so pretty. I saw a picture of you two the other day and I couldn't stop thinking how you're exactly the kind of girl I'd imagine Madden with. You look so good together."

"We're not—"

"She makes me look good," I say, while scribbling my name on a napkin, my attention focused on Natalie watching me.

"You're both amazing! Thank you. Thank you." She grabs the napkin and then drops some cash on the table, but I hand it back to her and grab her bill.

"It's on me to show my appreciation for your support."

"Oh, wow! I've always seen you getting in fights at

concerts and wondered if you'd be a dick in person. I'm so glad to find out you're not. You're the complete opposite. I'm not disappointed at all. Just another reason RISK is my favorite band, so thanks for being a good guy and not ruining my love for the band."

After the girl walks away, I smile at Natalie and we head back to our spot at the bar where our food is now waiting for us. "That was nice of you to offer to take pictures for her. Looked like you were having fun."

"I was. It made me happy to see you with a fan; just like the other night at the gas station. You're good with them."

"I have to be. They're good to me. If it weren't for them, I'd be nothing. RISK would be nothing."

She shakes her head and grabs a wing. "You could never be *nothing*, Madden. Don't ever think that."

Her comment has me feeling good inside, and I can't help the smile that takes over as I watch her relax with me. Natalie is good for me. I like the person I am when I'm with her, and truthfully, I'm already dreading giving her back to my brother soon. Not that she's anyone's property, but I know once we're back we won't have moments alone like we did in the woods or here at the bar.

"Are you having fun here?" I ask after a couple of beers.

"I am," she says, looking around the bar that is starting to fill up. "With work I never get a chance to just sit back, enjoy the silence, and think. There's always too much shit going on. It can get overwhelming at times, and it makes me wish I had said no when offered the management position. Things were so much..."

"Easier?"

She nods and takes a sip of her beer. "Yeah, but sometimes easier isn't always better. Paying rent was a struggle before, and now I live comfortably and can provide for myself without worrying if I'm going to overdraw my account for food before payday. If my car breaks down and I have an unexpected expense to pay for, I'm prepared."

"Why don't you and my brother live together?" I've wondered this for a while now. Two years together with hardly any time to see each other and they still choose to live apart.

"I don't know. I guess we've just never discussed the possibility of living together. It hasn't crossed my mind much to be honest. We both have so many other responsibilities to deal with just the idea of moving seems overwhelming."

"I don't think so." I finish off my third beer and hold it up, letting Myles know I need another. "I couldn't see myself not living with the girl I was in love with. Especially if we hardly see each other living apart. It makes sense to want to spend every free minute you *do* have together."

"Yeah," she whispers, seconds later. "You'd think so."

"What if my brother asked you?"

She laughs as if it's the funniest thing ever. "To move in with him?"

"What's so funny about that?"

"Me moving in with him is the last thing he'd ask me to do right now. Did you know that I sleep at my place at least two nights a week, per his request, so we don't disturb each other's sleep routine? I don't think he'd survive us sharing a bed every night."

"My brother is seriously fucked up. I'd want you in my bed every night if you were mine. He's crazy for wanting otherwise."

She stares at me for a few seconds before turning away. "I'll take another one too, please."

"Want to go back soon?"

"I don't know. I'm sort of enjoying this."

"What? Being alone with me?" I ask, just to tease her.

"What if I am?"

"Then I'd like that."

"Would you really?" she asks, her eyes curious as she tilts back her beer.

"I wouldn't say it unless I meant it, so... yeah."

She looks away and clears her throat.

"You don't have to feel awkward about that, Nat. It's okay to enjoy each other's company. It's not going to make you any less committed to my brother. It's not like you're going to fall for me before this trip is over."

"Which is *exactly* why I agreed to come. You and I would never work."

"Why's that?" I turn her stool around so that she's facing me. "What makes you so sure that the two of us wouldn't have ended up together instead had you not been dating my brother when I first saw you?"

"What? I don't know." She laughs nervously and downs the rest of her beer, before setting the empty bottle down. "Is that a serious question?" she asks when I keep looking at her.

"Yeah. I'm a little curious. Tell me just for the fuck of it."

"Because it'd be too hard not to see you every day."

"What if you could?"

She laughs. "That'd be impossible."

"What if I said I only want to tour two months out of the year and bring you with? Then what?"

"You'd do that for a girl?"

"I'd do *everything* for a girl I care about."

It takes a few moments before she finally says something. "Then she'll be one lucky girl once you find her."

The bartender pops over, interrupting our moment. "Another round?"

"Yeah. We'll take another." I grab the beers that he slides our way. "We'll be over by the pool table."

"Sure thing, man. I'll transfer your tab to Mia."

"Perfect." I toss a twenty down for him and nod at Natalie. "Up for a game or two of pool?"

"I'm not that great, but sure."

"Doesn't matter. Tonight is just about us having fun. If you don't sink a single ball in, that's fine."

She laughs. "I'm definitely down then."

I offer to let her break, but the balls barely move, so I let her take another shot and she sinks in a three.

"I guess that means I'm solids?"

"You can be anything you want to be. Just sink in any ball you have your eye on. No fucking rules right now. We both deserve it."

"Okay. Well if that's the case, then I think I'll take this one right here." She smiles and hits the eight-ball in that happens to be right in front of the corner pocket. "Does that count?"

"Sure." I nod. "Keep going until you miss."

"I might just win if you keep letting me choose which ball to hit in. Then what?"

I lean over her shoulder and whisper in her ear. "Then I'll congratulate you and we'll play another game."

"How many games are we going to play?"

I smile against her cheek. "As many as you want."

The flash on someone's phone has my attention going to the back corner of the room where a group of four guys is hanging out doing shots.

"That's going to end up on the internet. Think my brother will see it?"

She stiffens below me for just a split second before relaxing and taking her shot. "Well, if he does, then maybe he'll question why he was such a dick to let me go in the first place."

I back away when she misses her shot. "Do you want him to question why he let me take you on this trip?"

She's silent for a moment, watching as I sink a few balls in, before finally saying, "I don't know. Maybe. Maybe I become a little more pissed the longer I'm here."

"Why is that?"

She grabs her beer and takes a gulp. "Because the longer I'm with you, the easier it is to see why you're easy to fall for. He knows you better than anyone else, and yet, he let me go anyway."

I'm not sure if what she just said is the beer talking or not, but my heart races in my chest anyway. "Yeah, he did. Maybe he'll regret it after seeing us together on social media and start treating you better."

"Maybe," she says softly. "Or maybe it'll be too late." She said the last part so softly that I barely heard it. I'm not sure if she meant for me to, so I keep it to myself.

"Can we get next game?"

Two of the guys from the table taking pictures of us join us by the pool table, pulling my attention from Natalie leaning over the pool table. "Sure, man. No problem."

"Damn," the second guy mutters under his breath, his attention focused on Natalie's ass. "That's one fine ass. I noticed it from across the room."

I try my best to ignore his comment, but the moment he licks his lips and adjusts his dick, I swing out, hitting him across the face. Apparently, I've had enough beer for my reckless nature to come out.

He stumbles back and grabs his jaw. "What the fuck! Did you see that?" he asks the bartender. "The fucker just hit me. He thinks that just because he's famous he can go around punching people. You all see that?"

I get in his face after tossing a handful of cash down on the pool table. It'll be more than enough to pay for our drinks. "Next time keep your comments about my girl's ass to yourself." I reach my hand out. "Let's get the fuck out of here, Nat."

"Yeah, you better get the fuck out of here. Unless you want my friend here to beat your ass and then call the cops. You don't just come around here swinging at people."

Natalie pulls my arm when I attempt to confront the piece of shit. "Let's go, Madden."

"Yeah, listen to your girl, *Madden*. Your band isn't here to back you up. Go on now. Walk away."

"You, shut the fuck up!" Natalie seethes. "We're leaving." She pulls my arm again, and only because I don't want to end up in the back of a police car I let her lead me outside before I lose my shit completely.

"What the fuck?" she says once we're alone by my truck. Her chest is quickly rising and falling as she looks me over. "What was that about? Why did you hit that guy? You could've gotten arrested, or worse, those guys could've hurt you, Madden. There were two of them and only one of you."

"It was nothing. I just had a few too many beers." I toss her the keys. "You good to drive?"

She nods. "Yeah. But first I want to know why the hell you risked your ass in there. Tell me the truth. That wasn't just having a few too many beers."

"That asshole grabbed his dick while eyeing your ass. *That's* why I punched him, Nat. And I don't give a shit about getting hurt. That doesn't bother me. I can take a few punches. He's just lucky I walked out when I did."

She swallows, her eyes meeting mine. "You punched him because he was looking at my ass?"

"He wasn't just *looking* at it. He was imagining it in his hands and the fucker had a hard-on for you. He deserved to be hit."

"You didn't have to do that," she says quietly. "I could've

handled him. And besides, it's not your job to beat guys up for looking at me wrong."

"Well, my brother sure as fuck doesn't find it to be his job. One of us has to do it."

She runs a hand through her hair in frustration, before turning away. "Let's just get back to the cabin and forget this ever happened."

"I'm sorry." I open the driver's side door for her. "I shouldn't have said that. I'm an asshole and I wish I could take it back."

"Fine. I accept your apology."

"I mean it, Nat."

I help her into the seat. She looks at me while shoving the key into the ignition. "I do too." She flashes a small smile. "You did get that fucker pretty good."

"Yeah, I did." I smile and shut the door, before jumping in myself. "Let's just go back to the room and chill and watch TV. It's been a long day of pretending for you." I say once we pull up at the cabin.

CHAPTER SEVENTEEN

NATALIE

WHEN WE PULL UP AT THE CABIN I CONSIDER TAKING HIM up on his offer and going straight to the bedroom to hide away for the night. That would be the easy option for me, but instead, I motion for Madden to follow me around back.

This is his time with his friends, and even though he offered to have an easy night away from everyone for my benefit, I don't want him to miss out on time spent with his old friends. It's not fair to him and I won't do that.

"You sure you want to do this?"

"Yeah." I wrap my arms around his neck because I know we're within seeing distance of everyone now. "You don't have a lot of time left with your friends. As much as I'd love to hide out and not have to play pretend every second of the day, I can't and won't be selfish. I'm here for *you*, Madden. Besides, you just punched some dude for me. I didn't ask for it, but maybe I owe you one."

"Fuck, my brother is an idiot." He picks me up and wraps my legs around his waist, his smile widening as he grips my neck. "I believe that more now than ever." His lips press against my forehead and my stomach fills with butterflies. "Thank you."

"You owe me another cheesecake when we get back." I tease. "The biggest one."

"I'll buy you ten." He sets me down and whistles at Jake when he does a cannonball into the pool. "Nice one, dick!"

"Get the hell in, guys!" Seth holds up his drink, before tilting it back. "The water is nice and warm and we're about to turn the party lights on."

"Want to change first?"

I nod. "Yeah. You?"

He shakes his head. "Nah, I'll wear my boxer briefs. Fuck it, right? Not like I haven't already made a dick out of myself tonight."

I think on it for a second and say screw it. I spend every day being uptight and thinking too hard. I've had a few beers and things between Madden and I are feeling good right now. I'm ready to just let loose and have fun. "Let's go then." I smile and walk backward, stripping his jacket off. "Who needs a bathing suit, right?"

"Fuck yeah."

I barely wiggle his jacket free before he's coming at me, picking me up. He's jogging to the back with me over his shoulder, so I hold on tight, laughing as he sets me down next to the pool. "Your jacket. I dropped it."

"I'll grab it later. Drink?"

"Yeah. A beer will be fine."

He winks and heads toward the cooler where Walker and Jake are playfully arguing about who did what last year.

"You getting in?" Jess questions from below me in the water. "Strip down and jump in. Madden will bring your drink to you."

Alana is floating around on the flamingo, her eyes on

Madden and the guys talking. Her watching him reminds me of how she kissed him this morning and it has me wanting to play my part hardcore right now.

"Yeah. I'll be in in a second." Before I can talk myself out of it, I walk toward Madden, grab him by the front of his hoodie, and pull him to me. "Kiss me."

"What?" He looks surprised as I grip the bottom of his hair and stand up on my tippy toes. "You sure?"

"Yeah," I whisper. "Do it before I change my—"

His lips come down on top of mine and my stomach does summersaults, goose bumps spreading across my skin. His kiss feels less forced than the last few times—more natural—and it has my insides going crazy as I kiss him back.

"Perfect," I whisper when we break the kiss. "Is she looking?"

It takes a few seconds, but he finally pulls his eyes away from mine to look over my shoulder. "Yeah, she's watching."

"Then let's get in and have some fun. Strip."

He looks me in the eye and strips his hoodie off. "Damn. Remember what I said on the way here?"

"Don't even go there." I laugh and strip out of his T-shirt from last night. "This is just pretend with a friend."

"Oh, so I'm a friend now?"

"Maybe." I kick my jeans aside and jump into the pool, hearing him jump in right behind me.

"I like that." He wraps his arms around me from behind and whispers beside my ear. "Just two friends having fun. We can do that, right?"

"Right."

He spins me around, and instinctively I wrap my legs around his waist. It's when his hands move around to grip my ass that I stiffen up. "Boundaries, Madden."

"Just doing what comes naturally, Nat." He squeezes my ass and bites my neck, causing my heart to jackhammer in my chest. "She's still watching. I've got to treat you like you're *my* girl. If you're not going to fall for me then what's the big deal?"

"There isn't one." I wrap my arms around his neck and glance over his shoulder at Alana. She's pretending to be into whatever Jess is talking about, but I can tell she's still paying attention to us. "If you go any further though... I'll have to kick your ass."

He laughs and moves his hands up to my lower back. "Is that a promise?"

"Yeah and I keep my promises."

"I like that in a girl." He brushes my hair behind my ear and runs his lips along my cheek. "You look beautiful today, by the way."

I close my eyes, the feel of his lips on my skin causing my insides to heat. "You don't need to compliment me to get me to play the part." I open my eyes and lock them on his. "But thank you."

"I mean it." He grips the back of my head and rests his forehead to mine, his lips hovering just out of reach. The urge to kiss him has my breathing picking up. "All bullshit aside, you're the most beautiful woman I've ever met. I don't need alcohol to say that either, so don't even think it's because of the beer I've had."

His compliment has my chest feeling tight with emotions. "You're a smooth talker, Madden Parker. I can see why all the girls fall for you." With that, I swim out of his arms and over to where Jess is bouncing the volleyball back and forth with Seth. It seems like the safer option right now with how I'm feeling.

As soon as Seth notices me coming their way he hits the volleyball at me, so I quickly hit it back, my attention going to Madden every chance I get in between hits.

I don't know why I'm watching him, but I do know that I

shouldn't be. It's not because I'm playing the part of his girl-friend that I can't take my eyes off him right now. I'm finding that I like watching him. I enjoy being around him. It's starting to scare me, if I'm being honest.

"Did you two have fun at the bar?" Jess hits the ball away and swims over to me, her attention landing on Madden with the others.

"Yeah, it was nice. We had a few beers and just hung out."

"That's good. Did he have any fans there?"

"A few. He actually went over to one and said hi." I smile, loving how happy he made her. "You should've seen how excited she was. She was practically shaking."

"Sounds like Madden. Even when he's trying to get away from the fame for a bit and be normal, he ends up giving his fans what they want. I admire him. I'd go crazy with no privacy. I don't know how he does it sometimes."

"I admire him too," I admit. "He's a good guy. Everything about him is..."

"Perfect." She laughs. "I would hope you think so, because you're dating the guy."

"Right," I say, mostly to myself. "Want a drink? I'm about to grab another one."

"Sure, babe. I'll take one."

I'm treading through the water to get to the stairs of the pool when I feel a tug on my waist, before being pulled into Madden's hard body. "You look like you're having fun."

"How do you know?" I tease as we step out of the pool and head to the cooler.

"Because I've noticed. I like it."

"Me too." I hand him a beer before grabbing myself one. Then I search through the cooler for a Seagram's Escapes for Jess. "I really like your friends."

"They like you too." He steps in close and looks me in the

eyes. "Which means you have to come back. It may not be with me next year, but I want you to come again."

I swallow, not expecting to hear that. "I don't know if that will even be an option."

"I'll make sure it happens. Even if I have to drag my brother here myself. Okay?"

I nod, even though inside, the thought of not coming here with Madden feels... off. "Okay. I'd like that."

Once back in the water, I chill with Jess for most of the night while the guys talk around the picnic table. I'm not sure where Alana disappeared to a while ago, but I'm glad to not have to see her constantly watching Madden as if she's thinking up ways to win him back over before this trip is over.

That's something I won't let happen. Not if I can stop it, and not when things are going so well. By the time Madden leaves, Alana is going to believe we're in love. I'll make sure of it.

CHAPTER EIGHTEEN

NATALIE

Last night after the partying was all over and we went to bed, I couldn't stop thinking about what Madden did for me at the bar. Even after he fell asleep beside me, I laid awake, replaying the scene in my head.

I took my shot and turned behind me, proud that I'd sunk a ball in, just to catch Madden's fist flying into some stranger's face. It surprised me, and even though it shouldn't have, it also turned me on; which is why I was so angry to find out he did it because of me. Before I could think, I wanted to pull him into my arms and kiss him, but instead, I turned away before I could make that mistake.

I don't *need* a guy to fight for me—I'd never ask that of anyone—but he did. He protected me even though I'm not his, and that showed me just how much he cares about my safety. After that guy threatened Madden, my fear of him getting hurt showed me I care about his too.

I haven't seen Madden in over an hour now. After our morning walk in the woods, he grabbed his guitar and headed toward his truck to clear his head. I've been hanging out with Jess, Seth, and Riley, playing a game of cornhole, but every time Madden starts playing his guitar, I get distracted and daze off.

"Your turn, babe. All you gotta do is get one on the board and miss the rest and we win." Jess claps her hands in excitement before bumping Riley with her hip. "This is the winning game. You boys ready to lose?"

"Not really," Riley mutters. "Get it in the hole," he yells across to me, trying to trick me. "It'll feel so much better than just getting it on the board—"

I laugh when Jess's hand covers Riley's mouth. "Nice try but I don't plan to make one in."

"Oh, come on," Seth taunts from beside me. "You know you want to. Just do it for the sake of another game."

I think about it for a split second after throwing my first bag and landing it on the board. "Maybe later. Sorry, boys." I throw my other two bags toward Jess's feet, missing the board on purpose. Truth is, I don't think I can go another minute not walking around to watch Madden while he plays. "I'll be back in a few."

"Sure you will, babe!" Jess yells after me. "We all know you're not coming back. Not when our rock star is looking sexy with his guitar."

I laugh but don't say anything as I make my way to Madden's truck. The sight of him sitting in the back, guitar in hand, with his hair falling in his face as he plays has me stopping and taking a deep breath. I should've just stayed in the back with the others. I know this now because my heart is practically pounding out of my chest as I watch him play.

"Hanging by a thread, close to unraveling. I'm holding onto nothing, ready to let go. Just ready to let go."

"I like that." He stops playing to look at me. "Sorry. I

205

could hear you playing from out back. Hope I'm not disturbing you."

He smiles and pats the spot beside him. "You just couldn't resist watching me play. I get it. Come here."

"Funny." I climb up beside him and he bumps my shoulder to tease me. "I do enjoy watching you play, but to say I can't *resist* is going a little overboard. I wouldn't say I like it that much."

"It's fine, babe. You can admit it." He leans in to speak beside my ear. "I like that you enjoy watching me play."

"Is that right? Why is that?"

"Because I like you," he whispers. Those four words cause goose bumps to spread across my body unexpectedly.

Not wanting him to see my reaction to his admission, I turn away and clear my throat. "Just keep playing. I want to hear more."

"I don't have much written yet. I was just playing to clear my head and those words came to me. It's nothing."

"Well, maybe you should keep playing and see what other words come to you." I lay back on his hoodie and use it for a pillow. "I'm just going to relax here for a bit and clear my head too. Pretend I'm not even here."

"There's no pretending you're not here," he says gently.

"Is that part of the song?" I ask nervously, not even wanting to wonder what he meant by that. "Because I like those lyrics. Go with it."

He starts playing again, eyes on me. "There's no pretending you're not here creeping into my bones. You're crawling under my skin and it scares me in a way I've never known..."

I close my eyes, allowing myself to get lost in the sound of his voice, his words hitting me hard and deep. It has my breathing speeding up and me questioning my own emotions to these lyrics. I suddenly feel hot, leading me to sit up and take my jacket off.

"Where's my jacket?" he asks suddenly, as if just noticing I haven't been wearing it all morning.

"I don't know. I haven't been wearing it today."

"I noticed," he says, setting his guitar aside. "I decided not to give you a hard time about it, hoping you'd change into it later."

The truth is, I woke up wanting to slip into it. I didn't even second guess it. I just instantly went to where I usually leave it on the dresser. "I couldn't find it this morning. I—" I stop once it hits me. "I left it outside last night. Remember?"

He shakes his head. "I walked past that side of the cabin this morning and didn't see it. I would've noticed it."

My stomach sinks. "Do you think Alana has it?"

"For fuck's sake. There's nowhere else it would be." He jumps down to his feet, his expression tight. "I'll get it back from her."

I shake my head and climb down after him. "I'll get it from her. I think it's about time the two of us have a talk. We've been here for four days and she still treats me as if we're not together. I think it's time that changes."

"You sure you're ready for that? You don't have to confront Alana. I talked you into coming here, I should be the one to handle her."

"We want her to believe this is real, right? What's going to make it seem more real than me fighting for you? That's something I should've been doing this whole time. I'm ready to do that now."

He doesn't argue as I walk away in search of Alana. I haven't seen her since we came back from our walk this morning, which has me wondering if she's been snuggled up in his jacket all day thinking of ways to break us apart. That thought angers me to no end.

"Has anyone seen Alana?"

"Yeah," Jake says cautiously. "She just got out of the shower. Saw her in the kitchen making a sandwich."

"Is everything okay?" Jess asks as I walk past her.

"Yeah, everything is fine. I just think it's time we have a chitchat. That's all."

Jess looks a little nervous but doesn't say anything as I make my way past her and Jake, walking inside to find Alana.

The sight of her in the kitchen wearing Madden's jacket causes a surge of jealousy I wasn't expecting. She doesn't notice me at first, so I stand here and watch her, thinking about how many times over the years she's worn that jacket just like she is right now. She looks comfortable in it, as if it belongs to her.

I hate that with everything in me.

"The jacket, Alana. Take it off."

She puts the butter knife down she was using to spread mayonnaise and sets her attention on me. "Why should I? If you cared about the jacket I wouldn't have found it laying outside in the dirt."

"It was outside because—" I stop, realizing I don't owe her an explanation. Not even for a damn second. "Just take it off. You lost your right to wear it the second you hurt Madden." I step in closer until we're only about five feet apart. "You're done hurting Madden. I'm here to make sure you never get the chance to again. He might've loved you at one time—that I know—but what you did to him broke his trust in you. It broke him in the worst way. He never will trust you again. He deserves someone so much better than you. He deserves the fucking world. You had your chance, now back off."

"Despite what you might think of me, I care about Madden more than I care about myself. I'd never hurt him again. Not if my life depended on it. But here." She tosses the jacket at my chest and I catch it. "Don't come crawling to *my* friends when Madden realizes it's me he's still in love with and breaks your heart. It may not happen in the next few days, but it will happen. Every year we get closer to getting back together. That's proof enough that he still loves me. He's loved me his entire life. That's not an easy habit to break. You *will* get hurt. Don't say I didn't warn you."

I feel sick to my stomach when she walks away, her words on repeat in my head. I *won't* get hurt. That's not going to happen, because I'm not Madden's to hurt. But why does the idea of being hurt by him scare me?

"Maybe so," I say before she gets outside. "But I'll take that versus him hurting another day over you. He deserves anything he wants in this life. He deserves everything good, and I'm going to do what I can to give him that, so leave him alone. It's the least you can do after ripping his heart out. I won't ask nicely again."

The look on her face confirms my words meant something to her. As if they have her thinking, and that's all I wanted out of this conversation. For her to stop being selfish for once.

Without a word, she steps outside, leaving me here to think about my own words. He *does* deserve everything. Madden is one of the best people I've ever known, and this trip is quickly opening my eyes up to that. It's scary, yet exciting to get to know the real him; the side he hides away with alcohol and partying.

I stand in the kitchen for a good five minutes to get my haywire thoughts under control before changing into Madden's jacket and joining the others outside. Madden is sitting in one of the lounge chairs, and as soon as he sees me, he smiles and motions for me to come to him.

I climb into his lap as if it's natural, making me realize that it is. Being with Madden is becoming natural.

He rubs his thumb over my cheek. "You okay?"

I nod and lean my head back so that it's resting on his chest.

"I see you got my jacket back. You didn't have to do that. I could've talked to her."

"I did have to, Madden." I lean my head back to look into his eyes when he tilts my chin back. "I *wanted* to. Just like you wanted to punch that guy at the bar for me."

He kisses my forehead and whispers, "It looks better on you by a long shot."

"Yes." Jess plops down into the chair beside us. "You two have the right idea. Just chill and soak up the sun for a bit." She laughs when she notices me wearing Madden's jacket. "It's getting hot out here, babe. Might want to take that off before you have a heat stroke."

"I will." My eyes land on Alana's from across the pool. I'd rather that outcome than to take it off. "In a little bit."

I find myself running my fingers along Madden's arms when they tighten around me, taking in his smooth skin. Everything about this moment feels right. My frame of mind is good, as if I could just close my eyes and get lost with him, right here, right now.

Monday is our last full day here, and as I sit here in his arms, snuggled into his chest, I try to figure out just how I feel about that.

The pit in my stomach tells me I'm feeling anything *but* good about it.

CHAPTER NINETEEN

MADDEN

MY KNUCKLES ARE STILL SORE FROM THE OTHER NIGHT when I punched that fucker across the face, but I'd do it again when it comes to Natalie, no questions asked. The fact that my brother isn't willing to hurt someone over her has me sitting here in my thoughts, pissed at him for being such a fucking pussy.

It's not the beer talking either, despite how many I've already had tonight. It's all me—my real thoughts. I don't have to be sober to know that.

The girls are hanging out by the fire, so I've just been sitting back with Jake and watching Natalie talk and laugh with Jess. I meant it when I said I'd make sure she gets to come back next year. Even if I have to bring her as a friend. She deserves to enjoy this experience like Logan and I have been doing for years. She belongs here, and more importantly, I want her here.

"What's good, man? You've been stuck in that head of yours for a while. Things going according to plan?"

I pull my eyes from Natalie and tilt back my beer. "If not, we still have tomorrow. We'll step things up if we have to, but I think Alana is finally giving in to the idea of me moving on with Nat."

"I don't think anything needs to be stepped up, Madden."

"You think she already believes we're a real couple?" I turn my attention to Alana, who is watching Natalie and Jess bond. She looks jealous, which probably means she expects Natalie to return next year.

Jake lets out a humorless laugh. "Shit, *I* believe you guys are a real couple; even more now than our last convo. You sure you haven't been playing me this whole time? Tell me the truth. Are you and Natalie really together? There's no way your brother would be okay if he saw the way you two have been bonding."

I shake my head and set my beer down. "Why would you have to ask that shit? If I was dating someone your ass would be the first to know. You know me, Jake. Trust me, we're not dating. I'm not sure I could even handle a relationship with anyone because of how fucked up my head is."

"Could've fooled me, brother." He stands when Seth and the others head toward the girls. "You may *think* you're pretending, but at this point, I think it's a hell of a lot more real than you realize. You just haven't figured it out yet. And from what I can see, you're a lot less fucked up in the head than the last time I saw you. Maybe that's all Natalie's doing."

"Fuck off, Jake. I already told you she's with—"

"I know, dickhead, but I don't see him bringing her. Just because he's in the picture, doesn't mean she wasn't meant to be yours to begin with. I'm just saying... be careful before you start to believe that yourself. I'm just looking out for you. As your best friend, that's my fucking job."

Jake walks away and I remain sitting here, beer in hand, as I watch Natalie laugh at something Seth said. Her smile has my fucking heart about to burst. I'm starting to question if maybe Jake is on to something. If he is, then I'm totally fucked.

The timer beeping on my phone has me standing from the picnic table and heading inside to take dinner out of the oven. I'm not the best cook, but ever since I threw together a meatloaf years ago, the others have asked me to continue cooking it each year. Not that I'm complaining. It's about the only thing I can cook, and a home cooked meal is nice once in a while when you spend most of your time on the road.

"Smells good in here." Alana's voice has me tensing as I set the pan on the stove to cool off. "I've been waiting the whole trip for this."

I exhale and grip the kitchen island, my gaze meeting hers. "I *have* to make it, so I figured I might as well do it tonight while we're all still somewhat sober."

"Good idea." She brushes a blonde strand behind her ear and leans over the island. "The trip is almost over and I feel like we haven't gotten a chance to spend any time together. It's the first for that, and I don't like it."

"It's for the best, Alana." I release my grip and turn away to grab the plates.

"Why does it have to be this way?" She's hurt. I can hear it in her voice, and I don't feel good about it, yet I feel somewhat relieved.

"Because we're better apart. *I'm* better when we're apart." This time when I say it, I mean it. I realize that the moment the words leave my mouth.

"That hurts," she whispers painfully. "You should know I'd never hurt you again. You know me better than tha—"

"No," I cut her off to avoid the guilt trip. "I thought I knew you, and I was sure you'd never do what you did, but I was wrong. I won't be wrong again. Not when it comes to my fucking heart."

I'm grateful for the interruption when Jess and Natalie walk in, cutting this little moment short. Without thinking, I lift Natalie onto the kitchen island, spread her thighs, and then move in between them. "Good timing," I whisper against her ear.

"That's what I'm here for."

"Stay here." I grab a fork and dig into the meatloaf, before standing in between her legs again. "Try it," I pressure her, smirking when she makes a funny face at the meat.

She shakes her head and tightens her lips when I try shoving it into her mouth. "Stop," she says on a laugh, pushing my hand away. "I told you earlier, I don't like meatloaf. I've hated every single one I've tasted. I'll barf right on your hand. Don't test me."

"You'll *love* my meatloaf. I promise." I grip her hip and squeeze it, knowing how it works her up. I love that I know that about her. "Try it or I'll do *this* all night." I squeeze her hip tighter and she moans out, squeezing the island below her. "I don't think you want that, do you?" I whisper.

"I hate you," she whispers back, before looking into the living room where the others have gathered. When she realizes no one is watching, she turns back around. "Fine. One bite and you don't ever squeeze my hip again or I kick your ass. Got it?"

I scrunch my face up and set the fork aside. "No deal."

"What?!" She jumps down from the kitchen island and comes after me when I walk to the sink. "Really, Madden? Now you suddenly don't want me to taste it?"

She goes to reach for the fork, but I grab her hand, stopping her. "Not if it means me never squeezing your hip again. I'm good."

"Give me that." She stands on her tippy toes when I lift the fork up high enough she can't reach it. "Madden! Come on!"

I spin around, trying to keep it out of reach, but she bites my bicep. "Did you just bite me?"

"Why? Were my teeth digging into your skin not confirmation enough?" She grins and reaches for the fork again, but I toss it aside and pick her up, setting her back onto the kitchen island. Stepping between her legs again, I grip the back of her hair, exposing her neck for me to bite it.

"Don't bite me unless you want to be bitten back, Nat." I run my lips over the spot I just bit, knowing that we most definitely have an audience by this point. "You don't want to know all the places I'd *bite* you."

Her breathing is exerted as she lifts her shoulder to her ear, pushing my face away. "Let's not go there, Madden."

"Why?" I ask on a growl. "You afraid you'll like it? It won't hurt... much."

Her eyes meet mine, her chest quickly rising and falling. Hell, mine is too. It almost looks like she's about to move in to kiss me, but instead, she grabs the fork and shoves it into her mouth.

"My meat is good, right?" I grin when her eyes widen.

I expect her to push me or yell at me, but instead, she nods. "Surprisingly, it's good." She hands me a plate and tilts her head. "Maybe I like meatloaf after all."

"I could change your mind about a lot of things you think you don't like. Just give it time."

"I'm starting the movie!" Jess yells to us from the couch. "Bring both pans in here and join us."

"Movie?"

Natalie nods as I help her down to her feet.

Before joining the others, I fill Natalie's plate with food, wanting to make sure she gets enough, because I know how the guys eat. Which is why I cooked two pans, but it's still never enough.

I wait until Natalie is done eating before I pull her into

my lap and gently bite her neck just to tease her. When she playfully elbows me, I kiss the spot on her neck I just bit. This time, it's not for show. I did it for me, and that fucks with my head through the entire movie. It's still on my mind, even now that we're all back outside drinking again.

"Come on, fucker!" Riley hollers. "We're about to play a little game of Truth, Dare, or Drink. Get the fuck over here."

Exhaling, I stand from the picnic table. I was really hoping Riley would forget about this game this year. We've been playing it since we were old enough to come to the cabin on our own without Jake's parents. "I'm coming, dick."

When I take a seat next to Natalie, Riley is standing between the circle of chairs, deciding on who his first victim will be. He takes entirely too long, causing a few of us to groan before he finally turns to Jake. "Truth, Dare, or Drink, fucker?"

"Should I be nervous?" Natalie whispers.

"If you don't like to give lap dances, jump through fire, or kiss random people... then yeah."

She smiles and bumps my shoulder. "The trip is almost over. Might as well live it up a little, right?"

"Right," I whisper, eyes landing on Alana at the same time she looks my way. "Just know that I never back down from a dare. If they dare me to get down on my knees and lick your inner thigh, I *will* do it, so don't kick my ass and give us away."

She nervously tilts her alcohol back, taking a long drink, followed by a second and third. "It's too late to back out now, right?"

"Dare." Jake finally says.

"I dare you to strip down to your boxers and give Jess a lap dance, *but* you have to do it standing on your hands."

"What the fuck do you mean on my hands?" Jake stands and begins stripping down to his boxers.

"Stand on your fucking hands and give Jess a lap dance. Do you not understand the words coming from my mouth? On your hands."

"Dude, I've been drinking all day." He kicks his jeans aside and yanks his shirt over his head. "What makes you think I can stand on my fucking hands?"

"Just do it, baby!" Jess yells in excitement, looking him up and down. "Give me a sexy dance. Make it hot and you might get lucky tonight."

He shrugs. "Fuck it." It takes him a few tries to get standing on his hands, but he finally manages to do it, thrusting his hips in Jess's face. He's completely off rhythm to the music but keeps thrusting until he eventually falls over, cussing as he hits the ground with a thud.

Everyone laughs and whistles as he gets back to his feet and straddles Jess's lap, doing his best to move his hips seductively. Dancing has never been Jake's strongpoint.

"All right. All right. I think we've all had enough of watching your ass move out of rhythm," Walker says on a laugh, standing up. "I'll go next. Seth. Truth, Dare, or Drink."

"Truth."

"Seriously, fucker?"

"Yeah, I need a few more drinks before I do a dare. Especially from you."

"Okay, fine. Is it true that you got caught jerking off by Jake's mom Freshman year?"

"That's fucked up," Jake mutters. "Why bring that shit back up?"

"Because his ass never fessed up," Walker points out.

It's a few seconds before Seth finally grins and takes a drink. "It happened. And she liked it too."

"Fucker!" Jake tosses a stick at Seth's head, but he ducks right before it can hit him.

"I knew it!" Riley yells. "You lucky bastard. Jake's mom is ho—"

"Don't even go there." Jake gives Riley a warning look and he chuckles into his drink.

Seth grins and rubs his hands together. "Okay, enough about my ass. Alana. Truth, Dare, or fucking Drink?"

"Dare." Her eyes flicker my way as if she's hoping her dare will involve me. Seth better hope for his health that it doesn't.

"All right. You and Riley have been a little cozy this weekend. Kiss the fucker. Don't stop until I finish this drink."

"With or without tongue?" Riley stands and walks over to Alana's chair.

"What the fuck do you think?"

Riley grins and gets down on his knees in front of my ex. "Well, are you going to kiss me or what?"

Alana grabs the back of Riley's head, her eyes landing on me again, staying there as she leans in and kisses him. I don't know why the fuck she thinks kissing him is going to make me jealous. We've been playing this game for years—we've all practically kissed each other—and I've never once gotten jealous. It's a game none of us take seriously.

"Looks like someone is trying to make you jealous," Natalie says stiffly, as if the idea of me being jealous bothers her.

"That shit won't happen and she knows it."

"Why is that?"

"It's a game, Nat. None of this is real."

"Is that the only reason?" she asks.

Before I can respond, Seth claps his hands. "All right, you two. That's enough." Seth points to Jess. "Your turn to call a dare."

Jess stands and turns to me. "Madden... I dare you to..." She looks around, trying to think of something, before finally focusing her attention on Natalie. "Jake gave a little lap dance, so now it's your turn to give Natalie one. Make it *hot*. Use your hands and mouth on her. Show us how badly you want to fuck her tonight, because we all know it's happening."

I stand and remove my hoodie, before gripping Natalie's thighs and spreading them apart. "You ready for this?"

She swallows and nervously grips the seat. She's not ready for this; not by a long shot. "Go for it."

Cracking my neck, I grip the top of Natalie's chair and straddle her lap, grinding my hips into her. When my lips move along her neck, she lets out a little moan and her grip on the seat tightens.

"Hell yeah! Move those hips!" Jess yells. "Look at that ass move."

"Hey," Jake mutters. "Mine moves just as good."

"Ha." Alana mutters. "In your dreams."

Rolling my hips to the rhythm of the music, I move my hands around to grip the back of her hair, forcing her to look up at me while I grind against her. Her gaze is just as heated as I feel, and for a moment, I get so wrapped up in pleasing her I don't even realize I'm hard against her.

"Madden," she whispers.

"Shhh..." I run my lips along her jaw, doing what Jess asked me to do. She wants me to use my mouth and hands on her, so that's what I'm doing. When my lips reach her mouth, I capture it with mine at the same time I grab her hands and place them on my chest.

When they move along my abs, groping them as I kiss her, I bite her bottom lip a little too hard, things getting heated between us.

"Holy fuck, it's getting hot out here!"

"Yeah, lose the fucking clothes already and just fuck right here. Give us a show. I won't complain," Riley adds.

It takes my friends yelling for Natalie to remove her

hands from my chest and remember I'm not my brother. But I place them back on my body to remind her that he doesn't exist right now. "I'm yours right now, remember? Pretend you want me," I whisper.

Her eyes lock on mine and stay there as her hands explore my body, taking in my tight abs as I grind my hips above her.

"Touch me like you want me to *fuck* you." I yank her hair and scrape my teeth across her throat. "Make me believe it."

Grabbing the top of the chair, I step up so that I'm standing above her with my crotch in her face. Then I grab her head and slowly start grinding in her face. When her hands grip my ass, I bite my bottom lip and slow down the rhythm, getting so lost in Natalie that I forgot we're not alone until someone whistles at us.

Clearing my throat, I jump down from the chair and run my hands over my face, watching Natalie's chest as it heaves as fast as mine.

"It's about time that ended," Alana mumbles. "I'll go next."

I turn away and cuss under my breath, because I've been dreading Alana's turn since the game started. I know her well enough to know that she's going to try and get under my skin just because she's hurting.

"Natalie. Truth, Dare, or Drink?"

Natalie sits up straight in her chair, as if to show she's not intimidated by my ex. I don't like where this is going. "Dare."

Alana looks surprised she chose a dare, but then smiles as if that's what she was hoping for. "I dare you to let Walker kiss you. Time is up when I call it."

My muscles immediately tense as Walker stands from his seat and grins. I'm two seconds away from punching that grin off his face. He's already tested me enough this trip.

"Okay." Natalie stands right as Walker stops in front of her chair. "No tongue, though," she says firmly.

My heart fucking skips a beat when his hands grip her face and he moves in for the kiss. I can't tell if there's tongue involved, but he better hope for his safety that there isn't. Especially since she said no.

"Fucking call it," I growl to Alana after a minute.

She shakes her head. "I'm not ready yet."

Walker's grip on Natalie's face tightens, and when I see his tongue dip out to touch her lips, I grip him by the shoulder and yank him back, causing him to lose his footing.

"Damn, man. What the fuck?" Walker stands up straight when I get in his face. "It's a dare. Chill the fuck out."

"The dare didn't call for putting your fucking tongue in my girl's mouth, asshole." When I turn away from Walker, all my friends are looking at me. I'm too pissed to even give a shit that I just ruined the game. "Game fucking over."

Before anyone can piss me off more, I walk away.

I've been in the cabin for less than a minute when the door opens to Natalie joining me. Her face is red, and I can't tell if it's from embarrassment or anger over the way I acted outside.

"What was that about? I thought it was just a g—"

"Fuck it." Letting go of everything, I come at Natalie, wrap my hands into the back of her hair, and kiss her so hard that she falls against the wall. When she kisses me back, her tongue slipping into my mouth, I lift her up and wrap her legs around my waist, getting lost in the moment. Lost in us.

I can't think straight right now. All I know is that I want to erase Walker's kiss. I hate that she might've liked it and I want her to like my lips on her more. I *need* her to.

Growling against her lips, I tug the bottom one with my teeth, my hand moving to squeeze her hip. The little moan she releases has me growling out and grinding my erection against her body. I'm being reckless with my brother's girl and I fucking know it.

I want inside of her and from the way she's kissing me back, she wants it too. That thought has me kissing her harder, my tongue exploring her mouth as if it's mine to taste. Lost in the moment, I slide my hand up her shirt, my finger slipping under the fabric to graze her hard nipple.

Fuck, I want it in my mouth.

"Whoa, am I interrupting something?"

Jake's voice has me sliding my hand out of Natalie's shirt and setting her back down to her feet.

As soon as her feet hit the floor, she pushes at my chest to put some space between us and without a word, walks away.

"What the fuck was that?" Jake growls out.

I place my hands against the wall and bow my head, my mind all fucked up. "I don't know."

"*That* didn't seem like pretend," he points out.

"It was a mistake," I say stiffly. "I fucked up."

"Well then you should probably fix it and fast."

"Yeah. You don't think I fucking know that. I'll handle it."

"Let's fucking hope so."

Once I'm alone, I punch the wall, regretting it immediately once I see the hole I left. Just like I regret making out with Natalie. She probably hates me now. "Fuck!"

I don't know what the hell just happened a minute ago, why I slipped up and kissed her in private but what I do know is that I was *not* supposed to feel the way I did when seeing her kiss another guy. Far from it. I need to get my head straight before I fuck up majorly. This trip was supposed to solve my current problem, not cause a new one.

And that's exactly what's going to happen if I slip up again.

CHAPTER TWENTY

NATALIE

It's the middle of the night when Madden crawls into bed beside me. Even though I'm wide awake, I close my eyes, not wanting to talk about what happened tonight. I don't know what came over me earlier, but I do know how I feel about it, and that's what scares me the most.

It might've been a mistake, but it felt anything *but*; at least for that split second that I didn't allow my head to get involved. What the hell does that say about me? I have a boyfriend. I'm not just dating any random guy either, I'm dating his brother. His fucking brother. That's the lowest of lows.

I don't know what's on Madden's mind right now or how he feels about our kiss, and that's messing with me as he lies beside me. I'm not sure why, but I hate it. I shouldn't care whether he liked it or if he felt anything at all, but that's all I've been able to think about since it happened.

Panic set in earlier and I rushed to my phone and powered it back on. I knew there was no service here and it was pointless to text Logan, but I did it anyway, needing to remind myself that I'm his. I'm not Madden's, even though I've been playing the part. A role is all it is.

Natalie: I miss you. Can't wait to get home to you.

Of course, he didn't text back. He won't even receive the message for another day. It sucks, because I need some form of communication with him now.

I change my focus to Madden's heavy breathing, and I can tell he's struggling; probably just as hard as I am over our make-out session. There's movement behind me, and then suddenly, his arm wraps around me and I'm pulled against his body.

My heart is racing so fast that it's hard to catch my breath, but instead of moving away, I keep my eyes closed and pretend I don't notice the way he's holding me.

It's not until his fingers run through my hair and my entire body relaxes into him that I know I'm completely screwed. I've fallen for Madden Parker in the few days we've been together—having feelings I never had for his brother—and we still have another full day together before heading back to the real world.

I close my eyes, struggling with the fact that even though I should be happy, my heart hurts. I'm more confused than I've ever been before, and because of that, I need sleep to come.

WHEN I WAKE UP, the first thing on my mind is mine and Madden's make-out session. I can't just call it a kiss, because it was so much more than that, and if Jake hadn't walked in to see us, more could've happened. That thought scares me the most.

Sure, I'd had a few drinks and was feeling a bit tipsy, but that's no excuse for kissing him back or letting his hand explore my breasts. It's definitely no excuse for liking it either. I screwed up, and I have to own up to it with Logan. It was wrong. Knowing Madden, he'll probably try and take all the blame when we get home, but I won't allow that.

"You up?" Madden's groggy voice comes from behind me and I swear my heart skipped a beat at hearing it so close.

Despite our little fuck-up last night, I still slept in his arms the entire night. I'm not sure anymore if it was for Alana's benefit or mine. I should've moved away when he crawled into bed, yet I didn't.

"Yeah." I roll over to face him, running a hand through my snarled hair. "Haven't been able to sleep in hours."

"We should talk about last night." He sits up and reaches for his T-shirt, slipping it on. I hadn't even noticed that he'd taken his shirt off in the middle of the night. Knowing that he did makes my insides ignite. "I never should've kissed you like that. I'm sorry. Clearly, my head is fucked up right now due to all the time we've pretended. It's probably a good thing we're heading out tomorrow."

My stomach sinks from hearing him admit he shouldn't have kissed me. *Why does it sting when I should be relieved?* "Don't beat yourself up. It's done and over with. We were both drinking and not thinking clearly. If I had been, I never would've kissed you back." I exhale and attempt to crawl over him to get out of bed.

Before I can get off, he grips my hips and stops me right as I'm straddling his body. "Is that true?" His eyes settle on mine, and I swallow, knowing I'm about to lie. "Because you didn't seem drunk, Nat."

I press my hands to his chest when he squeezes my hips,

wanting an answer. "I wasn't drunk," I admit. "Just buzzed enough to let go, and that stupid dance didn't help any."

He smiles, causing my heart to jumpstart. I love that smile so damn much now. "So, you enjoyed my dance?"

"Shut up." I shove his chest and climb off him.

"That's not an answer," he whispers over my shoulder as I search through my suitcase for a change of clothing.

"Maybe I'd rather not give one."

I close my eyes, goose bumps spreading across my skin when he brushes my hair away from my neck. "Which is why I want an answer even more."

I slam my suitcase shut and turn to face him. "Yes. I liked the dance. Any girl with a heartbeat would've enjoyed that dance. There... are you happy?"

"Yes." He grins and hands me his jacket. "Put your jacket on. We're going on our morning walk."

After he's gone, I stare at his jacket for longer than necessary trying to figure out why Madden called his jacket mine. We've been here for almost a week and he's never called it *mine*.

By the time I throw my hair up, brush my teeth, and meet him outside, he's sitting on the picnic table at the tree line waiting on me. He's not looking in my direction, so I take a few minutes to admire his messy hair, ripped jeans and faded black T-shirt, and just how sinfully gorgeous he is. This is the last time we'll be out in these woods together and the feeling I get from that thought is anything but pleasant.

He stands and nods once noticing me. I meet him by the picnic table, walking straight past him and into the woods. I get this sudden urgency to get lost in the wilderness and not come out for hours. Everything seems to be hitting me at once and I feel overwhelmed.

"Nat, slow down. Talk to me."

"I can't." I speed up, dodging and jumping over branches

to get away, until finally, he catches me and pulls me into his body.

"What's going on?" He presses his forehead to mine and brushes his thumb over my cheek. "You can talk to me. I'm here for you."

"I don't know." I breathe out, my heart racing. "I guess the thought of going back home, to work, and back to..."

"My brother?" he questions. "Is what?"

"Stressful. Hard. Lonely. A lot of things. I don't know." I back away from his touch and lean against the closest tree, fighting to control my breathing. I didn't realize how trapped in my life I felt until getting a taste of freedom away from it all. "Being here is freeing—like an escape—and tomorrow morning we'll be leaving. I don't know how to feel. I'm being stupid right now. I'm sorry."

He shakes his head and pulls out a cigarette, lighting it. "You're being anything but stupid right now, Nat. I feel that way the day before leaving every single year. My life isn't what everyone thinks it is. It's just as hard and stressful as any normal person's life; probably more. I like the getaway too. Which is why I'm here. It's why I needed you here with me."

"What happens when you go back?"

"Well, I usually spend a week sulking in my fucking misery before going back to the band and sticking to a tight schedule. Between writing songs, practicing with the band, and dealing with our manager and all the shit he lines up for us, it's a lot to take on. Especially after getting a taste of being with my old friends like it used to be." He takes a long drag and slowly exhales. "Depression kicks in and I'm a miserable, drunk dick for at least a month or two."

"I don't want that for you," I admit, my stomach twisting into knots. "You can call me, you know... when you get back on the road. If you need someone to talk to, of course. Not that I'm the person you'd want to call, I'm sure, but I'm here for you. I want you to know that."

"You're wrong, Nat." He smiles and puts out his cigarette. "You *are* the person I'd want to call."

We stand here in silence for a moment and I notice Madden checking me out in his jacket. It reminds me of his comment from earlier. "Why did you call this jacket mine?"

He pushes away from the tree. "I want you to have it after the trip. It's yours."

I shake my head when he begins walking as if it's not a big deal, walking to catch up with him. "Wait, what?" I attempt to take the jacket off to give it back, but he stops me. "Madden, it's your favorite jacket. I can't keep it."

He pulls on the zipper and leans in against my ear. "And *you're* my favorite girl. It only seems right that you get to be the one to keep it."

At this point, I wouldn't be surprised if Madden feels my heart racing in my chest. That's how hard it's beating. "Thank you." I'm not sure why I said that, but I can't seem to form any other words. I should tell him no. I should tell him it's inappropriate and force him to take it back, but I can't.

"So, tell me something about you that my brother doesn't know. I want to leave here knowing something he doesn't." He starts walking again, heading back, and I follow.

"There isn't much to know," I admit. "I don't keep secrets from him. Wish I could say the same about your brother."

"There has to be something he doesn't know. Even if it's insignificant. I don't care. I just want to know."

I exhale and try to think of something I haven't told Logan. Truth is, there are a lot of insignificant things that Logan doesn't know about me, but it's not because I haven't told him. It's because he doesn't ask. "When I was eleven, I dislocated my right elbow. I was running to the neighbor's house and tripped in their driveway. I remember thinking my arm looked funny and I was afraid it would look like that forever."

"Did you cry?" he asks, curious.

"Actually, no. Not when I hurt it, at least. It wasn't until I got into the room and they were about to snap it back into place that I cried. I was so terrified it would hurt. Not that injuring my arm didn't already hurt. But the idea of them messing with it was scary."

"I had an arm injury once too. I broke my left arm when I was nine." He holds up his left arm. "My uncle had me on his shoulders and he tripped over something and I landed on my arm funny. I cried my ass off." He laughs. "I guess you're tougher than I am."

"You were younger," I point out.

"Yeah, I guess." His smile is contagious, making me smile too. I swear his smile is the best one I've ever seen, and it makes me the happiest. "What else?"

"When I was in the fourth grade, I was taking a drink from the water fountain and my whole class was in line behind me. The boy behind me lifted up my blue jean skirt. It was stuck over my butt until I felt a draft from the wind. It was embarrassing to say the least."

"Well, if I was in your class, I would've rearranged that little prick's face for you."

"Like you rearranged the prick's face at the bar?"

He brushes my hair behind my ear and nods. "Exactly. And I'd do it to the next guy who treats you with disrespect too."

"Why?" I suddenly ask, curious.

"Do I need to say it, Nat?" He stops once the cabin comes into view.

"Yeah," I say firmly. "I want to hear it. Tell me."

He hesitates for a short moment before opening his mouth to speak, but he gets interrupted by Jake doing some kind of weird catcall. "Looks like they're waiting on us."

I'm frustrated when we get back to the others, annoyed that I didn't get to hear his answer. I'm even more annoyed that I can't stop wondering what he was going to say.

"All right." Jake claps his hands one time. "It's our last day here together, assholes. Let's drink, play some games, and make the best of it. I'm going to miss you dicks once we leave." Jake punches Madden's shoulder playfully. "Especially you. I barely get to see you outside of a concert. Not that I'm complaining. I'm proud of you, man."

"Thanks, brother." Madden's gaze sways my way, where it lingers, before he says, "I'll miss you all too."

I know that he's talking to Jake and the others, but a part of me wishes it was meant for me. I want him to miss me, because I know without a doubt that I'll miss him once this is all over.

CHAPTER TWENTY-ONE

MADDEN

Fuck, this day has gone by way too fast for my liking. Jess has been stingy with Natalie all evening, basically telling me that I get the next few days alone with her, while it might be a year before she gets to see her again. If only she knew that once we leave here, I have to give her back to my brother. That shit burns more than I'd like to admit.

I've been thinking about her returning to his bed and imagining him on top of her. All it's done is put me in a shitty mood. Technically, she's his. I shouldn't want to protect her from my brother. I shouldn't want to rip his throat out at the idea of him putting his lips on her.

What the fuck is wrong with me?

"You're staring really hard right now, brother." Jake says, distracting me from where Natalie is dancing with Jess. She's finally letting loose and enjoying her time here with my friends, but in less than twenty-four hours, everything will change. "It's bad enough that I found you two making out last night. Get your fucking head straight before tomorrow."

I bring my beer to my lips and tilt it back, eyes on Natalie as she motions for me to join her. "It's already straight," I lie, standing up. "Doesn't mean we still don't have a show to put on until tomorrow morning. I know what I'm doing. Trust me."

He attempts to say something, but I set my beer down and walk away before he can. When I reach Natalie, I wrap my arm around her waist and pull her against me. "You look like you're having fun." I smile against her cheek. "I like that."

She laughs and runs her hand through my messy hair. She's out of breath from dancing with Jess and the sweat running down her chest has me feeling hot. "I am having fun. Thanks to you. Best vacation I've ever taken. Not that I've taken one before, but still."

I laugh and lift her up, wrapping her legs around my waist as we dance. "Me too," I admit. "Had it not been for you, this trip would've been ruined for me. I owe you big time, Nat; anything you want."

Her arms wrap around my neck as she looks down at me. "I already told you what I want—you not drowning yourself in alcohol after we leave." I can tell it's important to her, which makes it important to me too.

"I'll stay sober for you." I grip the back of her head with my free hand and press my forehead against hers. "Thank you. No one else could've pulled this off with me, Nat. No one."

"Why do you say that?"

Without a thought I say exactly what's on my mind. "Because you're perfect for me."

She smiles and wiggles her way out of my arms. When she goes to reach for her drink, I grab her from behind and pull her back to me, moving my hips against her ass to the rhythm.

Instead of fighting me, she melts into me, matching my every move so fucking perfectly. Getting lost in the moment, she reaches her arm back and grabs my head, her body grinding so painfully perfect against mine that my dick jumps.

She has to feel me hard against her, but Natalie stays in the moment with me, not giving a shit just like last night. At least for a few moments. That means she's getting comfortable with me. Maybe even a little too comfortable.

Gripping the front of her throat, I press my lips against her neck and kiss it, feeling Alana and everyone else's eyes on us. This is the most sexual we've been this entire trip and it's fucking with me. At this point, I'm not even sure if what we're doing is only for show. It sure doesn't feel pretend right now.

Her ass is pressed against my dick. One hand is on her throat and the other is on her waist as we move to the music. The need to bend her over and fuck her is so overwhelming that I have to take a step back and get my head straight.

My eyes land on my brother standing at a distance with his arms crossed, watching us. My fucking heart drops at the realization that I'm all over his girl in front of him. He's not supposed to be here. "Logan." I clear my throat and release Natalie, feeling her tense the second she hears my brother's name. "I thought you weren't coming."

Everything gets lost in the chaos of our friends jumping up to welcome him. I should be happy to see him. I've been trying to get him here for years, yet now that he's finally here, I want the opposite. It's my last night with Natalie, and him being here is going to make shit uncomfortable.

"I managed to get tomorrow off." He grips my shoulder, before offering Natalie an awkward, platonic hug, making it seem as if they've only met a couple of times, but the way he looks at her—in a way that only I can see—seems anything but. "Thought I'd come visit with some old friends I've been missing and hang out with my brother and his girlfriend. Who knows when I'll get to see you again."

"Hell yeah, man." Seth hands Logan the beer he just opened. "Glad your ass could make it. Even if only for a night. It's good to see you."

"Real good." Jake glances my way, his expression a warning. "Glad you could join the party."

Natalie's discomfort shows as she grabs a beer and takes a sip. I don't want the others to notice, so I wrap my arms around her from behind and whisper in her ear. "Nothing has changed. You're still mine. Don't forget that. My brother agreed to it. Remember that."

Logan is talking to Riley, but his attention keeps landing on me and Natalie. He needs to get his shit together before he ruins everything we worked for on this trip. I know I'm probably a dick for doing this, but as a reminder that he needs to back the fuck off, I press my lips to Natalie's neck, my eyes on him. Hopefully he'll get the hint and stop staring.

He tenses but then turns away, just as I had hoped, his attention going to Alana, who seems to be staring at him awkwardly as she sips her drink. I'm sure the shit she put me through has her feeling uncomfortable, knowing that Logan took care of my ass. They haven't seen each other since the year we split.

Since it's the last night, we all settle down around the fire so we can reminisce on old times.

I keep Natalie close to me, my arms around her waist despite my brother flexing his jaw my way every chance he gets, telling me to back off. He's the dickhead that decided to show up, knowing what the deal was. It's not my fault he has to see me all comfy with his girl and shit now. If anything, I should be the one pissed.

"You okay?" I whisper against Natalie's neck when I

notice how tense she is against me. "He knew what he was getting into by agreeing to let me borrow you. He can't get pissed now."

"I'm just trying to figure out what he's doing here," she whispers back after a few seconds. "He agreed to me coming alone with you and pretending to be your girlfriend and then he just shows up unannounced? He chooses *now* of all the times he could've come, especially after telling me no the past two years. Seriously, it pisses me off. I could've been here as his girlfriend like I should've been all along, but he didn't want that. Now that I'm *your* girl, he decides to show his face."

I pull her tighter against me for comfort, because I can hear the frustration in her voice. He's a dick for doing this and he knows it. "He probably just misses you," I say, wanting to make Natalie feel better for my brother's fuckups. "I know I would."

"Maybe," she whispers back, finally loosening up in my arms and getting comfortable. "When it comes to your brother, I don't know anymore. Not after everything he's kept from me that I've learned about him this week."

"...that was three years ago. Remember that?" Seth jumps to his feet and slaps Jake on the shoulder. "You woke up beside the fire pit with your boxers pulled down to your ankles. That shit was not a pretty sight to see."

"Fuck you." Jake laughs. "You dicks kept feeding me shots even after I could no longer walk straight. What the hell did you expect?"

"Oh, that's nothing!" Jess says excitedly. "Remember that one time when Alana walked outside to find Seth floating around on the flamingo in one of her thongs? His balls were hanging out each leg hole."

Everyone bursts into laughter, Natalie included. I could've lived without the memory of that. I'm sure everyone could've.

"There was that one time when Logan blacked out and ended up in bed between Jess and I." Jake shoots my brother a hard look. "I thought it was Jess caressing my leg the entire fucking night until I rolled over and was face to face with that dickhead."

Logan's face turns red as he tilts his drink back. "To be fair, your leg was smooth. I thought it was Jess's."

"Funny, dickhead!"

"What about that time Madden was brave enough to fuck me in the pool while everyone else was sitting right here talking just like we are now?" Alana's eyes land on Natalie at the same time she tenses in my arms. "It was a long night. A very long one."

"What the hell?" Jess says in surprise. "That's not cool to talk about, Alana. It's rude and inappropriate."

"What?" Alana shrugs and sets her drink aside. "We're all talking about memories from past trips. It was fine to bring it up and laugh about it two years ago. What's the problem now? Am I just supposed to forget it ever happened?"

"Alana," I say firmly. "Drop it."

"Why? So, I'm just supposed to forget the way you pushed my bikini aside and sunk between my legs as if you needed me to breathe? Or did you forget how that felt? Did you forget how much you needed me then? Because I haven't."

"If he hasn't already..." Natalie says, surprising everyone. "He will soon. I'll make sure of it. Now I'd shut my mouth if I were you."

There's an awkward silence after that; although, my brother gives Natalie a look of disapproval that I notice out of the corner of my eye.

"Okay." Walker turns the music louder. "Maybe we should take a break from talking and just chill for a bit."

"Yeah," Logan adds. "Probably a good idea."

Natalie is staring in Alana's direction as if she's fighting something back, before finally standing and walking toward the cabin.

I get ready to stand and go after her, but my brother stands first. "I'll be back. I left a six-pack in my car."

It's an excuse to get some alone time with Natalie. Our friends don't know that when he disappears into the cabin he'll most likely be kissing and touching her, but I do, and it has me anxious as shit. After a few minutes and them both still gone, I can't take it anymore, wondering what he's saying and doing to her, so I leave the others and head toward the cabin.

I walk inside, their voices catching my attention from the hallway. I can't see them, and like a nosey dick, I stand here and listen, wanting to know what they're talking about.

"...what do you expect, Logan? How do you want me to act when I'm supposed to be here with your brother? Of course, I'm not jealous of Alana." Her voice shakes. "It's an asshole thing of you to ask. You can't just show up here five days later and all of a sudden act like the jealous boyfriend."

"Well, it sure sounded like it out there." He pauses for a second, before adding. "It sounded real to me, and hell yeah it has me jealous. In case you've forgotten, just five days ago you barely tolerated my brother. Now you two are all cozied up together as if you're in love. What the hell am I supposed to think? Was it real? Outside in front of everyone. Tell me the truth."

"What?! No. I'm just... I'm playing my part. That's it. Am I not supposed to act like the jealous girlfriend? Here you are playing the part of the jealous boyfriend for the first time ever and *you're* the reason I'm here in the first place. You decided it was okay behind my back without talking to me first. Don't forget that."

"Dammit, Natalie. I told you I never thought you'd agree to it. That's the *only* reason I agreed."

"If you say so."

"It is," he says a little too sternly for my liking.

"Everything good in here?" I make my way around the corner to see Logan pinning Natalie against the wall. His body pressed against hers has a surge of jealousy taking over. "You might want to take a step back before the wrong person walks in. You're lucky it's only me."

My brother exhales and takes a step back.

"What are you doing here, Logan? You said you weren't coming. Why show up now on the last fucking night?"

He lets out a humorless laugh and walks to the kitchen to grab a beer from the fridge. He shuts it and leans against the door, his eyes hard. "I saw a picture online of you two at a bar looking a little too cozy. Then I got a message from Natalie that she missed me. So here the fuck I am. Guess I should've just stayed home."

My stomach drops at hearing Natalie text my brother that she missed him. "When did she text you?"

"Last night. Or at least that's when the message came through."

When I turn to look at Natalie she looks guilty, as if she wishes she'd never sent it. I wish she hadn't either, because for some reason, it feels fucking shitty. Like my girl betraying me. "I didn't think you'd get the text. I figured you'd get it when we were on the road back home."

"Well, apparently you're the only one with cell service here. Good to know." I try my best to hide my disappointment, but my voice hardens at the end. "I guess I'll let you two catch up since you miss him so much."

I walk away before I can do or say something I'll regret. Shit, I don't even know why her missing him hurts so fucking much, but it does. I go out the side door that leads to the hot tub, wanting to avoid our friends.

If I take off into the woods, they're going to know something is wrong. So instead, I grip the edge of the hot tub and squeeze. I'm on edge right now and seconds away from making an ass out of myself.

The longer I'm out here and they're inside alone, the harder I squeeze, wishing it were my brother's throat instead. Talk about fucked up.

CHAPTER TWENTY-TWO

NATALIE

I DON'T KNOW WHY I'M SO ANGRY WITH LOGAN FOR showing up, but I am. I thought I'd be happy to see him. I'm supposed to be happy to see him, since he's my boyfriend, but all I can think about is how this could screw things up for his brother, and I've become protective of Madden.

If Alana or the others notice Logan's discomfort with me and his brother being close, they're going to catch on that something isn't right. We've worked too hard this entire trip to make Alana believe we're really together just for Logan to show up and possibly threaten the progress we've made. I'm pissed. Then there's the fact that I've been practically begging him for two years to bring me here and he's refused every time, with the excuse that he can't take off of work.

"You should go home, Logan."

His eyes widen with disbelief and he sets his beer down. "Are you serious, babe? I drove all the way out here to see you, and now you're telling me to go home?"

Anxiety fills me when he moves in and grips my hip,

giving it a slight squeeze. Without thinking, I yank his hand away like it's not supposed to be there. My reaction is so natural that it confuses me. "I'm sorry," I whisper, taking a step back. "You being here is only going to complicate things for your brother. You know more than anyone how much he needs things to work. Are you really willing to risk his one chance at getting his life back just because you saw a photo online and decided you wanted to see me?"

He tenses his jaw and looks me over, taking me in wearing Madden's jacket. "You're wearing his jacket. It's the first thing I noticed when I walked up aside from you grinding your body against his. That's his favorite jacket," he adds.

I swallow and reach into the fridge for a water bottle. "It's actually mine now. He gave it to me."

"What the fuck? Are you serious?" He cracks his neck, before gripping the counter with both hands.

"Yeah. He seemed serious about it."

"That asshole," he spits out. "I know exactly what that means."

"What?"

He stands up and rolls up his sleeves, clearly angry. "That he's falling for you."

My chest tightens, but before I can figure out how I feel about Logan's words, Jess and Alana join us in the kitchen.

"Hey! Where's Madden?" Jess asks. "He's not in bed already, is he?"

I shake my head and force a smile. "He's by the hot tub waiting for me." That might not be true, but that's the door he left out of. "I'm going to join him. I'll see you guys in a little bit. I'm sure you guys have some catching up to do."

I expected Alana to give me a nasty look or have some snide remark, but when I glance her way, she's looking at Logan. I can't tell if she hates him or has a thing for him, and instead of waiting around to find out, I walk away in a hurry to get to Madden. I need to see that he's okay. I hate that he walked away like he did.

When I step outside and close the door behind me, he's leaning against the hot tub, his arms crossed over his chest. He looks up, his amber eyes meeting mine, causing my stomach to sink when I see the pain in them. "Everything good with my brother?"

"I don't know," I admit. "He's mad at me for telling him he should leave."

Madden pushes away from the hot tub and grabs my shoulders to look at me. "You told him that? Did he do something to hurt you?"

I shake my head. "I just want to get through this last night together. I think it's best if we avoid the others for a bit and let Logan catch up with them. I don't think he'll be leaving, and if we're going to get through this, we can't have him watching us the way he has been since arriving. It's making me nervous."

"We'll stay away all night if you want. I'm all about making you happy. Just tell me what you want."

Butterflies fill my stomach from the way he's looking into my eyes. The urge to lean in and kiss him has me clearing my throat and turning away instead. "A dip in the hot tub?"

He smiles and yanks his shirt over his head. "I'm down."

I smile back and strip down to my bra and panties. "Just a nice relaxed night in the hot tub."

"Sounds good to us." Logan's voice has me stiffening the moment I step into the water. "Alana and I just had the same idea. Well, I did, and she followed."

He can't be serious.

"It's the last night and I haven't been able to enjoy the hot tub yet," Alana says, climbing inside and taking a seat in her own little corner. "You guys had it to yourselves the other night. You can share the last night."

Anger courses through me and I cast a hard glare in Logan's direction. He did this on purpose and he knows it. If he wants to see me and his brother together, then it looks like he's going to get his wish. As if he hasn't done enough, to top it off, he brings Alana with him. That's so low.

"I guess we don't have much of a choice." I wait for Madden to sit down before taking a seat between his legs. His arms instantaneously wrap around my waist, causing my heart to speed up.

"You comfortable?" he whispers against my neck.

I nod and wrap my arms around his. Logan has no one to blame but himself right now. *He's* the reason I'm in his brother's lap putting on a show. *He's* the one who decided to play this little game because he's being selfish.

"How's your girlfriend enjoying our friends?" Logan steps into the water and takes the seat closet to us. The way his gaze lands on me has me becoming angrier with him. He's being a complete dick right now and it has me wondering if this is the *real* him; the version I've been learning of but haven't seen yet. "Fitting right in as far as I can tell."

"Yeah." Madden pulls me tighter to comfort me. He makes me feel protected, as if he has my back. "Everyone loves her. In fact, we were just talking about her coming back next year."

"I think planning a year from now is thinking a little too far ahead," Alana says, tensing, her eyes landing on Madden. "You don't know if you'll even be together then. You two could break up tomorrow for all you know."

"I do know," Madden says sternly. "Natalie isn't going anywhere anytime soon. I won't fucking let her."

"I agree with Alana," Logan chimes in, giving his brother a pissed off look. "It's a little early to be making plans for next year. Maybe you should take it easy, brother, in case things don't work out. Alana is right on this one."

I shoot Logan a hard look, unable to believe the shit coming out of his mouth right now. "I think I've changed my mind. I'm not in the mood to be in the hot tub anymore." I stand and grab Madden's hand, showing him I want him to come with me. "You two have fun."

"Come on, guys." Logan stands and watches as we grab our clothing. "We just got in. Get back in."

"No thanks." I narrow my eyes at him, being careful not to make it noticeable to Alana. "You two enjoy each other's company since you both believe things won't work out between Madden and me. I'd rather *not* listen to this shit tonight and ruin the good vibe our last night here."

"I agree, *brother*. Natalie is right on this one." Madden places his hand on the small of my back and guides me to the door, opening it for me. "I'm sorry about him," he says once we're alone. "My brother is being a fucking dick tonight."

"Yeah, he is." I slip my dry clothes over my wet underwear and run my hands through my hair in frustration. "I want to kick his ass right now."

Madden grips my face and bows his head to look at me. "Me too. Trust me. He's lucky our friends are around. He should've never put you in that uncomfortable situation."

"What about you?" I meet his gaze, my stomach sinking at the idea of him still hurting over Alana. "He never should've brought your ex into the hot tub knowing how you've been struggling over her. That's what I'm the most pissed about."

"I'm not anymore."

My heart stops at his admission. "You're not?"

He shakes his head and smiles. "Nope. *You* helped me realize that. I'm over Alana. I think I have been for a while and just didn't notice. Being here with you, I've realized what makes me the happiest."

"What's that?"

"Being around someone I can trust and have fun with; someone who is playful and feisty and makes my fucking heart go crazy whenever I look at her." He pauses, his gaze landing on my lips. "Someone who makes me feel good and happy. Someone like you, Nat. I want someone like you."

I can't breathe, my emotions taking over. I don't know why I'm reacting this way over something so simple as him saying he wants someone like me, but it's doing something to me that I can't control. "I need to take a walk." I back away, putting space between us. "I need some air."

Before Madden can stop me, I walk away and rush out the front door to escape. I need to breathe and being around him is making it hard right now, especially after hearing what I just did.

I take off around the side of the cabin and press my back against it in a hurry. I'm standing here breathing heavily and trying to calm down when I hear Logan's voice come from the front. He must've just come outside.

"...of course I didn't fucking tell him. We already discussed this, Alana."

My eyes widen at Alana's name, my heart racing even faster.

"Then why is he acting so cold toward me? He's barely talked to me this entire trip. You're trying to tell me it has nothing to do with him finding out about us?"

I suck in a breath, my hands clinging to the cabin behind me over learning the truth. Logan and Alana. He's the reason Madden has been so broken? He's the reason Madden almost drunk himself to death! Logan didn't agree to me coming here because he thought I'd say no. He agreed to me coming out of guilt.

"Do you really think I want him knowing, Alana? Does that make any fucking sense?"

"No. But neither does your brother showing up here with

another girl either, yet here he is ripping my fucking heart out."

"You should've thought about that before you crawled into my bedroom that night and undid my pants, wanting to discover what was below the belt."

"Fuck you," Alana spits out. "Clearly, it was the biggest mistake of my life. Your brother will never forgive me for cheating in the first place. Just imagine if he knew it was with you."

It's quiet for a second before Logan says, "Maybe he should know."

"I'll never speak to you again, Logan. I swear. You better not."

"I'm not going to. I need some fucking air to think. Go back inside before someone gets suspicious and finds us out here arguing. I told you not to follow me in the first place."

I don't hear anything for a few seconds and then Logan comes into view. I consider pretending I didn't overhear his conversation with Alana, but I can't. I'm so fucking angry that I push away from the cabin. "It was you?"

Logan stops dead in his tracks, his back tensing. "You weren't supposed to hear that," he says, turning to face me. "It was a stupid mistake that I regret."

I shake my head and push him back when he reaches for my shoulders. "How could you do that to Madden? To your own fucking brother?" I shove his chest, anger taking over. "Huh? Tell me!"

"I don't know," he says gently. "It just happened. And then it was too late to take back."

"Tell him," I bite out. "He deserves to know the truth. You need to tell him."

"I can't, Natalie. I can't do that."

"You can and you will." I look up to meet his green eyes,

wanting him to see how serious I am. "Either you do it or I will."

"Drop it, Natalie. It's not happening."

"Wrong answer." I go to walk away, unable to look at him right now, but Logan grips my arm, pulling me backward.

"Let me go," I grind out. "Now."

"Let's talk about it, Natalie. Please."

I get ready to tell him to fuck off, but Madden coming at us has me shaking Logan's grip off and taking a step back.

Madden looks ready to murder his brother and I don't blame him one bit. I feel the exact same way.

CHAPTER TWENTY-THREE

MADDEN

"What the fuck are you doing, brother? Huh?" I slam Logan against the side of the cabin, my hand moving up to grip his throat as I turn to look at Natalie, who looks emotionally wrecked. "Go inside. Now."

She shoots Logan a hard look, her chest heaving and her hands shaking at her sides. "We're through, Logan. I'm done with you."

"Nope." I slam my brother harder against the cabin when he attempts to go after Natalie as she walks away. "Don't even look at her right now. What the fuck is going on? That's not how you treat women. You don't grab them that way. I know you."

He squeezes his eyes shut and swears under his breath, before gripping my hand and yanking it from his throat. "This isn't the time to talk about it, Madden; not here with all of our friends. I just need to get to Natalie and talk. I didn't mean to be so rough with her."

"No. Fuck that. It's the perfect time to talk about it. Give

248

her some space." I motion around the darkness. "There's nobody out here but the two of us. Everyone else is out back by the fire. Now talk. To me. Not her. I'm not letting you anywhere near her until you calm the fuck down."

When he doesn't start talking, I slam him against the cabin again, my anger taking over. "Talk!" I growl out, digging my forearm into his throat.

"Madden, stop!" I feel Alana's hand pulling at my arm, before I see her beside us. Her eyes are rimmed red like she's been crying. "It's not all on him. It was me too. *I* fucked up too. Let him go." Her voice shakes when I turn to face her. "I'm sorry, Madden. I don't... I don't know what else to say. You weren't supposed to find out this way."

It takes a second before it clicks, my arm digging harder into my brother's neck. "You?" I question, seeing red. "You and Alana? All this fucking time I thought it was someone that meant nothing to me—just some piece of shit out to get laid—but instead it was my own fucking brother."

I growl out and punch the wall beside Logan's head. He closes his eyes in shame. "You were never supposed to find out."

"Clearly." I remove my arm from him and turn away, hurt that my own fucking brother, of all people, is the one who destroyed me. The one person I thought I could trust. "What? You just planned to keep it from me forever?" I ask, after turning back around. "Was that your plan? Just keep me in the dark like a goddamn fool."

"Madden, calm down." Alana steps in the path of my brother when I take a step toward him. "Please. I don't want you two fighting over me. I love *you*, not him. Sleeping with him was the biggest mistake of my life. I've regretted it every day since, and I regret ever saying I was confused. I never was. It was always going to be you over him."

I narrow my eyes at her, surprised that she thinks me

wanting to hurt my brother has anything to do with her. "It's not about *you*, Alana. Fuck, why can't you see that? It's about family. It's about trust. It's about the one person who is supposed to have my back betraying me." I lean in so that we're face to face. "I'm over you, Alana. I think I was a long time ago and just didn't see it until now. I. Don't. Love. You. Anymore. Get that through your head and let me live my life. No more texts. No more calls. Nothing."

"You mean that?" Her bottom lip trembles as she looks me in the eyes, and I know she's trying hard not to cy. "Do you? Fucking tell me and you better mean it, because once I walk away, it's for good."

"I'm over you, Alana. I want *nothing* to do with you. Is that clear enough?"

"Fuck you, Madden!" she spits out, shoving my chest as hard as she can. "I *hate* you." She shoves me once more, before storming off, leaving me alone with my brother.

"Madden, we can talk this out."

I shake my brother's hand off and shoot him a warning look. "Go the fuck home before I do something I regret."

"Come on. I'm your fucking brother. At least give me a chance to explain."

"Yeah, my *brother*, which is exactly why there shouldn't be shit to explain." I place both palms against the side of the cabin, fighting to get a grip before I fuck my own brother up. "Is that why you agreed to let me take Natalie on this trip? Don't fucking lie to me either."

"Yes," he says, after a few seconds of silence. "I was trying to make up for my mistake. I didn't want you hurting any—"

"Fuck off and leave. If I have to look at you, I'm going to hurt you. Walk the fuck away. You owe me that at least."

He stands still for a few moments to weigh his options, before finally walking away. Seconds later, the door to his SUV closes and he drives off.

"Fuck!" I yell out, before running both hands through my hair. I'm pissed—really fucking pissed—and all I can think about is getting to Natalie. I *need* her right now.

I make my way through the cabin to mine and Natalie's room. When I walk inside, Natalie is angrily packing her suitcase, tossing everything inside as if she's in a hurry to escape this place. I can't let that happen. I need her here; especially right now.

Closing the door behind me, I stalk toward Natalie, grab her waist, and pull her against me. The moment her body connects with mine, I grip her face and crush my lips to hers, walking her backwards until her back hits the dresser.

With a growl, I slip my tongue into her mouth, my hand moving around to tangle into the bottom of her hair. It takes her a second before her hands are on me, gripping the front of my shirt. "You're not going anywhere," I whisper, picking her up to carry her to the bed. "I fucking *need* you, Nat."

When I lay her back, her eyes meet mine, taking them in, as if to see if I meant what I just said. Fuck yeah, I did. She must've realized she heard me correctly, because she's pulling me to her by my T-shirt.

I roughly slam my lips against hers, my insides burning to be inside of her. I've never felt like I needed anyone the way I need Natalie right now. I never felt the need to touch every inch of another person before. Not until now.

With my lips on hers, I reach in between our bodies and yank Natalie's jeans off, before sitting up just long enough to pull her shirt off next. Her staring up at me, her big blue eyes filled with need, has me yanking my T-shirt over my head and lifting her up the bed until her head is against the headboard. Gripping her panties in my left hand, I swallow and lock my eyes on hers. "If you don't want me inside you, I need you to tell me now." I grip them tighter and squeeze. "Tell me, Nat.

Tell me you don't want this as much as I do and I'll fucking walk away right now."

"I can't," she whispers, her chest quickly rising and falling as she studies my face, her gaze stopping on my lips. "I want it, Madden. I wouldn't be underneath you half naked if I didn't." She closes her eyes and leans her head back when I pull her panties down, slowly lowering them a couple inches. When she still doesn't change her mind, I yank them down her legs and spread her thighs to move back between them.

"Fuck, everything about you is perfect, Nat." I can barely catch my breath as I reach behind her to undo her bra next. "So fucking beautiful." I toss her bra aside and grab her hand, placing them on the button of my jeans, letting her know I want her to undo them.

Looking up at me, she undoes the button, before slowly lowering the zipper. "You're perfect too, Madden." She lowers my jeans, her eyes taking my body in as my erection springs free. "Everything about you. I've thought this since the moment I laid eyes on you on that stage. *That* is why I've found any and every reason to dislike you over the years. It's because I was attracted to you and afraid of showing it. I'm not afraid anymore."

"Is that true?"

She nods her head.

"Fuck taking this slow." I yank my jeans off, climb back between Natalie's thighs and line my cock up with her entrance. "I'm sorry if I hurt you but..." Gripping the back of her head, I look into her eyes as I slowly enter her, inch by inch until I'm buried inside of her.

She softly cries out, her nails digging into my shoulder when I begin moving in and out, taking her deep each time. She's so tight and wet and that mixed with the fact that it's *Natalie* I'm inside of, has me wanting to come within minutes, but I keep it together, needing as much of her as I can get.

"Fuck babe," I whisper against her lips, my hand moving to grip her throat as I move in and out of her. She moans out, her mouth opening as I playfully bite her bottom lip, before dipping my tongue into her mouth, tasting her as I fuck her. I don't even care that she was just my brother's minutes ago. In this moment, she is mine and I'm going to take her as if she's mine to keep.

"Madden..." She digs her nails into my flesh and throws her head back when I accidentally thrust too hard, going deeper. "Don't stop," she says when I pause to see if she's okay. "Don't ever stop..."

I move her leg and flip her over to her stomach. She grips the sheets and moans out as I immediately slide back into her. I'm deep—so fucking deep—yet I want more of her. I want to own every inch of her beautiful body.

Pressing my lips against her neck, I gently grip the front of her throat and thrust into her repeatedly, filling her deep over and over. Each time she cries out for me, I thrust harder and faster, unable to get enough. I've waited and wondered for too long what it'd be like to be inside of her, and I don't plan to stop until she's fully pleasured and shaking below me from multiple orgasms.

My free hand moves around to find her clit, and the moment I begin rubbing circles over it, she moans out and buries her face into the bed as she squeezes my dick from her orgasm.

I almost lose my shit and come, but I'm not done with her yet. Pulling out of her, I stand beside the bed, grab her and flip her over, before yanking her to me.

She lets out a surprised gasp when I pick her up and wrap her legs around my waist as I enter her again. "Hold on, babe."

Once she's holding on tight, I grip her hips and fuck her hard and fast. Her body is slick and wet against mine, every inch of our bodies covered in sweat as I make her quietly scream into my neck. Everything about this moment says that she's mine. That may change once we leave, but I push that thought aside and capture her mouth with mine.

A few more thrusts and her pussy squeezes my dick again, my mouth catching her moans as she comes for me. I can't hold back anymore, coming seconds later as I bite her bottom lip, before I growl out and kiss her neck.

"Holy fuck." I breathe out, fighting to catch my breath, before I grip her hair and kiss her long and hard. "Sorry if I hurt you," I whisper.

She shakes her head and kisses me, before wrapping her arms around my neck. "I'm fine," she says breathless. "A little sore, but I'll be fine."

I smile and lay her back on the bed, before slowly pulling out, watching as my cum spills from her pussy. It's the hottest thing I've ever seen, and I have to fight back the urge to take her again. "Hang on." I reach beside me for my T-shirt and clean her off, before cleaning myself.

The way she looks at me as I climb into bed beside her and pull her into me has me feeling a way I've never felt before. It scares the shit out of me, but I hold her anyway, wanting her as close to me as humanly possible.

I don't know what the fuck we just did or what's going to happen next, but I do know that I've never felt this way inside a woman before; not even with Alana.

"I wasn't expecting that," she whispers.

"Expecting what?"

"Us having sex. Or feeling the way I do. None of it."

I smile, running a thumb over her cheek. "I didn't either."

"Did we make a mistake?" She sounds worried, and I hate that with everything in me."

"I don't think we should think too hard tonight." I move in and kiss her, before pulling her closer onto my chest. "I just want to hold you tonight and not think about shit. Not my brother. Not you and him. Not how I feel about what he did. Nothing. Can we do that?"

She grabs my neck and pulls me in for a kiss. "Yeah, I think we can do that."

Closing my eyes, I pull her tighter, secretly terrified of what will happen next. She may not want my brother tonight, and she may think she hates him now, but what about tomorrow when we go back to reality? Will it be like it never happened when we go back to our old lives?

CHAPTER TWENTY-FOUR

NATALIE

I wake up to an empty bed, Madden nowhere in sight with his suitcase already packed. My heart sinks at the notion that he took his morning walk without me. After what happened between us last night, waking up with no idea of how he feels right now has me feeling queasy.

We both got lost in the heat of the moment, in the animosity we both felt toward his brother, and we ended up naked and sweaty and out of breath on top of each other. I have no idea what it means for us or our future or if it means anything at all, and I despise that feeling more than anything.

I move, and the slight pain between my legs reminds me just how deep Madden buried himself inside of me. My insides instantaneously ignite from the memory of how hot and passionate it was. I've never felt that way during sex before, not even with his brother, and I know without a doubt that Madden has ruined me for all other men.

After a few minutes pass, I climb out of bed and slip into some clothes, before heading out of the bedroom to see if

Madden is somewhere inside. Once I realize that he isn't, my chest fills with anxiety.

He did go on his walk without me.

Exhaling, I reach into the fridge for a bottle of water and head back to the bedroom to pack. I'm in the middle of shoving everything back into my suitcase when the bedroom door opens. My heart jumps, expecting it to be Madden, but when I turn around, it's Jess.

"Hey, babe. Have you enjoyed the trip?"

I nod and plaster on a bogus smile, not wanting her to see how hurt and confused I am. "Really good. Thanks again for having me. I had a lot of fun."

She smiles. "Me too. I'm glad you came, and I hope to see you again next year. Hopefully by then things will calm down with Alana. Sorry you had to deal with some of the stuff she said and did."

My smile fades, because from the looks of it, I'll probably never come back here again. Logan and I are through, and Madden probably won't want anything to do with me now that he's had time to think about what we did. "Yeah, me too."

"I heard what went down last night," she says after a few moments of silence. "We all heard what went down between Madden and Logan. Is that why he took off so quickly?"

I nod and zip up my suitcase, my body tense, hoping she didn't hear anything else. "Yeah. What did you hear?"

She looks disappointed as she takes a seat on the bed. "That Logan was the asshole Alana cheated on Madden with. It took us all by surprise. We planned to come talk to Madden last night and make sure everything was okay, but based on the noise coming from this room last night..." she trails off, a small smile taking over. "I thought it'd be best to wait until this morning." She looks around, as if just noticing I'm alone. "Where is Madden, by the way?"

"On his morning walk."

"Without you?"

"I was sleeping pretty hard. He probably didn't want to wake me." I try to convince myself that's the case, but my stomach still feels empty. "Had a late night," I add, hoping to make it more believable.

"Sounded like it." She stands and wraps her arms around me, squeezing. "Tell Madden to give you my number before he hits the road, okay?"

I nod and smile, happy that we'll still be friends after this. Jess was my favorite part of this trip aside from getting to know the real Madden—the version I fell hard for. "I'll be sure to do that. I'll send you a text so you can save my number too."

We both look over when Jake pokes his head through the door and smiles. "Morning, ladies."

"Morning."

"I have the car mostly packed up and everyone else is almost ready too." He nods to my suitcase. "Need me to carry that to Madden's truck?"

I shake my head. "No, thanks. I've got it."

"I've got it." Madden's voice has my insides gushing with excitement, making me feel like a damn teenager with my first crush. "We'll meet you guys outside."

"Okay, cool. I'll help Jake grab the rest of our stuff. I want to make sure none of my makeup gets left behind."

Once we're alone, Madden hands me his jacket and kisses the top of my head, his lips lingering. I wait for him to say something, anything at all, but he doesn't. It gives me anxiety as we head outside with the others.

Seth and Walker look hungover as shit. It's a good thing they apparently rode with Riley, who is looking perky and ready to hit the road.

"I'm going to miss you all so much." Jess walks around

giving everyone hugs, and so do the others; all except for Alana, whose attention has been on Madden the entire time.

Her sunglasses are on, but it's still easy to tell she's been crying. Now she has to live with the fact that Madden knows she cheated on him with his brother. That's the worst betrayal of all. I'm sure she's worried he'll never talk to her again, and a part of me hopes he doesn't. She doesn't deserve his time and energy.

After Jake whispers something in Madden's ear, everyone goes their separate ways, him opening the door for me once we reach his truck. His eyes meet mine for a split second after I climb inside, before he shuts the door and walks away without a word.

The silence still lingering after we drive off has me feeling even sicker, and the fact that my phone goes off multiple times with texts from Logan once we're in an area with better service doesn't help.

After the sixth ding, Madden glances my way, his grip on the steering wheel tightening. "Is that my brother?"

I nod and flip my phone over, not wanting to read his messages right now. The way I'm feeling toward him, I just can't deal with him.

"You're not going to read his texts?"

"No. I'm not interested in what he has to say right now."

The ride is silent for a good hour before he asks, "What if he wants to get back together? Then what?"

I shake my head even though he's watching the road. "It doesn't matter."

"Why?"

"Because I don't want to get back together. I meant what I said at the cabin."

"Which part?" he asks firmly.

"*Everything* I said at the cabin, Madden. I meant all of it.

But what about you? Maybe you said and did stuff you didn't mean. Did you?"

"I never say shit I don't mean, Nat. That's not who I am."

"Then why are you being so indifferent toward me?" I ask angrily. "Why sleep with me if you don't have feelings for me? Was it only because you wanted to get back at your bro—"

"Fuck no." He exhales and grips the steering wheel, his knuckles turning white. "Don't say that shit, Nat. Of course, I have feelings for you. Why do you think I'm so fucked up right now and unable to act right?"

"Oh, I don't know. Maybe because you decided sleeping with me was a mistake? Or getting back at your brother for something in the past was stupid and now you regret it. I don't fucking know, Madden. You tell me."

"Because I'm falling for you and I'm fucking terrified, okay." He turns to face me, my heart sinking to my stomach from the anxiety in his eyes. "I'm terrified that after a period of time you'll realize you're still in love with my brother; that you only slept with me because you were angry with him. I'm fucking terrified that you'll go back to thinking of me as the reckless rock star and realize you can't be with me because of shit I've done. That's why I'm unable to act right, Nat. Is that a good enough explanation for you?"

I remain silent, trying to process everything he just said as I sit here. He just confessed that he's falling for me, and I'm just as terrified as he is.

"You don't think I'm scared too?" I ask once we're close to Logan's. "That I don't have my own fears of you realizing that you can't be with your brother's ex and rip my heart out? Huh?" I become angry just thinking about it. "Or that you'll realize you're still in love with Alana just like you always have been? I'm scared too."

"That won't happen." He pulls up in front of my car and shifts his truck into park. "I'm over Alana. That's the one thing I'm sure of, but Alana and I haven't been together in a long time. You and Logan are fresh, and until I know that you're sure about us, I think I should stay away. As much as I fucking hate it, and trust me, I do, I think you need time to figure things out without me in the picture as a distraction. I can't take getting my heart broken again, especially when it comes to you. After this trip, I know I wouldn't survive."

"I already told you what I want, Madden. What more do you want from me? What do I have to do to prove to you that I want you? I wouldn't have slept with you otherwise. Tell me," I say, my voice fading to a whisper, my exhaustion getting the best of me.

"I need to know that in a week or two you won't regret what happened between us during this trip. That you won't go running back to my brother. And in order to ensure that, we need time." His words come out pained and it breaks my heart. "I'm sorry, Nat."

"Fine. If time is what you want, then that's what you'll get. Enjoy your life as a single rock star. I'm sure you'll have plenty of women to pass the time. Maybe it's best we part ways now so neither of us get hurt. Have a great fucking life, Madden."

I hop out of his truck and slam the door behind me, hurrying to grab my suitcase. I shouldn't have said it, knowing I didn't mean any of it, but he's not playing fair. I'm in the middle of trying to pull it over the bed of the truck when Madden reaches over me to help.

"No! Don't. Just leave me the fuck alone."

"Nat, please don't get angry," he pleads when I put my hand out, putting space between us. "It's not what you think. I don't want to leave shit this way."

"That's too bad, because I'm done talking." I yank my car door open and toss the suitcase into the back, before jumping inside and quickly starting the engine. When I reach for my seatbelt, I notice Madden reaching for the door handle, so I

VICTORIA ASHLEY

lock it. I'm hurt and thinking irrationally right now. I know I
need to calm down, but I'm too far into my emotions to stop
my actions at this point.

I shove my foot against the gas as I peel out of my
parking spot, glancing into the rearview mirror when I drop
it into drive. Leaving Madden standing with his hands in his
hair, I drive away, my heart shattering as I watch him through
the rearview mirror until he disappears.

He wants time apart. Time apart is what he'll get. No
matter just how much it hurts me. And it does. It hurts so
much more than walking away from Logan—a man I've been
with for two years. It's not Logan who's left me broken, it's
his brother—Madden—the heartbreaking rock star.

CHAPTER TWENTY-FIVE

NATALIE

I'VE BEEN LYING HERE STARING AT THE CEILING FOR I don't know how long when the door opens and Kayla steps inside. I don't need to look at her to see the pity on her face. She's had that same look since I returned to work six days ago.

"What are you doing in here, honey?" She gently closes the door behind her, as if too much noise is going to set me off or something. "You've been in this room for over an hour. Are you sure you can handle being at work right now? I'm sure we could get someone to cover your shift for a few days."

"What?" I question, barely listening to her.

Truth is, I haven't been able to concentrate on anything since leaving the cabin. All I can think about is how Madden has probably gone back to his usual business, partying and having fun without even a thought of me. I doubt I've even crossed his mind. When this all started, I wasn't necessarily happy but was fine. He was miserable. He got what he wanted. He's finally over his ex, and in the end, I'm the one that ended up hurt.

"You need to take some time off work to clear your head. It's okay to need a mental break after all that went down." She walks over to sit on the edge of the bed. "I'll talk to—"

"I'm fine." I sit up and force a straight face, even though it feels like my insides are being crushed. "I'm fine, Kayla. I'll be down in a few. I've gotta fix the TV first."

"Is that what you came in here to do?" she asks cautiously. "Because I can take care of it if you're not in the right mind frame."

"I said I'm fine," I say a little too snippy. I'm not fine. I'm anything *but* fine, but if I admit that out loud, I'm afraid I won't be able to ever get over this crushing feeling, and I don't want to feel another second of this pain. "I wouldn't be here if I couldn't do my job, Kayla. I'll handle it."

"All right. I'll be around if you need me." She stands and walks out the door without another word, and I can't help but feel guilty for being such a bitch to her. I've been trying so hard not to take it out on her or anyone else around me, but the more time that passes without a word from Madden, the closer I feel to exploding. I've never felt this crushing weight on my chest before and it's breaking me.

Running my hands over my face, I lay back down and close my eyes. Why the fuck did I agree to that trip to begin with? I must've asked myself that a hundred times now, and every single time I come up with the same answer: Madden Parker.

I went knowing I'd have to get close to him. I knew we'd have to kiss, and I also knew there was a slight possibility I'd fall for him in the end, yet I still went, because I didn't want to see him hurt anymore. I wanted to be the end of his pain, and by the time it was all over, he ended up being the beginning of mine.

Not only has Madden been ignoring my calls since Tuesday, but also, Logan has been texting nonstop apologizing to me about sleeping with Alana, as if it's *me* he should be making it up to. Him being sorry for hurting Madden isn't going to get me back. It's not going to change the way I look at him now that I've learned the truth. He hid a huge part of himself from me.

Six days was all it took for my entire world to fall apart around me, and I blame Logan for that. If it weren't for him, his brother would've never spiraled down a dark road and needed me to save him. And if Madden didn't need my help, I never would've fallen for him and gotten tossed aside. I hate him right now. I know that feeling will change, but not yet; not today, and probably not next week or the week after.

I finally sit back up and take care of the problem I came in here over an hour ago to fix. Then I plaster on the best content expression I can muster up to get me through the rest of this day.

"SORRY IT TOOK SO long to get here." Carla says, shutting my apartment door behind her. She looks me over, before handing me a bottle of Disaronno and a slice of cheesecake. "Figured you could use this right now."

"Thanks." I plop down on my couch and grab one of the empty glasses from the end table to my left, handing her one. "You really didn't have to come here on your only day off and join me in my pity party. Like I said over the phone, I'm fine."

"It's okay *not* to be okay, Natalie." She holds her glass out for me to pour her some amaretto. "Shit, you just broke up with your boyfriend of two years, fell for his brother, and then lost him too. This is Madden Parker we're talking about here, babe. I know for a fact you're *not* fine."

"Maybe not," I admit. "But I will be. It's only been days. I've heard it takes what..." I tilt back my drink. "Years? I can survive that long. Or at least do my best. Which is what I've been doing since I got home."

"Babe, you haven't left your house other than to work. And don't think I haven't heard from Kayla about you disappearing at the hotel for hours at a time." She stops to take a sip of her drink, before continuing. "Do you know where he is?"

I shake my head, my heart sinking to my stomach. "Not at Logan's. That's about all I know."

"Do you want to know?" She stares at me, waiting for an answer I'm not sure I want to give.

"I don't want to know," I rush out before I can think on it too hard. "I can't think about what he's doing. All those girls... I can't handle that. The thought of him going back to his old lifestyle *kills* me. It literally makes it hard to breathe."

"Do you honestly think that Madden is with other girls right now, partying away as if you don't exist after what you two went through?" She shakes her head and sets her glass down. "Girl, you haven't seen the way that boy loves. When he loves, he gives his all. He's one hundred percent committed."

"What makes you think he loves me?"

She's quiet for a moment. "Because he had sex with you *sober*, babe. The moment you told me that the other night, I knew he was in love with you. You're the first and only girl since his ex. Trust me, he's not hooking up in a hotel room with some random girl right now."

The words 'hooking up' and 'hotel room' make me feel sick to my stomach as I think back to all the photos of him leaving with random girls in the past. "I wish I could believe that. I really do. But even if so, *he* shut things down. He told me we needed time and now he's ignoring me. He didn't even give me a choice, Carla."

"That was him trying to protect you, Nat." Her using Madden's nickname for me has me setting my glass aside, my stomach hurting too much to drink any more. "You were his brother's girlfriend for two years. He probably knew you'd feel guilty for hurting Logan and wanted to give you the proper chance to figure out if you made a mistake breaking it off with him. It's a sticky situation. What would've happened had you two left together and then a week down the road you decided it was a mistake to leave Logan for his brother? That you couldn't handle his lifestyle. Or that you just simply didn't love him and walked away?"

"It would've been bad," I whisper.

"Worse. It would've been devastating for both of you. This is the time for you to think extra hard and figure shit out. Go talk to Logan. See if living without him is something you can really do."

"I can," I whisper, staring at the photo of us on the wall, before I stand and take it down, tossing it into the box with the rest of Logan's things. "But can Madden live without him is the true question. Because he might very well have to if I end up switching teams."

"That's something the boys need to work out, babe. Logan hurt Madden first. I think he owes Madden a real chance at true love again. If Logan doesn't see that and support his brother, then he's an asshole. And an asshole isn't what I see when I look at him. He's just someone who made a mistake and needs to make it up to his brother. I think he will. Logan is a good guy."

"Do you truly believe that, Carla?" I swallow, my chest aching, because I want to believe it too. I want to believe that Logan would give Madden that chance if he chose it. "That Logan is a good guy after what he did to his brother in the first place? He didn't give a shit about hurting him in the past, so what makes you think he'd step back now and allow him to be happy with me if that's what he chose?"

She grabs my face, a slight smile playing on hers. "Because that's what he told me last night at the bar. You didn't think that you and Madden were the only two stopping in from time to time for advice, did you?" She shakes her head. "Are you absolutely positive that Madden is what you want?"

"Without a doubt," I whisper. "He's all I can think about. It hurts so bad being without him. I've never felt that crushing pain before in my entire life; not even when Abel cheated on me, and you know how badly that hurt me."

She nods. "Your high school sweetheart. He hurt you really bad. I remember how hard that made trusting Logan in the first place. Just remember how long it took for you to fall for Logan. It took what... six months before you said you loved him?"

"Yeah," I whisper. "And even then, I was terrified I was making a mistake."

"You spent what, a week with Madden, and you're so fucking sure you love him that you can barely function without him." She stands and pulls me to my feet. "Go after him, Nat."

"I'm scared."

"Of what, babe?"

"That he doesn't feel the same way. I'm fucking terrified, Carla. I don't think I can handle knowing the truth if that's the case. I can't."

"You'll never know how he feels unless you find him and tell him the truth. Do you really think you can live with that?"

I think on it for a second, already knowing the answer. "I need info on the band." I swallow, my heart racing at the idea of seeing him. "Think you can do that for me?"

She joins me in the kitchen, where I'm tossing dirty dishes into the sink. "Of course, babe. I'll text the band and let you know what I find out."

Carla has been gone for a while now, and I can't sleep, because all I can do is stare at my phone. Every five minutes I pick it up and look, as if a message from Carla with an address will pop up any minute. After hours of struggling to sleep, I grab my phone and walk outside on the patio.

There's something I need to do before going after Madden. I'm not sure Logan deserves a conversation after what he did, but I need to know for Madden's sake that he won't lose his brother.

I don't know if Madden will say yes or what I'm even going to ask him, but I'm willing to take a risk when it comes to him. Carla is right. If I don't at least let him know how I feel, I won't be able to live with that.

I'm going after the man I love. Screw my job, my ex, and everything standing in my way. It's time for me to be the reckless one.

CHAPTER TWENTY-SIX

MADDEN

MY CHEST HURTS, THE TIGHTNESS IN IT MAKING ME FEEL AS if I'm suffocating. It's been this way for over a week now, the constricting feeling growing more with each day I'm away from Natalie.

We might've gone to the cabin *pretending* she was mine, but by the end, that's what she was to me: mine. At least, that's what I let myself believe toward the end. And those last nights together, with her in my arms, were the best I've had in a long time. For the first time in years I was truly happy and felt whole inside.

The hardest part of walking away from the trip was knowing that Natalie was happy too. I filled a void in her that my brother has been unable to fill in the two years they've been together, and like an idiot, I let her drive away due to my fear of being hurt. I had my shot at happiness with her—I could've made her mine—yet I didn't, because I was too fucking terrified of losing her.

She might've been happy with me on the trip, but what

about when it was over? My fear of what would happen once we got back home and back to reality took over. I couldn't risk making her mine, losing my brother over it, and then losing her too if she realized she'd made a mistake with me. I'm not strong enough for that; not even fucking close.

To ensure that could never happen, I said the things I felt I needed to say that day. I told her we needed time even though that's the last thing I wanted.

"Do you know how bad sleeping alone feels after you've been sleeping with someone?" I take another drag off my cigarette and slowly exhale, leaning my head back. "It fucking sucks. I haven't had a solid night's sleep in over a week, man. What I wouldn't give to have Natalie in my bed every fucking night, wrapped up in my arms... It doesn't feel right—being without her. You know?"

"Baa."

"Tell me about it. I don't know what to do."

"Baa."

I laugh and turn to Pixy, feeling silly that I'm out here spilling my guts to a goat. "You tired of listening to me yet? Yeah? I feel ya."

Pixy lets out another long "baa" before walking away.

Apparently, even a goat is tired of my shit.

"Mate, would you go after her already? All you've been doing since you arrived at our doorstep is mope around and spill your guts to the goat."

I put out my cigarette and turn to Chance, who just got home from a landscaping job. I've been crashing at his and Aubrey's place since leaving the cabin. I should've been back with the band days ago, but I couldn't stomach going back to the same old shit. Not just yet.

"I can't."

"Why can't you?"

"Because I can't fucking have her as mine just to lose her. I won't survive it."

He runs a hand through his messy hair and exhales. "Mate, what makes you so fucking sure that you'll lose her?" He pulls a Pixy Stix from his pocket and pours it into his mouth, waiting for an answer.

"I can't risk it, Chance. Not when it means I could lose everyone I love for good, her included."

"Have you talked to Logan since the night at the cabin?"

"No. My phone is broken."

Chance shoves his empty wrapper into his pocket and then hands a cake cone to Pixy when the goat "baas" again, as if to complain about not getting a snack. "I can't tell you what to do, but you should figure things out soon. You can't hide from life in our guest room forever. It'll find you at some point. Like Aubrey and I said before, you're welcome to crash here for as long as you want, but is staying here really what's best for you, your brother, or Natalie?"

"I don't know shit right now. Why else would I be out here talking to a goat?"

He laughs and pulls out another Pixy Stix, ripping the wrapper open with his teeth. "That's when you know you need to step up your game and take care of what you want. Pixy hears enough of my shit as it is. He doesn't need your shit to deal with on top of it."

"Da-da."

Chance smiles and picks up my niece, before grabbing the back of his wife's head and kisses her long and hard. The whole time I've been here he's never *not* kissed her with full passion. "Miss me, Princess?"

Aubrey laughs when the goat "baas" as if to answer, and little Bree giggles and bounces up and down in Chance's arms as if it's the funniest thing ever. "Apparently, someone did. Maybe even more than I did."

"Uncle Madden." Little Chance runs up out of nowhere and kicks a Soccer ball my way. "Come on."

Deciding to forget about my problems for a little bit, I kick the ball around with my nephew for a while before sitting down for dinner with the family that I offered to cook for.

I owe them that much after letting me stay here for as long as they have, so I cooked my famous meatloaf before finally going to the nearest cellphone place to replace my broken phone. I've been staring at it ever since, my head all fucked up.

"You call her yet or are you just going to sit here in my junk art room staring at your phone all night?"

"It's past midnight. I thought you were sleeping?" I point at the wall where one of the posters he had printed hangs. "You going to keep that shit up?"

"Why wouldn't I?" He laughs while messing around with something he made. I'm not even sure what the hell it is. "I needed something to fill the empty walls. I was even thinking about adding a few more."

"You would too. Just so you can laugh at my ass while you work."

He leans against the wall and crosses his arms across his chest. "Seriously, though. You need to stop talking to my fucking goat and start talking to the girl you love. I fought for what I wanted. It wasn't an easy journey—far from it—and look how it turned out for me."

"I might not get so lucky." My chest aches at the thought of Natalie not wanting me. "Not everyone has a fucking Australian accent to help them with the ladies."

He chuckles and uncrosses his arms. "My mouth might've had something to do with it, but I can tell you now that it wasn't the accent coming from it."

I crack a small smile at his dirty remark. "I'm heading out

tomorrow morning. I need to get back with the band. I won't have time to drive back to Temecula first."

"Sure, you do, mate." He pushes away from the wall. "If you want her as bad as I think you do, you will figure it out. No more excuses."

I nod.

"Goodbye, Mate." He offers me a wide smile before yawning. "I don't want to see your ass when I wake up. I don't think the goat does either."

"I believe that," I say on a small laugh. "I think he tried kicking me today."

Chance laughs as he makes his way toward the door, leaving me alone.

I sit here for a while, still staring at my phone thinking, before I jump to my feet, quietly gather my shit, and leave a note for my cousin and his family thanking them for letting me crash here. I'll thank them properly the next opportunity I get.

Chance is right. I need to go after what I want, no matter how hard the fucking journey is. I'll deal with my brother after. He'll just have to understand, because I know for a fact that there's no happiness in my life without Natalie. These past eight days have proved that.

CHAPTER TWENTY-SEVEN

MADDEN

MY HEART POUNDS HARD AGAINST MY RIBCAGE AS I WALK toward the hotel entrance. I was hoping to find Natalie at home, but after waiting around for a few hours and calling her twice, I figured she must be working and is unable to check her phone; either that or she just doesn't want to. I wouldn't blame her at this point if it was the latter.

I was without a working phone for over a week, and I regret being a goddamn coward now just in case she tried reaching out to me. The only voicemails were from my band-mates and manager, so I finally sent them a text telling them I'd be back in time for the concert tomorrow night.

The thought of leaving here without Natalie—or at least winning her back—has me feeling sick to my fucking stomach. As much as I'd like to get piss drunk and just disappear like I normally do after a trip, I made a promise to Natalie to stay sober and I plan to keep it.

"Fuck. Here goes nothing." I step into the hotel, my

stomach sinking when I see Kayla at the desk instead of Natalie. "Is she here?"

Kayla looks up from the computer screen, her eyes widening when they land on me. "Holy shit, Madden. No, she's not here. After moping around for a fucking week, she asked for a few days off and is now ignoring my phone calls. So, I have you to thank you for that. Thanks a fucking lot for breaking her heart."

"Tell me where she is, Kayla."

"Did you miss the part where I said she's ignoring my calls?" She rolls her eyes and gives me the dirtiest look. Apparently, she's not a huge fan of me anymore. "So I don't know where she is, but when you find out, tell my bestie to call me. I'd appreciate that. Now, if you don't mind..."

"Fuck!" I grip the counter and squeeze, feeling like the dick that I am, before turning away and rushing outside to my truck. There's only one other place I can think of that she'd be, and if that's the case, I need to get to her before I lose her for good.

When I pull up in front of my brother's, neither of their vehicles are parked outside, so I head toward his office, anxious to get to her. It's been over a week since we've spoken, which is more than enough time for my brother to win her back. That's my biggest fear.

A sense of relief hits me when I pull up at the office to find my brother's vehicle in his usual spot and Natalie's nowhere in sight. I sit here for a minute, considering going in to talk to Logan, but the longer I sit here, the more anxious I become to get to Natalie. I shift my truck into park and get ready to drive away when I notice the driver's side door of my brother's SUV open.

My heart races when Logan steps out, his focus on me in my truck. Looks like this conversation is going to happen after all.

"Hey," he says when I step out of my truck and close the door. "You've been ignoring my texts for over a week. I've apologized a million times for my fuckup. I don't know what else to do, Madden."

"I haven't had a phone until late last night. I wasn't ignoring anyone." I cross my arms and exhale, getting impatient. The last thing I want to hear is his apology for fucking me over. I'm ready to get straight to the point. "I'm not here for your excuses as to why you fucked my ex while we were together. I'm here for Natalie. I'm sorry if you don't like that or if it hurts you, but I want her, and I'm not leaving town without her knowing that. I've lost too much over the years and I refuse to lose her too. I'm in love with her, Logan. I won't apologize for that either. Either accept it or don't. I couldn't care less at this point."

He looks taken aback by my confession. His green eyes meet mine as he begins rolling up his sleeves. I don't know if he's preparing to fight me or just nervous like he gets easily. "Yeah, well, Natalie isn't here. Unlike you, she *has* been ignoring my calls and texts." He exhales and runs a hand through his unusually messy hair. "Except for late last night when she showed up at my house to give me an earful and tell me we're through indefinitely. Apparently, she fell for my younger brother. Who would've fucking guessed that shit? But what can I do? I fucked up. There is no going back, and evidently, you two have a bond that we never developed in the two years we dated. She made that clear as day before driving away."

My heart speeds up over hearing my brother say Natalie has fallen for me. Here I was expecting to have to fight my brother to win Natalie back and she's been mine all along. I just didn't know it. "Where is she, Logan?" I push away from my truck and yank the door open, eager to get to her. "Tell me where she is. Now." I'm getting really impatient at this point.

"I have no clue. She left last night saying she had somewhere to be. From the looks of it, she had her suitcase in the back of the car. I didn't get a chance to ask before she peeled out of the driveway on a fucking mission."

"Fuck!" I jump into my truck and reach for my phone to call Natalie. When she doesn't pick up after the fifth try, I start the engine and slam the door shut, ready to go after her. I don't bother taking the time to say goodbye to my brother. I hit the gas and head toward Natalie's house again, hoping to find her there. I'm not sure why, though, since my brother said her bags were packed.

After driving around town for a couple of hours with no luck, I pull off into a parking lot and beat the shit out of my steering wheel like a goddamn idiot. Once my knuckles are bruised and split open, I head toward the hotel in Vegas where my bandmates are staying, just as promised.

I hate leaving Temecula without Natalie, but what can I do at this point? She's gone, and although my brother seems to think she's fallen for me, apparently that's not enough for her to answer my call.

Maybe he was wrong; that or he just wants to get back at me for going after Natalie. Either way, leaving without her is a shit feeling I never want to experience again.

CHAPTER TWENTY-EIGHT

MADDEN

LAST NIGHT WAS ROUGH AS SHIT, AND SLEEP DIDN'T COME no matter how hard I tried to force it. I kept looking at my phone hoping to hear from Natalie. Once three a.m. hit, I threw my phone across the hotel room and cracked the screen to shit.

"You sure you're good, man?" Landon questions, giving me a concerned look. "You haven't touched liquor since you got here, and you always have a couple of shots before going on stage. I don't know whether to be concerned or happy."

"Leave him be, fucker." Hendrix slaps our drummer's shoulder. "Clearly, he's in his head about this Natalie chick. Don't stress him out right before we're about to go on stage. He's good."

I stand from the couch and empty half a water bottle, my nerves causing my hands to shake. I've been trying to reach Natalie since last night and she's yet to return my calls. Going on stage to perform for a bunch of screaming fans is the last thing I want to do right now.

"I'm ready." I look down at my busted-up phone in my hand one last time before tossing it onto the couch, walking away when there's still nothing from the girl I love. "Let's get this shit over with."

I ignore the flashing of cameras and random screams of admiration as we head toward the stage. I'd rather smash this guitar than play it right now, but I place the strap over my shoulder anyway. It's just a few hours, and then I can get on the road and head back to Temecula. I don't care if I have to wait a week for her to show back up at her house. I'll sleep in my goddamn truck if I have to.

The moment we hit the stage the screams are so loud they're deafening. Usually, I'd at least be buzzed by this point, and on some nights, halfway to fucked-up. Being on stage sober is a new experience for me, and my nerves are going crazy as I look around at the hundreds of faces, realizing the one I want to see the most is nowhere to be found. Not that I expected her to be here. I haven't seen Natalie at a concert since that first one two years ago.

"What's up, Vegas! Make some noise if you guys are ready to party tonight." The screams grow louder, girls close to the stage jumping up and reaching out in an attempt to touch me, so I bend down and hold my hand out letting a few of them grab me as they scream out that they love me. "Hell yeah! Let's get this night started with a little something you guys know well."

More screams and whistles fill the room as the band begins playing "Without You" but starts to die down the moment I begin singing, everyone joining in.

The lyrics leave my lips effortlessly; although, my attention is elsewhere in the crowd, my concentration shot as I scan the faces for Natalie again. It's fucking stupid, yet I can't stop myself from doing it, my anger growing toward the end of the fifth song at not finding her.

Chances are she's gone for good. I might've fucked up that night by pushing her away. What I should've done is fought for her. I should've followed her to her house and knocked down her door to get to her. If I had the chance to do it all over again, I would've taken the chance and risked my heart. It might've gotten broken, but at least then I could've said that I tried instead of letting her drive away like the pussy that I am.

When I look Landon's way, he gives me a nod, as if to make sure I'm cool. Hell no, I'm not. I'm anything but cool, but I nod back anyway, before grabbing a water bottle from the stool and slamming it back, wishing it was something else. But not only do I *want* to stay sober for Natalie, I know that drinking will only numb the memories of her. I'd rather feel the excruciating pain I've been feeling than block out the way I feel for her. That'll only hurt more.

"Dude." Hendrix meets me at the middle of the stage, his face full of frustration. "You're fucking up the lyrics, Madden. Get it together. Just until the end of the show at least. Can you do that shit?"

"I always do, don't I?" I toss my empty water bottle at him, my asshole mood kicking in. He looks down and shakes his head as it bounces off his chest. "Worry about yourselves. I can take care of me. Got it?"

"Yeah. Sure, you can."

I walk away and stand at the end of the stage, my jaw flexing as I run a hand through my wet hair. I've never felt so close to walking away before. In fact, I don't even want to walk at this point, I want to fucking run out of here and go after Natalie. My nerves are completely shot, and Hendrix is right, I've messed up the lyrics multiple times hoping nobody caught on. Apparently, I did a shit job hiding it.

"You know what? Stop the fucking music." I turn around to face my bandmates. "I need a minute." The crowd goes

281

quiet as I remove my guitar and drop it, walking away, but before I can get too far, I turn back around and grab the mic again. "Fuck it. I'm sorry guys, but I've got a girl to go after. I haven't stopped thinking about her since the moment she drove away and left me standing in the driveway feeling like a dumbass for not fighting for her. I've regretted it ever since, and I can't fucking function without her. It wasn't supposed to be that way. I wasn't supposed to fall for her but I did. I'm an asshole for falling for my brother's girl, but I did, and I don't regret a second of it."

There are mixed reactions from the crowd, some booing me for stopping the music and others cheering me on to go after my girl, and some are yelling out that they'll date me instead.

"Fuck being scared. Fuck my heart. Fuck everything. I'm in love with her and I'm going after her. I *need* to go after her." As the words leave my mouth, I realize that I'm about to walk away from a concert for the first time. I'm going to let down hundreds of people—my bandmates and manager included—but for Natalie, I have to be selfish. I can't wait another fucking second without losing it. "Wish me luck." I drop the mic and walk off stage, not giving two shits that I just fucked up.

"Where the fuck are you going?" Jason grabs my arm, but one look at my face and he releases it. "You can't just walk away during a show, Madden. Hundreds of people paid good money to be here tonight."

"Are you going to stop me?" When he doesn't say anything, I add, "I didn't think so. Make sure everyone gets a refund. I'll pay them back out of my own pocket."

A shit ton of flashes go off as I hurry through the building and out the back door, finally able to breathe the moment I step outside and head for my truck. I usually don't drive to concerts, but I knew the moment I got off stage tonight that

I'd be going straight to my truck and driving away. I just didn't know it'd be this early.

With shaky hands, I reach for a cigarette and light it, before closing my eyes and leaning against the side of my truck. I need a moment to calm my nerves before getting behind the wheel.

My jaw tenses when I hear footsteps, but I keep my eyes closed, because I know I'll lose my shit on whoever the fuck decided to follow me out here.

"Did you mean what you said inside?"

My heart jumpstarts at the sound of Natalie's voice. I open my eyes to see her standing in front of me in a pair of ripped-up jeans and a white shirt with the leather jacket I gave her. Her hair is pulled into a side braid just like the first time I saw her, and for a moment, I forget how to breathe.

"Did you?" she questions again, taking a step closer. "I need to know, Madden."

"Every fucking word, Nat." I toss my cigarette and cup her face, my eyes meeting hers. Fuck, how I've missed looking into them. "I never should've let you drive away that day. I should've gone after you and showed up at your doorstep." I step in closer until our bodies are touching. "I was a fucking asshole for not stepping up and fighting for you. I let my fear of losing you get the best of me and I made the biggest mistake of my life. I don't want space. I never fucking wanted space. All I want is you."

"Then why didn't you answer my calls?" She attempts to put some space between us, but I step in close again, not willing to let her go. "I called you for days and sent texts and got *nothing* in return." Her voice is shaky, her emotions taking over. "I thought maybe you didn't feel the same way I do. It hurt, Madden; really fucking bad. Do you realize how hard it was to function with those thoughts in my head, haunting me day and night? Do you? I'm pissed at you. I'm pissed that you couldn't just pick up the phone and talk to me like an adult. I'm pissed that I wanted nothing more than to hear your voice and your laugh and it was nowhere to be found. I *hated* it so much."

"I didn't have a phone." I move my hand around to grip the back of her neck as I rest my forehead against hers. "And fuck, Nat, do you think I wasn't hurting too? That my heart didn't fucking ache to think you didn't want me back. I was terrified you'd realize I wasn't good enough for you. It killed me. Every goddamn day." I pause, my lips moving to brush hers. "I love you, Nat. I'm *in* love with you, and I just confessed it to a room full of people and walked out in the middle of a concert. That's how much I love you. I'm willing to risk it all to be with you. I want you. Fuck that. I *need* you, and I'm not afraid to fight for you until you realize you want the same. If you need time..."

"Wait. What?" She shakes her head, her hands moving up to grab my face. "I walked out the moment you said you had a girl to go after. I wanted to catch you before you left." She pauses for a second, before asking, "Did you really just do that? Tell a whole room full of people you're in love with me?"

"Yes," I whisper, gripping her neck tighter. "I'd do it again too; a million fucking times."

"Dammit, Madden."

I grip her face and hold it steady. "What? Are you mad at me for that?"

"No." She stands on her tippy toes and wraps both arms around my neck. "I'm mad that I'm about to fucking cry, because I love you too. I'm so in love with you that it hurts when you're not close. I wasn't supposed to fall for you. I wasn't supposed to switch brothers. I was supposed to continue pretending that I wasn't attracted to you. That I didn't secretly have a thing for the famous rock star that millions of girls have already fallen for. You made it hard to pretend. You made me love you, and I'm scared. I'm scared to lose you. I won't survive it."

"Me too. But I'll risk it all for you, Nat. I don't care what it takes, I want you as mine. Tell me what you want me to do and I'll do it."

"I want you to not hurt me." Her eyes study mine and the fear in them breaks my fucking heart. "I know how that feels."

"I'll never hurt you, Nat. Fuck. Come here." Grabbing the back of her head, I capture her lips with mine, my heart feeling full for the first time in over a week.

Her kiss is just as desperate as mine, her hands gripping my hair as I lift her up and wrap her legs around my waist.

"I love you," I whisper against her lips, before gently biting the bottom one and tugging. "I want you here with me. Will you stay?"

She smiles against my lips and nods. "I might've quit my job to be here, so I don't have to be back for a while."

"Are you serious, Nat? You're not fucking with me?" I gently grip her chin, forcing her to look me in the eyes. "You're staying?"

"I'm staying. For as long as you want me to." She pauses to kiss me. "I'm yours, Madden. I'm not going anywhere."

"You have no idea what you've just gotten yourself into by becoming the rock star's girlfriend." I grab the back of her head and crush my lips against hers, climbing onto the tour bus and shutting the door behind us. "You sure you can handle that?"

"I guess we'll find out."

She truly has no idea. Because I don't plan to leave her side unless I have to. Fuck, I might even bring her on stage with me. Natalie is mine; so fucking mine.

CHAPTER TWENTY-NINE

NATALIE

I IGNORED MADDEN'S CALLS AND TEXTS THE LAST DAY needing our first interaction to be in person. I needed to see his face for our conversation to see how he truly felt. The last thing I expected was for him to walk off stage to come after me. My plan was to show up dressed like the first time he saw me and wait for him to spot me out in the crowd.

I didn't expect the concert to be as crazy and packed as it was, but apparently, RISK sells a lot more tickets now than two years ago. I should've known that when I bought a concert ticket and the show was nearly sold out.

It was easy to tell something was off with Madden on stage. He was even singing the wrong lyrics, and for a second, I was worried he'd spiraled into his old habits of getting so wasted he can't function.

My heart was racing the whole time, waiting for something bad to happen. When he stopped the music and began talking to the crowd, I swear my heart stopped. I couldn't breathe the whole time I waited to hear what he had to say that was so important he stopped in the middle of a performance.

We can't keep our mouths and hands off each other as Madden carries me to the back of the tour bus, past four bunks and into a private bedroom. The moment the bedroom door shuts behind us, he tosses me onto the bed and climbs on top of me.

My entire body is on fire with need as he yanks his leather jacket off of me and hurriedly undresses me as if he'll die if he isn't inside of me soon. I feel the same way. I want him inside of me and all over me. I want everything that is Madden Parker. I'm in love with this man and I never want to go without him again.

"Take it off, Madden." I smile up at him when he rips his shirt over his head and tosses it aside, amused. "You don't think I've noticed that hashtag trending?"

He smirks and sits up, teasingly undoing his jeans just to mess with me. "How badly do you want me to take these off?"

"Really fucking bad, rock star." He grins and undoes the zipper, before grabbing the back of my head and kissing me hard. "I'm desperate at this point," I tease, nibbling his bottom lip. "Take them off. Now."

He bites his bottom lip and lets out a small growl. "Fuck, I love it when you give me orders." Standing up, he kicks out of his jeans and climbs back on top of me, his muscles bulging as he holds his weight above me. "I missed the shit out of you, babe. Don't be surprised if we stay in this room for a couple of days. I have some making up to do."

I close my eyes and moan when he trails kisses over my stomach and breasts, before pulling my bottom lip into his mouth. Everything he does is so sexy. The head of his dick against my entrance has me thrusting my hips up, desperate for him to sink into me. When he does, slow and deep, I cry out and bite his arm.

"Fuck," he growls out, resting his forehead against mine. "You feel so damn good. All mine."

After a few seconds, he begins moving in a slow, steady rhythm, every hard inch stretching me for him. He's right. I'm his and there's nothing I wouldn't give for a million more moments with him like this. He has ruined me for all other men, because no one will ever come close to comparing to Madden. He's my rock star and I plan to keep him.

His teeth scrape across my neck as he rotates his hips. This man knows what he's doing, and I'm seconds away from an orgasm if he keeps moving his body so perfectly.

"Come for me, Nat," he growls against my ear. "Show me that you're mine. Only mine."

Two more deep thrusts and my pussy clenches around his dick as an orgasm explodes through me. It's so intense that I scream out and grip the sheet, my body thrashing below him.

"So goddamn beautiful when you come for me, babe." His lips capture mine, before he pulls me onto him so that I'm straddling him. He's careful at first—barely moving—before he grips my hip just the way I like and moves me up and down, hard and fast until he fills me with his cum.

The way he looks at me as he fills me has me losing my shit and coming for a second time. Just it being Madden is hot enough, but knowing that he's in love with me too does something to me that I've never felt before.

I know without a doubt that I made the right choice. Madden is the right Parker brother for me. He's *my* Parker brother, and I'm here for the long run. "I love you," I whisper against his lips, wanting to reassure him that I've made up my mind. "Only you."

"Fuck, babe." He grips the back of my head with both hands and roughly kisses me. "I love you so much. It's me and you. Whatever it takes I'll make it work, and I'll always put you first—before myself, before my band, and before anyone else in my life. You're no longer an afterthought for someone else. You're my number one. I won't hurt you, Nat. That's a promise."

"I trust you," I whisper, running my hands through his sweaty hair. "That's why I'm here giving you my heart. I'm not going anywhere. No more breaks. No more time. I know what I want and that's you. Always."

His lips crash against mine as he lays me on my back. He's still hard inside of me, and when he begins moving again, taking me slow and deep, I hold onto him for dear life, enjoying every second of his hands, mouth and body on me.

I don't think I'll ever get used to this feeling—having someone love me the way Madden does. I know it may not be an easy road ahead, figuring things out with his lifestyle, but I'm all in and ready to see what the future holds.

CHAPTER THIRTY

NATALIE

TWO MONTHS LATER...

I SWEAR I'LL NEVER GET USED TO SEEING MADDEN ON stage surrounded by hundreds of screaming fans. It's so much different than experiencing on a screen, which is how I've been watching their concerts over the years. I never imagined I'd be here, backstage, watching from a few feet away. Eight concerts later and it still feels surreal.

What is even more insane to me is that the moment the last song ends and he says goodnight to the crowd, he's going to walk straight to me, pull me into his arms, and tell me how much he loves me. He's done this after each concert, and every single time I fall more in love with him.

I never knew I could love someone the way I love Madden. I never imagined I'd need to be with someone every minute of the day or I'd miss them, but I feel that with Madden. I don't see that changing anytime soon either.

"All right, Chicago! It's been a fucking blast, but we have

to call it a night soon. Make some noise if you want one last song!"

The crowd goes wild as Madden, Landon, and Hendrix throw their arms up to hype up the crowd. The screams and whistles are deafening as I join in making my own noise. It feels so good to be able to cheer them on and show my support. I wasn't lying when I told Madden at the cabin that RISK is one of my favorite bands. I meant it, and they still are.

"Hell yeah, Chicago! That's what we like to hear." My heart races when Madden turns my way, his eyes locking on mine as he continues. "This next song is something I wrote with the help of my girl—the love of my life. This woman is the world to me. I need you all to show her some love!"

The crowd starts chanting "Natalie" repeatedly, and just like every time, my face turns red with embarrassment and I feel like I'm overheating. Especially when all attention is locked in my direction as if they all know where I stand at every concert. I swear he does this on purpose.

Another thing I'll never get used to is random strangers stopping me in the streets, asking for a picture with me and fangirling over me because I'm Madden's girl. It's complete insanity if you ask me, and not something I ever wanted, but for Madden I'll live that life. It'll take some getting used to, but I'm sure it'll die down eventually, when they all get bored of our relationship and it's not so fresh.

Madden laughs into the mic as he begins playing his guitar, warming up for the song. "That's a lot of love there. I think you earned it."

The noise slowly dies down once the band joins in. Every time they perform this song I think back to our trip. I miss the week we spent there together walking in the woods and playing games. I even miss the bickering we did. It was nice having some privacy with him, and I'm already looking forward to the next trip.

"...hanging by a thread, and close to unraveling. I'm holding onto nothing, ready to give in. Even when I knew I shouldn't want you, my heart wouldn't let me stop. 'Cause there's no pretending you're not here creeping into my bones. You're crawling under my skin and it scares me shitless, in a way I've never known..."

By the end of the song, Madden is covered in sweat, and when he grabs a water bottle from the stool to pour it over his head like he always does, he smiles and winks at me. My heart jumpstarts just like every time he smiles in my direction.

"That's all for tonight, Chicago!" he yells into the mic. "Who wants to see us next year?" The crowd screams at the top of their lungs and a few of the women in the front row start jumping up and down and reaching out for Madden as he walks by. "Fuck yeah, Chicago. You'll be seeing us soon. Until next time..."

"Thank you for coming out tonight," Landon adds. "We wouldn't be here without your love and support."

"Hell yeah!" Hendrix says next. "Who will we see in Wisconsin next weekend?"

A good portion of the crowd screams, which isn't surprising. It seems a lot of their fans follow them around from show to show when they play close enough to their home state.

The other bandmates are still talking to the crowd, but the moment Madden gets free he walks directly to me, lifts me into his arms, and kisses me long and hard. My body ignites into flames when his tongue dips into my mouth and he lets out a little growl to show me how much he needed this kiss.

"You guys were incredible, as usual," I point out when he sets me down to my feet.

"Is that right?" he whispers against my lips. "Did you see how the crowd went wild after our song?"

I smile and nod. "I don't know why you still give me credit. I didn't do anything other than—"

"Inspire it. You're the reason I wrote the song, Nat. You deserve credit. You had me in my feelings and confused as shit, because I knew even then that I wanted you. Scared the fuck out of me."

"I was scared too, Madden. I still am at times."

"Why?" He squeezes my hip and moves in closer.

"Because I've never loved anyone the way I love you. I'm scared shitless of these feelings I harbor inside me. They're so overwhelming at times that I can't breathe. Do you know how that feels?"

He smiles against my lips. "Yes." His lips brush mine before he tugs the bottom one between his teeth. "Every fucking day."

"You two lovebirds ready?" Landon asks, hurrying past us with his drumsticks. "We've got some autographs to sign."

Hendrix squeezes his way in between us and smiles. He's full of sweat and water just like Madden. "Miss me?"

Madden palms Hendrix's face and pushes him out of our space. "Fuck no, she didn't miss you." He laughs when Hendrix kisses me on the cheek and runs away. "I guess we should hurry and get this night over with so we can be alone. You down for that?"

I nod and wrap my arms around his neck. "I'm always down for being alone with you. How quickly do you think you can sign those autographs?"

"Depends..."

"On what?" I tease.

"On what you plan to do to me once we're alone?"

"Careful, rock star," I tease. "I might have my taser in my back pocket."

"Mmm... kinky..." I laugh when he picks me up and throws me over his shoulder. "Let's hurry this shit up then."

Camera flashes go off numerous times from every direction as Madden rushes to meet up with his bandmates. I can't even count the number of photos I've found myself in on social media since that concert where Madden walked off stage to find me. I try my best not to look at them all, but I get curious and find myself saving all the ones of Madden and myself.

The merchandise table is so crowded by the time we get to it that the security team has to separate the fans to give Madden room to walk to his seat. Usually, I stand off somewhere in the back and give them their space, but Madden pulls up the extra chair and sits me down in it. When he moves in to give me a kiss, my anxiety fades and I find myself interacting with the fans just as much as the band is. Some of them even ask for my autograph, which makes no sense to me, but Madden and the boys just laugh and include me as if I'm one of them.

After doing autographs and posing for hundreds of pictures, the band, Jason, and the security team pile up in the tour bus for drinks to celebrate and unwind. From the way Madden keeps eyeing me over and kissing me, I know it won't be long before he's dragging me back to our hotel room. Not that I'm complaining...

"Fuck, I love you so much," Madden whispers into my neck. "You sure you can handle living this lifestyle with me? It's like this all the time. It never stops."

I look down at my phone to check the time. It's already past midnight, just like every other weekend. They live a chaotic life but that's part of who Madden is. I want that to be part of me too. "Yes." I grab his face and kiss him. "I love you too much not to."

"I swear you two never stop to breathe," Hendrix jokes. "Let me guess... you're going back to the hotel room soon?"

"You know it, fucker. Don't be jealous."

I laugh when Hendrix rolls his eyes and the boys start bickering back and forth. The band has become like a second family since I've been on tour with them, and although the boys give Madden shit, I know we have their support one hundred percent.

I'm ready for this new adventure with Madden no matter how crazy it gets. I'm a girl in love, and I only see myself falling more and more with time.

EPILOGUE

MADDEN

ONE YEAR LATER...

WE PULL INTO THE DRIVEWAY OF THE CABIN, AND JUST LIKE last year, all our friends are already out back hanging by the fire. This year, some things are different—we're not pretending, there are no lies, and Natalie doesn't belong to my brother. She's mine for real this time, and there's nothing I've wanted more than to bring her back to the cabin so we could enjoy it as a real couple. I've looked forward to it all year.

"You sure you can handle being my girl for the weekend," I tease, leaning in to kiss her bottom lip. "We're going to have to be all over each other, kissing and doing lots of other things... Dirty things."

She smiles playfully and grips the back of my head, pulling me in closer. "I'm not sure I could handle *not* being your girl. I never want to know that feeling again."

"Good," I whisper, my thumb tracing her lip. "Because you'll never have to."

"Is that a promise?" Her lips brush mine, and to answer her question, I kiss her, my hands digging into her hair. "I like that answer," she whispers when our lips part. "A lot."

"You'll get that answer every fucking time, babe. I'm never letting you go." Figuring our friends can wait, I pull Natalie into my lap so that she's straddling me. Gripping her hips, I squeeze while rocking her above me. "You sure you don't want me to make love to you right here? It's been a while since we've fucked in my truck."

She squirms above me and laughs when I reach for the button of her jeans. "Madden," she warns. "Everyone knows we're here. They're going to wonder why we're taking so long."

"Then we'll lie," I whisper against her ear, before gently biting it. "We'll tell them we took a walk in the woods to Axe throw."

She looks as if she's almost considering it when a knock at the window causes us both to jump.

"Fucking, Jake." When I look over, he's grinning and making thrusting motions while biting his bottom lip. "Sometimes I wish I wasn't friends with that fucker."

Natalie laughs and crawls out of my lap, quickly reaching for the door handle when Jess comes running up to greet her.

"Oh my god, girl!" Jess screeches. "Tell me everything that's happened since last year. Don't leave anything out."

The girls take off toward the cabin and Jake and I stay back while I light up a cigarette. "You two look good together," Jake points out. "You look happy. *Really* happy. It's been a while since I've seen your old self."

"I am." I take a long drag and slowly exhale the smoke into the air. "I'm happier than I've ever been, Jake. It might've taken stealing a girl that didn't belong to me, but I wouldn't change anything about the way things went down to get to where we are."

"Good. That means you have no regrets." Jake smiles and hits my arm. "I guess you heard that Alana started dating a new guy and decided to skip this year?"

"That's what Jess told Natalie last week. I'm happy for her. I hope things work out better for them than they did for us."

"She seems happy. I guess only time will tell." Jake nods toward the cabin. "Seth and Riley are out back and Logan will be here soon. Walker's dumbass forgot to request off work, so he won't be here until Saturday night."

I take one last drag off my smoke before tossing it and following Jake around the cabin. The girls are sitting across from each other talking and the guys are playing a drinking game.

"Landon and Hendrix will be here tomorrow night; possibly even my cousin Chance and his wife Aubrey, depending on if Adele can take the kids."

"Sweet. Sounds like we have a fun six days ahead of us. Hell yeah."

Coming up behind Natalie, I wrap my arms around her neck and kiss the side of her face. "Want a drink?"

She nods and turns her head back far enough to press her lips against mine. "Can you make me Jess's specialty drink?" she asks hopeful.

"Shit. I think I remember what's in it."

Jess laughs. "Why don't you make us both one then and I'll be the judge."

I'm up for the challenge, so I head into the cabin and begin mixing together random shit that I somewhat remember Jess throwing into her specialty drink. I'm in the middle of sticking straws into the cups when my brother walks in.

Although we've talked since everything went down last year, we haven't seen each other face to face. Not gonna lie,

I'm a bit tense right now, not knowing what to expect. Whether he likes it or not, Natalie and I aren't going to hold back on our relationship just because he's here.

"Hey, little brother." Logan grips the counter and nods at the drinks in front of me. "Wanna make me one of those?"

I laugh and grab an empty cup. "It's probably going to be sweet as shit."

He smiles. "That's okay, because it's for my girlfriend."

I pause making the drink to look up at him. "Since when the fuck do you have a girlfriend? You didn't mention dating anyone to me last time we spoke."

He crosses his arms over his chest, his smile widening. "I wasn't sure things were serious between us until a couple of weeks ago. Wanted to take things slow and see where things went."

"Right on." I smile, happy for him. "I'm glad you brought her for us to meet then, brother." I hand him a drink and slap his shoulder. "Let's join the ladies outside then."

When we walk out back, I stop dead in my tracks when I spot Carla sitting with the girls.

"It's not Carla," he says on a laugh. "She hitched a ride with us once she realized we were going. Her name is Danika and she's friends with Carla. I met her at the bar when I was spilling my guts to Carla one night."

It takes a second before I notice a platinum blonde sitting on the other side of Carla. I've seen her a few times over the years, and she seemed nice the times I've talked to her. I just wouldn't have remembered what her name was had he not told me. "Leave it to Carla to fix everyone's problems," I say amused. "And thanks for bringing Carla along. The girls will have a lot of fun this year."

"They deserve it," Logan says from beside me. "After putting up with my shit all three girls deserve some fun."

I laugh and head toward the girls, handing Jess and

299

Natalie their drinks before giving Carla and Danika hugs to greet them.

A few hours later, everyone is lying around the fire, telling stories and enjoying each other's company, but unlike last year, there's no tension. Everything feels fucking perfect. Jake and Jess are happy. Logan seems really into his new girl, and Carla is getting along well with the boys. She doesn't seem to mind their constant flirting, but I doubt either of them will get anywhere with her. Then again, who knows? Maybe one of them has a chance.

"Wanna go for a walk?" I stand up and grab Natalie's hand, pulling her to her feet. "There's a special spot I want to take you?"

Natalie smiles up at me when I yank her into my arms. "Is that right? Does it happen to be in the woods with two spotlights?"

"Maybe," I say against her lips. "Wanna find out?"

"You know I do." She stands on her tiptoes to kiss me, before pulling me toward the woods. "We'll be back, guys!"

The moment we're alone and out of sight, I back Natalie against a tree and kiss her long and hard, wanting to take her right here in the woods. I don't give a shit who hears us. I'm proud to take my girl anywhere she'll let me.

"Madden..." Natalie bites my bottom lip, causing me to jump back. "Are you ever *not* horny?"

"Is that a serious question?" I joke, pressing my erection into her. "Because here's your answer."

"How about this? If you can hit the bullseye three times in a row without looking, I'll let you take me out here in the woods. Anywhere you choose."

"Fuck me!" I bite my bottom lip and growl out in satisfaction. "Challenge accepted."

I don't think I've ever walked these woods so fast in all

the years I've been coming here, but within minutes we're at my secret spot. *Our* secret spot.

I get ready to turn on the lights, but Natalie stops me and slips my new leather jacket off. "I just wanted to get you alone," she whispers. "Don't plan on joining the others for a while, rock star. You're mine until I'm done with you."

"Fuck, I love you."

She laughs against my lips and whispers, "Love you too babe," before I lift her into my arms and press her back against the plywood.

Fucking shit, I love this woman more than life. I never thought I'd feel happiness again after what I went through with Alana, but here I am, the happiest I've ever felt before. I have Natalie to thank for that. And for that reason, I'll spend every day making sure she's the happiest she's ever been too. I might've borrowed her to begin with, but I knew after that first night that she was meant to be mine all along.

Want to keep up with all of the new releases in Vi Keeland and Penelope Ward's Cocky Hero Club world? Make sure you sign up for the official Cocky Hero Club newsletter for all the latest on our upcoming books: https://www.subscribepage.com/CockyHeroClub

Check out other books in the Cocky Hero Club series: http://www.cockyheroclub.com

Author's website: https://victoriaashleyauthor.com/

Made in USA - Kendallville, IN
1202274_9798682508433
02.10.2021 1652